THE LAST ONE TO DIE

TERRI GREENING

This is a work of fiction. Names, characters, places, and incidents are products of the author's imagination or are used fictitiously and are not to be construed as real. Any resemblance to actual events, locations, organizations, or persons, living or dead, is entirely coincidental.

World Castle Publishing, LLC
Pensacola, Florida

Hardback ISBN: 9798266343818
Paperback ISBN: 9798891264755
eBook ISBN: 9798891264762
First Edition World Castle Publishing, LLC, October 14, 2025
http://www.worldcastlepublishing.com

Cover: Cover Designs by Karen
Editor: Karen Fuller

CHAPTER 1

I first met Cameron Talbert in a musty, corner bookstore in downtown Blue Haven, not far from the beach. He was looking for a present for his mother, I later found out, and I had stopped in on my way up north to Cove Pointe to pick out a hostess gift for my old, college roommate, who I planned to stay with for the remainder of the summer.

I knew right away we were destined for each other and not solely because of his dreamy, blue eyes and the tousled, sandy blond, surfer hair that made him look like he'd just ridden a big wave in on the lake. He had an aura about him that made my arms tingle, and that didn't happen very often.

We both ended up in the sweltering mystery section after I casually followed him there from the cookbooks. He wasn't going to get away with just nodding in answer to my clever "Nice day, isn't it?" question. When the book I was reading next to him inexplicably tumbled to the floor, he seemed surprised, even though I wasn't, and bent over to retrieve it. As he did so, his wavy locks ruffled in the cool air from a floor fan that whirred and spun in our direction. It took everything I had to keep from smoothing them out for him.

"Agatha Christie, huh?" he asked, straightening and handing the novel back to me. He brushed a light dusting of sand from his tanned forearm.

"Yes. She's one of my favorites."

"Mine, too," he said, smiling.

I stared, dumbstruck. His twinkling eyes and pleasant demeanor after his previous seeming aloofness caught me off guard.

"I'm Cam," he said, after a moment.

It was my turn to nod. "Faron," I choked out as I tucked a long strand of my silky, blonde hair behind my ear.

He looked at me quizzically, then replaced a book on the shelf before turning back at me. "Haven't I seen you somewhere before?" he asked.

Great line. Even better than my "nice day" comment. I gave him a big grin and hurried to answer. "No. I'm sure you haven't. I'm only visiting the area for the summer."

He nodded. "I see."

Hopefully, Cam hadn't seen my picture in the paper in the spring when my husband, Gill Chevalier, suddenly passed away. I didn't want to talk about that right now. I wanted to move on with my life and not dwell in negativity like this one annoying private investigator, at least I think that's what he was, who'd been on my proverbial case for a while after the funeral and kept following me around. Luckily, he'd gotten lost like I told him to and stayed that way. At least I think so. Kudos to me.

I was good at moving on. I'd had a lot of practice. And I certainly didn't have time to cry in my milk over something like my husband's death that I couldn't do anything about. I suppose I missed him, but who knows? I'd dealt with enough grief during my relatively short life as compared to Gill's, and I was good at covering up my feelings, especially when I found someone, like maybe Cam, to help me numb my pain.

"Guess I'm mistaken then," he continued. "Sure you're not a supermodel?"

Did he really just say that? Time for a snappy response.

"Umm. Yeah," I replied instead, slightly tongue-tied at the audacious compliment, although I had modeled a little bit once to help pay for my fine arts in music degree, which was mostly but not completely covered by my flute scholarship.

He grinned and turned back to the bookshelves while I concentrated on coming up with a killer line of my own.

The news story about Gill had been splashed around pretty far, including to the upper part of the state where I was now. A photo from the society pages of the two of us on our honeymoon two years ago in Bermuda had shown up occasionally, in addition to a more recent picture of him, but my hair was shorter back then, with a different style. I hoped by now, three months after Gill's death and the resulting publicity, I wouldn't be recognized.

The wide coverage probably had something to do with how much money and power my husband had accumulated over his sixty years. People seemed to like to read about people like that for some reason. I didn't. I wanted to get away, but I couldn't run to our place in Florida because Gill's lawyer said I shouldn't leave the state.

He wanted me to stick around until my husband's beneficiary information with the life insurance company was ironed out, which would take a few more months. He said my presence in the state was mandatory. I don't know what that means or what his deal is. But I pay him good money, so I listen to him.

I thought of another line and glanced at Cam. But he was concentrating on his book, so I looked away quickly before he looked up and thought I was staring at him. He probably had women staring at him all the time, and I wanted to be different. He sure was cute, though.

If things weren't worked out by the end of the summer,

'one way or the other,' like Gill's lawyer, Jay, said they would be, in his enigmatic manner, because that's the way he is, I was leaving regardless to spend some time down south in another home that I treasured. That was the deadline I set with him.

And if I got arrested or something for crossing the state line, Jay had better find a way to get me out. I didn't like the feeling of being controlled by the system, and I shouldn't have to put up with this nonsense, given the large amount of money I was sure I was coming into.

"Maybe you were in a movie or something?" Cam asked, looking up from his book. "You're pretty enough."

"No," I said, shaking my head. "Were you?" I smiled as I returned the compliment. He had that movie star look about him.

"No." He gave me an irresistible grin and returned to reading.

I shivered and pressed my lips together to keep from responding too quickly. He was devastatingly handsome, and I wanted to play this right.

I had married Gill, who had been a widower for several years, for the lifestyle and to keep from being lonely, and he knew it. We got along fine, most of the time anyway, but I didn't love him. That's just the truth. I only ever truly loved one man, and he didn't love me as much as I loved him. Isn't that typically the way it is with couples? One is always more in love than the other. I closed myself off after losing him. He was gone just like Gill.

Anyway, I hoped people outside the city I lived in wouldn't have paid much attention to the story about my husband and wouldn't know who I was. Also, I hoped a more rural town wouldn't have security cameras all over the place and people constantly taking cell phone photos. They made me feel like I was always being watched. I needed more privacy after all the hype.

I replaced my book and selected another one from the shelf while stealing another quick glance at Cam, who was still buried in a thriller.

Belatedly reading an article about Gill's death was the way my former roommate, Summer Dixon, found out about what happened and why she had invited me to spend the rest of the summer at her year-round bed and breakfast on a small, inland lake in Cove Pointe with her and her husband.

I had jumped at the chance even though Noble Dixon, Summer's husband of more than six years, was a former fiancé of mine. He'd married her on the rebound from me, I think, which was a little weird. But I could deal with it. That was a long time ago, and I still managed to keep in touch with Summer even though I didn't go to their wedding and didn't tell her much about me.

Noble definitely had to be over me by now, even though our contentious breakup at college had been hard. Besides, the alternative was to mope around an empty house at home, and that wasn't in my DNA.

"So, do you live around here?" I asked. I cringed. So much for originality.

"Not too far. I live in Cove Pointe, which is about twenty minutes north, driving along the big lake," Cam answered, looking up from his book.

"Really?" I bit my lip to keep from grinning.

"Yeah. I'm spending the day at the beach here because my office is closed until next week. They're redecorating."

"Your office?"

"Yeah."

"What do you do?"

"I'm a lawyer. I handle legal issues for people around the area. Paperwork, mostly."

"Hmm." If he hadn't been standing so close, I might have been able to think of something more alluring to say. As it was, the fresh scent of suntan lotion mixed with musky, male perspiration and some sort of beachy cologne made me swoon. "Maybe I'll call you sometime. I might need advice."

He laughed. "Go ahead, if you want. Here. Here's my number." He pulled a wallet out of his navy board shorts and handed me a business card.

"Thanks," I said, casually adjusting my yellow sundress strap, which had slipped off my shoulder.

"Sure," he said.

We gazed at each other for a moment before bells jingled when the bookshop door opened, seeming to startle us both.

"Hey, I've gotta get going. Some friends are waiting for me by the lake. I have to buy this cookbook and sub in a beach volleyball game before I head home," Cam said.

"Yes, of course. Nice to meet you."

"You, too. Maybe I'll see you around."

"Yes. Maybe."

He eased by me, and the light brush of his arm electrified my own. As he walked toward the front of the store, I appraised his sculpted movements like a master connoisseur, taking in his broad, bronzed back and muscular shoulders. He didn't look like any litigators I'd met. He looked more like a football player. I trembled and grasped his card firmly. I foresaw some sort of legal problem in my future, even if I had to make one up.

After Cam left, I waited a few minutes before heading to the counter with my cookbook. I offhandedly mentioned to the cashier that I was on my way to the Hidden Glen B&B in Cove

Pointe.

"Really? The Dixon place?" she asked.

"Yes."

"Summer comes in here once in a while. She and her husband run a nice place up there."

The cashier looked quickly down at the register. Was she frowning?

"So I hear," I said. I waited a moment. "Something wrong?"

"No, not at all. Just making sure the price is right. This book's on sale."

"Oh. Thanks."

She continued frowning as she rang up the purchase, then smiled and handed me the bag. "Here you go. Have a nice day and enjoy your stay in Cove Pointe."

"I'm sure I will," I said, taking the book from her. I paused for a moment, trying to think of something to say to draw her out. "The B&B's right outside Cove Pointe, right, and easy to drive to?"

"Yeah. Sure," she said. "Take a right on the second dirt road after you go through town. Drive down past Wild Blueberry Bog, and you can't miss it."

"Wild Blueberry Bog?"

"Just a local name for a big peat bog on the side of Cove Lake there. Don't worry, though, if you hear any rumors. They're not true."

"Rumors? What kind of rumors?"

She shook her head. "I'm not one to say anything. You'll find out soon enough. Just remember, they're not true." She turned away.

"What's not true?" I asked.

She didn't move.

"Okay. Got it," I said. I stared at her back for a moment before awkwardly walking away. I pulled open the jingling door and stepped out onto the sidewalk. What could she mean by rumors? My internal radar jumped to high alert, and I planned to keep it that way until I found out what was going on.

I walked down the block to my car. The big lake shimmered beyond the boardwalk, and sailboats fluttered down the channel in the fresh breeze. Lake towns were so beautiful. I hopped in and threw my bag on the passenger seat. Time to head north.

After driving through downtown Blue Haven, I picked up the highway again. The route had already narrowed to two lanes on my way north, and it remained the same as I drove toward Cove Pointe. The only difference was the burgeoning forest of pines on either side of the road that eventually blocked off views of the big lake and much of anything else. The name "Hidden Glen" for my bed and breakfast destination took on a new meaning. I hoped I'd be able to find it.

A pertinent exit sign eventually appeared along the road through a light misting of rain, and I pulled off the highway to drive through the small town of Cove Pointe—a fishing town, apparently, from the look of the boats anchored in the big lake's harbor. A few storefronts, a historic library, and a Chamber of Commerce dotted Main Street, and several people stood in line under an awning at a small ice cream shop, escaping the increasingly heavy precipitation—altogether a seemingly pleasant community.

Following the directions the bookstore cashier had given me, I turned right at the second dirt road after driving through Cove Pointe. The sky had darkened considerably. Lightning zigzagged through a thick, gray cloud bank that loomed over the trees lining the road, followed by a loud crack of thunder, which made me jolt straight up. Cam probably wasn't playing beach volleyball anymore if the storm was as bad as it looked.

I turned on my wipers and rubbed out a spyhole to see through as plump drops of rain pelted the steamy windshield, and I almost drove into a ditch to avoid a massive puddle. I wished I drove a Jeep and not my favorite old, sporty Lexus, which was getting splattered all over its silver paint job, so I could better navigate the shallow, muddy ruts.

Something suddenly ran across the road in front of me. I slammed on the brakes. What the heck was that? My car slid forward through the slick mud, and I desperately twisted the steering wheel to correct the trajectory. The Lexus careened around and stopped sideways in the middle of the road.

I let out a breath and peered through the driving rain at the wetlands area in front of me. Maybe this was Wild Blueberry Bog. A black shape shambled through the surrounding woods and disappeared behind a far tree. Was the creature a small bear, perhaps, or an animal of some sort? I rubbed a bigger spot in the windshield to look through, but the shape was gone. At least I hadn't run over the perilous thing, whatever it was. I turned my sights back to my car.

After accelerating slightly and straightening out the tires, I inched the Lexus forward. What had frightened me so? Animals ran across the road all the time, didn't they? But was it an animal? I continued on through the downpour and banished the incident from my thoughts, even though the hairs on the back of my neck bristled as a reminder. The sign for "Hidden Glen B&B" appeared another half mile down the road, and I sighed with relief as I gratefully pulled into the gravel driveway. I made it.

I sat still for a moment in the charming spot nestled in the trees to relax and get my bearings. Also, the rain was still prevalent, and I wanted to wait for a lull. The B&B looked pleasant enough, from what I could make out, with its wide front porch and wedgewood blue shutters on pale yellow siding. Several blue Adirondack chairs sat on the porch with generous pots of red impatiens between them, and an American flag waved on a pole near the door. I could see myself spending time here.

The front door opened abruptly, and a slim woman in a pink flowered shift ran across the porch. Summer. I'd recognize her anywhere with her flowing, Titian red hair reminiscent of a water nymph painting and, of course, her wide smile. She skipped down the steps and ran over to the car, seemingly unbothered by the rain. She tapped on the window and gestured frantically for me to get out. Seeing no other option, I grabbed my purse and my bag and hopped out into the downpour to race with her back up the steps to the porch.

Once inside, I set my things down and hugged Summer, who was effusive in her welcome.

"I can't believe you're here," she gushed. "It's been forever." She stepped back and squeezed water out of her hair.

"You're right," I replied. "I'm glad to see you, too. Here." I brushed raindrops off the reusable bag and handed her the cookbook. "I thought you might like some new recipes."

She peeked inside. "Thanks. Great. I'm always on the lookout for additional items for our menu. I'll definitely use this."

"Good."

"Come on in, and I'll put this away."

"Sure." I followed her through the hardwood foyer to the farmhouse-style kitchen, where she set the bag on the counter and turned to me.

"So how have you been holding up?"

"Oh, you know," I said evasively.

"I know. It must be difficult to talk about. What a terrible thing to have happen. Do they have any more details yet?"

"No."

"Hmm. No conjectures or anything?"

I shrugged. "I don't know. Maybe."

"Okay. Well, we're so glad you came. You can stay as long as you want, and we don't have to mention what happened again."

"Thanks. You're a good friend," I said. And I meant that. Not too many people had let me get away without saying anything after Gill's death. It seemed like I was constantly being cornered and peppered with inane questions like "Who found him? What room was he in? Where were you?" So annoying. Summer, though, seemed to intuitively recognize my limits. I hoped to find respite in this cozy dwelling.

"Of course. Let me show you to your room. We have amenities in the bathroom for you to freshen up. We'll bring your suitcases in later."

"Wonderful," I said, starting to follow her.

I looked up when the side door opened. Noble stood in the doorway. I'd know him anywhere. He had the same dark hair and piercing, green eyes that I remembered from when we were engaged, although he now sported a trimmed beard and mustache, as well. Before Summer or I could react, he slammed the door behind him and strode over to stand in front of me.

"Well. Look who showed up," he belted out. "If it isn't the little lady who murdered her husband."

CHAPTER 2

I winced at Noble's statement or maybe at the thunderclap that rattled the windows.

Summer's mouth dropped open. "How could you say such a thing?" she asked, sounding horrified.

She and I both stood stone still in front of him. I had no idea how to respond. Obviously, Noble wasn't over our broken engagement, or he never would have blurted out something like that.

"Nice to see you, too," I said sarcastically, after recovering my composure.

"Ha, ha. I'll bet," he said. "Looks like I escaped your icy clutches just in time."

What? Although completely taken aback, I scoffed at the familiar insult. After all these years, he was still accusing me of being cold and distant? He didn't even know me anymore.

"What's gotten into you?" Summer exclaimed. "You'll drive her away."

"Well, he's dead, isn't he? Chevalier's stabbing has been in all the papers," he said.

"They didn't say she did it," Summer said, sharply. "Faron needs our love and support, not your feeble attempt at humor. She's been through a harrowing experience, and her husband has passed away."

"Ah. Give it a rest," he said. "She's still here, isn't she?"

"Yes, she is, and we want to make her feel welcome. I'm sorry, Faron," she said, turning to me.

I raised an eyebrow and tilted my head slightly in response. Apparently, Summer wasn't jealous of my previous relationship with Noble. She seemed more protective of me than anything else, the same way she was in college.

"Yeah, alright," Noble said, sourly. He headed toward the sink. "Stay if you want."

"Gee, thanks," I said. How could I politely pivot and bolt out the door?

Summer seemed to read my mind. "Come with me," she said, quickly, taking my arm. "I'll show you to your room. Noble, can you make sure the window in the laundry room is shut? The rain is really coming down out there."

He nodded without turning around, and I walked toward the stairs with Summer. I had trouble remembering now what I saw in Noble. He had been attentive and caring toward me once, but he obviously still held a grudge over my leaving him if he blamed me for my husband's death. I'd gotten that vibe before, but mostly from malicious gossips in my community.

"I don't know why he's acting like this," Summer said in a loud whisper on our way up the stairs. "He only gets this way when we talk about you, which I try not to do, and he wasn't like this before we were married. I'm so sorry."

"What he does isn't your fault," I said firmly. "I'll deal with him in my own manner."

"Are you sure?" she asked over her shoulder.

"Yes, of course." I grasped the banister. I had no idea how I was going to handle her husband's unexpected attitude toward me.

"You must have enough to deal with grieving your husband. I hope you'll be able to rest and recover here," Summer said. She was as solicitous as ever, which probably made her good with her guests.

She looked up the stairs and then glanced back at me. "You're not upset that we're married, are you? We haven't talked about it much, but you two were quite an item in college."

"No, of course not. As you can see, Noble and I never really got along despite the fact that we were engaged for a while."

"Yes. I noticed the tension," Summer said, dryly. "He's actually a wonderful man, and he doesn't usually behave in this manner."

"I know. You said that. Don't worry about it. I can't thank you enough for inviting me here, and I'm sure we'll have a wonderful time even if things started out badly with Noble." Obviously, Summer didn't realize how pushy and obnoxious her husband could be, and I didn't want to be the one to illuminate her.

"I'm positive this will work out," Summer said, confidently. "By the way, you're our only guest for now because a few people canceled. But that could change anytime."

"Okay."

I tried not to take the cancellations personally because I had no reason to believe Summer had alerted anyone but Noble to my arrival. But I did seem to have a distancing effect on people lately. We reached the top of the stairs, and I followed her to a room a few doors down the hallway.

"Here we are," she said, leading me into a spacious bedroom with a large canopy bed against the back wall. "This is my favorite guest room. I hope you enjoy staying here."

"What a beautiful space," I said, looking around.

Vintage wallpaper displayed tiny sprays of lavender flowers, and an antique, canopy bed covered with a fluffy, cream comforter made me want to dive right in. The room held a complementary light fragrance of lavender, which probably emanated from the glass bowl of potpourri on the nightstand.

I walked over to the window. The large backyard was basically a clearing surrounded by pine and spruce trees with a red maple here and there, all of which were bending and swaying in the wind and rain.

"I wonder when this will let up," I said.

"Soon, probably," Summer said. "Outbursts spring up suddenly around here, but they just as quickly fade away."

She was probably referring to the sudden squall, but I couldn't help but draw a comparison to the outburst from Noble we'd experienced earlier. He was turbulent like a summer storm.

"The lake is on the other side of the trees," Summer said, joining me at the window. "Cove Lake, I mean. The town is on the big lake. But here on the smaller lake, we have a rowboat, a sailboat, and a motorboat tied up at the dock for the guests. You walk through the woods and down a few steps to the beach. Oh, and we even have a canoe. If you want to take a boat out sometime, simply mention it to one of us."

"Thanks. I might do that," I said, thinking I might ask Summer's permission but not Noble's. I preferred to keep my conversations with him few and far between.

After a moment, I stepped away from the window and looked around the room. Summer and Noble's stunning wedding photo, enhanced with an engraved silver frame, stood on a nearby dresser, and I picked it up and perused their smiling faces before setting the keepsake back down. I glanced out the window again.

"You know, I think I'll run down and grab my things out

of the trunk."

"Now? You'll get soaked," Summer said.

"No I won't. The rain's letting up a bit."

"Really?" Summer squinted and leaned toward the window.

"Yes. I'm sure it is," I said, heading for the door.

The real reason I insisted was that I didn't want Noble rifling through my belongings and bringing in my suitcases as a ploy to do so. I hadn't locked the car doors, and he could easily reach in and pop the trunk. Maintaining the solid distance we'd built between us over the years seemed important for both my and Summer's sake. I paused for a moment.

"Oh, by the way, do you have any bears or bear cubs around here?" I asked, thinking of my encounter with the strange creature on the road.

"Bears? A few. In the forest. And all sorts of animals live in the bog. Why?"

"I nearly hit something that ran in front of my car on my way here, but I couldn't make out what it was."

"Hmm. What did it look like?"

"Black or dark brown. Hunched over. Scurried across the road. I couldn't see much more in the rain. Oh, and the movements seemed awkward in a side to side kind of way—almost a limp."

Summer looked away, then back. "Could have been a bear. Probably a raccoon or something."

"Didn't look like a raccoon." Why did she seem evasive?

"I wouldn't worry about it. Whatever you saw is probably long gone by now."

"Yeah. Probably." I studied her taut expression. Something bothered her.

"Let's go get your stuff," she said, perking up.

"Yeah. Sure. Lead the way."

I followed her out of the room and back down the stairs. We passed Noble on the way out. He glanced at me and grimaced. Or maybe he purposely made a face. I wouldn't put it past him. I congratulated myself for not sticking my tongue out in return.

Summer stopped at the porch railing, and I stopped next to her, breathing in the sharp scent of pine. We stood together quietly in the warm, humid air, watching the slowing rain.

"You know, I'm glad you're here for another reason besides just visiting," she said, after a moment.

"Oh? What's that?" I asked.

"Umm. Nothing, really." She glanced at the door and back. "Only that I'm looking forward to having a friend around," she said, sounding wistful.

I looked at her. "Don't you have many friends around here?"

"I do now," she said, smiling.

I smiled back. "Yes, you do. I'll always be your friend."

"And I'll always be yours," she said. "Through good times and bad, although I hope the bad times go away for you soon."

"Thanks," I said. "That means a lot, especially now that I'm alone once more." I swallowed hard and pushed down the memories of previous times I had ended up by myself. No use wallowing in bad karma.

She nodded. "I know. I can't believe this happened to you again."

The silence this time was more awkward. The fact that Summer had said "again" brought up the memory of my first husband, Daniel, and the reference to his analogous loss seemed to hang in the air between us. I concentrated on thinking of something else—anything other than my checkered past.

"Well, shall we grab your things? Looks like the rain has dissipated," Summer said, breaking me out of my reverie.

"Sure."

"I hope you brought something you can wear to a birthday party," she said, as we walked to the car.

"Probably," I said. "Here?"

She shook her head. I opened the trunk and handed her a suitcase before grabbing another one and slamming the trunk shut. "Where's the party at?"

"The Talbert place down the road a piece."

I almost dropped my bag. "Cam Talbert?"

"His mother. He lives there with her and his twelve-year-old daughter, Kasey. Do you know him?"

"No, not really. Go on," I said, dumbstruck at the coincidence. But then, it was a small town and everyone probably knew everyone else. I walked with her up the porch steps.

"Cameron's the talk of the town with the local girls. His family made their money in lumber way back when. Ever hear of Talbert's Lumber Company?"

"I shook my head.

"Well, anyway, he's been a confirmed bachelor around here for quite a while."

"Really?" I asked. Somehow, I didn't doubt that he was popular, given how charming he was.

"Yes, and Eleanor Talbert is the director of the music camp down the road on the other side of the bog. Noble teaches music theory there in the summer."

"I see. I may have passed the sign at the end of their driveway on the way here," I said. "I didn't catch the name in the rain."

"Cove Pointe Music Camp," Summer said.

"Okay. He only works there in the summer?"

She nodded. "The camp is only open seasonally. He drives around the state the rest of the year, selling paper products to businesses to supplement our B&B income. Anyway, he's one of Kasey's teachers, and Eleanor was once a teacher of mine."

"Is that right?"

"Yes. Eleanor's quite a talented violinist, and Kasey occasionally comes over and helps me bake pies, especially blueberry, our signature dessert. The last time she did, she invited us to a birthday party for her grandmother tomorrow night at their cottage on the lake. We'd love to have you join us."

"Well, then, I'd love to come," I said, stepping through the front door after her.

I didn't see the need to mention my interest in Cameron or the fact that I'd met him. In my experience, people expected at least a year's wait after a death before accepting a new relationship, even laid-back friends like Summer, and I didn't intend to wait that long. I never did. I hated being alone. I glanced around the foyer. Thankfully, Noble was nowhere in sight. I'd determine how to deal with him later. We headed back up the stairs.

"I don't suppose you brought your flute with you," Summer said.

"I did. It's in my suitcase."

"No kidding. You'll have to play with us like old times, with Noble on the piano and me on the violin."

"Sure. The Dixon duet plus one," I said, laughing.

"Or the Dixon trio, like before."

"That would work, too," I said.

We got back to the room and set the suitcases near the bed.

"Come down when you're ready. Dinner's at 7:00. I'll go start something right now," Summer said. "Maybe I'll use a recipe from my new cookbook."

"Great," I said.

After she left, I sat on the bed, relieved to be in a new location hours from home. I hoped I was safe here. What if a murderer was coming after me, too? I had no way of knowing one way or the other.

If he wasn't, at least I'd be away from that snoopy private investigator with his piercing, dark eyes and furtive glances. I'd had enough of that in the weeks after the funeral. Why didn't he concentrate on helping the police find out who really killed my husband instead of bothering me? What a dolt.

I myself had had to go through the mill with the cops after finding Gill's body and calling 911, and that wasn't any picnic, let me tell you. I suppose the worst outcome for me would have been going to jail. But I have too much money to be locked up. I mean, were they serious? What was so odd about me reporting him dead in our own home? I was his wife, and I lived there. And that's what he was. So what if I wasn't emotional? Seeing the crime scene in our beautiful mansion would have shut anybody up. They let me go.

Gill's three children, who were all older than me, had treated me in a similarly rude fashion, barely looking at me and sneering when they did. I'll bet they hired a P.I. to harass me. I don't know why I thought that, but it seemed to be the only thing that made sense. Why else would someone be following me around asking questions?

And his children never liked me. They probably wanted Gill's money and saw me as an interloper, but I'd let the lawyers figure that out. Could they have contested the will? I wasn't too worried about that or how much I would get in the end if they had. Gill loved me a lot, and I was sure he made that evident through what he left me, even though I still didn't know all the particulars.

I spent the next few hours putting my things away in the antique dressers, freshening up, and changing into a pressed skirt for dinner. I wanted to look my best for my new hosts. Hopefully, Noble had changed his attitude toward me in the intervening time, although I had no reason to think that he had. But I could always wish for the best.

"Dinner's ready," Summer called as I was heading down the stairs.

I walked down the rest of the way and met her in the kitchen.

"We're having roast with potatoes and carrots," she said, picking up a platter filled with savory-looking food.

"Smells wonderful," I said.

"The recipe was in the cookbook. Follow me. I'll show you into the dining room."

I did as she asked and found Noble already there, lighting a candle centerpiece.

"Another beautiful room," I said, taking in the delicately flowered wallpaper and antique dining set. "I think you're in the right area of work if you can decorate and cook like this. People must love to come here."

"They do say that," Summer said, smiling as she set the platter on the table. "Won't you sit over there, and I'll sit here." She sat down across from me.

"Sure," I said, pulling out a chair and sitting. If people loved to come here so much, why wasn't anyone staying but me?

The seating arrangements were not what I would have envisioned, given that I had to sit next to Noble, who had taken a seat at the head of the table. But I could handle anything for an hour or so. After all, I only had to make small talk.

Noble stood and expertly carved the roast, giving each of us thin, juicy slices while Summer doled out roasted potatoes and carrots. When she was done, she handed me a basket of warm yeast rolls, and I eagerly took one. The food around here was shaping up to be exceptional.

While we ate, Noble smugly asked how long I was staying.

"Hard to say," I answered, vaguely. I didn't want to recommit to the whole rest of the summer in case things didn't work out. I turned to Summer. "I was thinking of heading down to the beach and taking a walk after dinner."

"By yourself?" she asked.

"Unless you want to come with me," I said.

She glanced at Noble. "I have things to do around here to prepare for possible guests this weekend."

Was that really the case, or did Noble forbid her from talking to me? I wasn't sure what the dynamic was.

"That's alright," I said. "I can go solo."

Summer continued. "I mean, you could go to the beach by yourself, but you might want to return before dark."

"Okay," I said, slowly. "Any reason for that?"

"Only that we've had some disappearances around Cove Pointe, and staying safe is of the utmost importance."

"Disappearances? Of course, I'll stay safe, but what do you mean by disappearances?"

Summer glanced at Noble again. He stared at his plate and forcefully cut up his slices of roast.

"Well, I don't know if I should tell you this, but in the last several years, a few people in Cove Pointe have disappeared without a trace, and no one knows why or where they are," she said.

"What?" I asked.

"Yes. And all of the disappearances happened in the summer, so I hope you can see why I'm warning you."

"I do. Thanks for telling me," I said, slightly unnerved. This was a surprising turn of events.

She nodded.

The corners of Noble's mouth turned up. "She didn't scare you, did she?" he asked, snidely.

"Maybe a little," I replied. "I might wait until tomorrow to check out the beach."

"How about some blueberry pie with whipped cream?" Summer interjected, a little too brightly. "Noble, would you help me in the kitchen?"

When they left the dining room, I stood and pulled aside a sheer, lacy curtain to look out the window. The evening light was pale from a pastel sky and breathtakingly pretty, and the tree leaves remained somewhat shiny from the rain.

My car looked forlorn and abandoned in the driveway, or maybe I was thinking about myself. Should I make a run for it? I could head back home and hide in my house to seek the privacy I craved. Or should I stay in this small, northern town and attempt to deal with Noble's childish cynicism, along with the missing persons situation and the odd creature that ran across the road?

I glanced up at the few, small rain clouds persisting overhead and thought of Summer, a stalwart friend, and also of Cameron, a seemingly new friend, with whom a future encounter seemed probable and rich with possibilities.

I juxtaposed that with an unknown murderer who could be after me, Gill's callous children who were probably after me, and a nosy private investigator who was definitely after me back home. Then I remembered Gill and Daniel and the other ill-fated men from my past. And even though I had an eerie feeling about Cove Pointe and an overpowering desire to take off, I decided to stay.

CHAPTER 3

After a delicious breakfast of fresh waffles and strawberries with Summer the next morning, I headed for the beach. I wanted to check out the waterfront before doing anything else because Summer had told me how beautiful and calming the lake was. I could certainly use that—if I made it through the forest alive, that is. Summer's warning about people in Cove Pointe disappearing in the summertime had done nothing to assuage my frayed nerves and had, in fact, added to them. Summer stayed in to work up a new menu for the B&B, and Noble had already left to teach at the music camp. So I went alone.

The woods were surprisingly dark and cool, but then, the sun had only recently come up. My toes in their sandals were damp and chilly from having navigated the dewy grass in the backyard. I meandered down a dirt path through the trees, glancing around nervously with my thoughts running wild.

Conversing with Noble the night before had been more distressing than I imagined, and I'd made sure to lock my bedroom door just to be safe. Still, memories of my past, especially Noble's despair when I'd broken off our engagement years ago, had haunted my dreams, and I'd slept fitfully.

Also, the diabolical way Gill's children, especially his oldest son, Paul, stared at me at the funeral stayed with me, too. Did they simply not like me? Or was there more to it? How fervidly did his sons and daughter covet a cut of their father's vast accumulation of wealth, and how long had they wanted it?

I suppose they'd expected me to cry at the funeral, but like I said, I'd cut myself off from my emotions years ago. When Daniel died, the softer side of me died as well. And no one, not even my next husband, was able to change that, as much as he tried. I shook my head to clear the racing thoughts from my mind and descended several wooden steps to the beach.

The scenery was breathtaking. The lake's surface was glassy with a purplish hue, and the shallows mirrored the deep greens of surrounding evergreen trees. Wood ducks and geese floated near a rustic dock where the small boats Summer had mentioned were moored. A loon wailed mournfully in the misty distance.

I slipped off my sandals and pressed my toes into the cool sand before walking to the water's edge and wading in while holding my chambray skirt above my knees. The brisk chill of the lake refreshed me and awakened my senses as ripples of water around me lapped quietly to shore. I breathed deeply of the crisp, piney air.

After a moment, I turned, waded to shore, and put my sandals back on. Then I strolled along the beach and out to the end of the dock. A fisherman waved from a rowboat drifting serenely near a cottage on the side of the lake, and I waved back. I understood now why Summer wanted to live here in this peace and tranquility.

A sudden thump and then another trounced me from my reverie, and I grabbed a nearby metal pole attached to the dock in reflex. What in the world? Before I could continue my thought, a true marching band rendition of a Sousa song with a bass drum beat resonated through the forest. Oh, that's right. A music camp operated nearby. I looked toward the muted sound but saw only trees obscuring the property on the other side of Wild Blueberry

Bog. A few, solitary docks on the side of the lake could belong to a camp hidden in the woods.

Most of the geese and ducks had moved to the other side of the dock on which I stood. And as they seemed surprisingly undisturbed, the music must be a usual occurrence. Since the band sounded pretty good, I tapped my foot in time to the melody until it ended. Then I looked back toward the lake. The fisherman, somewhat to my dismay, had rowed his boat nearly to me. He looked over his shoulder.

"Hello," he called out in a familiar voice.

"Cam?" I replied, startled.

"Yeah, it's me." He pulled up to the dock and held on to the side, resting his oars on the boat. "Are you staying at Hidden Glen B&B here?"

He was as handsome as ever, although his fishing hat and gear gave him more of an outdoorsman appearance than he'd had when I met him. He fit right in with the surroundings.

"Yes. How nice to see you again," I said.

He had no idea how nice it was. Seeing someone, anyone, in this secluded wilderness helped cast my fears away, especially someone who knew nothing about me or my past. What a refreshing change from last night. I hoped my recent background would remain a secret around here for a while—at least until Cameron got to know me and vice versa. Forming a relationship under a cloud of suspicion, which Noble's crude assertion that I'd killed my husband made clear existed, at least with him, would be difficult. And I didn't want to deal with the consternation. But I did want Cam.

"Nice to see you, too," he said in reply.

I thought I should give him a heads-up on my impending visit to his residence. "I'm actually here visiting Summer Dixon.

She's an old roommate of mine," I began.

"Is that right?" he asked. "Maybe if you're free tonight, you can come to my mom's birthday party with her and her husband. I live in that cottage over there."

Cam pointed to a home nestled in the trees on a slight hill, and I nodded to affirm my recognition.

"We're having some of my mom's friends and my daughter Kasey's friends from the music camp over to celebrate. The camp's by the lakeshore there." He continued to point, but this time in the direction of the two solitary docks.

"I'd love to," I replied. He'd read my mind, which confirmed my hunch that we were simpatico. "Summer did mention something about that."

"Good. I'm not too musical myself, but I plan to hang around for the party anyway," he said. "I'm in it for the cake." He grinned in his irresistible manner.

I found it impossible not to grin back.

"Did you catch anything?" I asked, glancing at the empty hook on his fishing line.

"Not yet, but I usually reel in some good-sized trout in this lake. I'm staying out here for at least another hour. Do you want to join me?"

"Oh, I don't fish," I replied.

"Everybody fishes," Cam said. "You can learn in a snap. Hop in, and I'll show you. I have another pole you can use."

Was he serious? I'd never fished in my life. I paused to contemplate his offer.

"C'mon. You'll have fun."

"I suppose I could try," I said.

"Great. Let me help you in."

Cam took my arm and helped me climb into the boat,

and I sat in the front behind him. Just then, the band struck up another tune.

"Won't the music scare the fish away?" I asked.

"I hope not," Cam said, handing me a life jacket. "That's why I didn't use the motor."

"Oh, I didn't think of that."

"I don't think the band will practice much longer outside anyway. When I'm around in the morning, I usually only hear them for about half an hour during which time, I think, they're going over their choreography."

"Good to know," I said.

He pushed away from the dock and dipped the oars into the water. He turned the boat, and I turned to look behind me at the lake. With the rhythmic push and pull of his rowing, he guided the boat expertly sideways straight toward Wild Blueberry Bog.

"Where are we going?" I asked, startled at the trajectory.

"Don't worry. I'll take us farther out in the lake to fish. I just want to row by the peat bog for a moment. I thought I saw something in the woods."

"Something in the woods?" I asked, feeling a chill from his thinner tone of voice. I had walked through the woods near there moments ago. "Like what?"

"Not sure. That's why I want to take a look."

The music abruptly ended, leaving only the sound of the oars lightly splashing in the lake. The boat slowed as we neared the bog. Trees on shore grew closer together here, and the forest appeared dark and unwelcoming. Was the air colder, too? A few slimy-looking black logs marked the beginning of a wide, greenish brown expanse of muck and moss that was visible behind cattails swaying in the shallows.

"Do you see anything?" I asked, shivering and thinking

again about Summer's warning that people disappeared around here.

Cam stopped rowing and turned to look. He scanned the shoreline from our position parallel to land, then concentrated on the bog.

"No. I guess not," he said after a moment. "Darndest thing. I could have sworn something moved earlier. Kasey's taking lessons right next to here, so I wanted to check the area. Looks okay, though."

"What do you think you saw?" I asked. I recalled the creature I'd seen run across the road on my way to the B&B yesterday.

"Could have been a person. Some people say an older woman lives in the bog. But I don't know."

"An older woman?"

"Yes, but I don't put much stock in that. Rumors about Wild Blueberry Bog circulate constantly around Cove Pointe."

"What kind of rumors?" I asked. The woman in the bookstore in Blue Haven had said something similar.

"Nothing important. I probably saw an animal," he said, offhandedly. "Shall we catch some fish?"

I nodded and tacitly dropped the subject even though I was still curious. Cam turned away and started rowing again, and we headed toward deeper water. The boat glided seamlessly through the still lake, and I had a clear view of the shore from my seat. I looked up and down the beach, searching for what Cam may have seen.

Suddenly, I saw movement in the pines near the bog. It was a man. Or was it? I squinted and leaned forward. Noble. I sucked in a breath. That couldn't be him. I looked again. It was him. What was he doing there? Was he watching us? Why would he do that? He was supposed to be teaching at the music camp.

"Look," I said, raising my hand and pointing.

At the same time, Noble disappeared behind the trees.

"Did you say something?" Cam called over his shoulder while pulling on the oars.

Cam was facing away from me, but he also had a view of the shore. He obviously hadn't seen what I saw. I reconsidered telling him. I didn't want anything, especially Summer's husband, coming between Cam and me getting to know each other. And I certainly didn't want to explain my past with Noble or his odd behavior when I was around, and possibly cast a shadow on Summer's marriage.

Besides, Noble had every right to stand in the bog and the woods if he wanted to. And who would believe me, a stranger, saying how strange he was when he appeared to be such an upstanding member of this small, close-knit community—something I, unfortunately, had no experience with.

"No, nothing," I said. I folded my hands together in my lap to control their trembling.

Cam rowed us out to where he was fishing before, then rested the oars in the boat and grabbed a pole and a tackle box.

"Here. I'll start you out with a worm for bait. That's what I use. I like to keep things simple."

"Sounds right to me," I said. I had no idea, so I let him take charge.

"Here you go," he said after a moment. He handed me a fishing pole. "Drop your line in the water and wait. That's all there is to it."

"I can handle that," I said.

I relaxed a bit. Cam had a casual way about him that made me feel better. I accepted the pole, making sure to avoid contact with the worm, and tossed the line over the side.

"Wow. You look like you know what you're doing," Cam said.

"Story of my life," I answered, glancing over at him. "I pick things up quickly."

"I noticed," he said.

The sensuous smile he gave me this time made my pulse race. We fished for a while in quiet companionship. The band must have retired inside because no more music interrupted the morning.

"Have you lived here long?" I asked, eventually.

"About seven years," he said. "My wife passed on when Kasey was five, and we moved here then so my mom could help take care of her."

"I'm so sorry. That must have been hard for you. Was your wife unwell?"

He paused for a moment. "She died giving birth to our second child, who didn't make it, either," he said, softly.

"Oh, no. I don't know what to say," I said.

"Don't say anything," he said. "The past is the past. I'll always miss my wife and baby and love them, but Kasey and I have moved on with our lives."

"Yes. I can see that you have," I said.

Gazing at Cam's lonely, bereft expression, I felt a tug on my heart at a soul level I hadn't felt in a long time. Daniel had engendered that same feeling in me. He understood loneliness and grief, too, having tragically lost his family in a plane crash as a child and being the only one in his family to survive. Reality can change, he always said. And he was right.

But Daniel's reality was based only on universal truths like life and death and good and bad, whereas my reality was based also on perceptions people had about who I was—perceptions I couldn't refute because of my shaky identity and background. These vacillating perceptions often made people pull away and even leave. So my reality could change on a whim, in addition to real time, while his reality changed only in real time. The result was the same, though—overwhelming grief and loss.

"How about you?" he asked, after a moment. "What's your story?"

"I don't really have a story," I said, evasively. "I'm just passing by."

He grinned. "Passing by, huh? I hope you'll stop and stay a while."

I glanced over at him, feeling suddenly shy. "Thanks. I might do that," I said.

I looked away quickly, feeling my eyes well up with tears, something that hadn't happened in a very long time. I gazed out at the peaceful lake and eventually brushed my wet cheek with my fingers. Little did Cam know how much I hoped to stay awhile. That was the real story of my life. My life goals had always been simple and hadn't changed since I was a child. I only wanted to find a safe place to be and someone to love me. But people kept dying.

We fished a while longer, but didn't catch anything, which was probably because the bass drum had scared all the fish away, but I didn't say that. Cam took me back to the dock at Hidden Glen and dropped me off.

"See you tonight?" he asked, after helping me out of the boat.

"Yes. I'm looking forward to the party."

"Good. Me, too," he said. He pushed away from the dock. "We'll catch some fish next time," he said.

"Next time?"

"Sure. I'll come pick you up again when I have a day off." He paused. "That is, if you want me to."

"Alright," I said. Did he just ask me on a proverbial second date to see if I'd go out with him? I hoped so. "That'd be fun."

"Okay then."

He waved before rowing away. I waved back and walked down the dock to the beach. I turned and waved again, happy that he did, too, before walking to the wooden steps and heading back to the B&B.

Walking through the forest didn't take me long. I jogged more than walked to alleviate my qualms about possibly being the next one to disappear around this town. I entered through the side of the B&B and found Summer humming to herself while working in the kitchen.

"I'm back," I said. The screen door slammed behind me.

"Oh, good. You can help me with this new blueberry pie recipe I'm trying."

"I'd like that," I said.

"You can grab an extra apron from the pantry, if you want to," Summer said.

"Okay."

I didn't mention running into Cam or seeing her husband in the bog watching us. Was he keeping tabs on me, or maybe Cam? For some reason, I found it prudent to keep my whereabouts to myself. I didn't want anything getting back to Noble. He wouldn't have known for sure that I saw him, and I wanted to keep things that way. Sometimes, having a possible enemy think you were a friend was a better ploy than revealing your suspicions outright.

"How was the lake?" she asked when I returned to the kitchen, tying my apron.

"Beautiful, just like you said," I answered. "And very relaxing."

"I think so, too," Summer said. She grabbed a paring knife out of the drawer. "Here. You can use this to peel the apples."

I took the parer from her, and she closed the drawer.

"I'm glad I found an extra one since you're here," she said. "I misplace things like that in the kitchen sometimes, and I don't find them until weeks later. We'd have had to share. I'd probably lose my head if it wasn't attached to my neck."

I laughed at the odd analogy, which was just like Summer to say.

We spent the rest of the morning and into the afternoon baking pies that gave off a wonderful aroma, which we left to cool on a rack on the counter. Spending a few hours with her was just what I needed to help me feel normal again after Gill's death. Summer was one of the few people I could relax with, which was probably why she knew more about me than almost anyone else. That wasn't saying a lot, though. I didn't tell her much.

Not many people knew the real me or anything about my past because, for the most part, I didn't feel comfortable talking about myself. Who would want to know that no one ever wanted to adopt me or that I spent my formative years in foster care and never knew, or at least didn't remember much about my parents? I did, though, have a vague memory of a funny, bearded man who used to read me stories, who could have been my father, that I loved very much. Anyway, pretty boring stuff.

After sharing a light lunch with Summer, I went up to my room to return a call to my lawyer. Rhonda, Jay Morrison's legal secretary, answered the call and told me in no uncertain terms that Gill's children were contesting the will. I shouldn't have been surprised, but I was. I don't know why they harbored such ill will toward me.

According to Rhonda, Gill's kids wanted the house in Florida and also wanted to cut me out of most of the money Gill left me because we hadn't been married very long. But the short marriage wasn't my fault. And if Gill left me something, he only did so because he loved me, which meant to me that I deserved whatever the will said.

Rhonda said they'd get back to me about the will later, and Jay only wanted me to know what was going on. She took down my address at the B&B in case they needed to send me any documents to sign and asked me to keep my location up to date with them. Maybe things were beginning to move along. I hoped so. I thanked her politely and hung up, fuming.

What a crock. At least I wasn't still in Fenton City with those money-grubbing kids who—did I mention?—were actually older than I was and should know better than to scrabble over money. I could have wrung their necks.

I stayed in my room reading one of the novels I'd packed to bring with me until the front door banged shut. Noble must be home. Sure enough, a few minutes later, Summer called up the stairs to say we were leaving for Eleanor's birthday party in about half an hour. We were driving over in their car.

I placed the book on the nightstand and walked over to the dresser to pick out an outfit. Maybe I'd curl my hair, too. I had to look good, not only to raise my spirits, but also to make an impression on Cam. Hopefully, no one would recognize me from the publicity photos that circulated after Gill's death and possibly ruin my chances for romance. I'd been alone too long already, and I was looking forward to a very interesting and worthwhile evening.

CHAPTER 4

Driving to the party in the car was as awkward as I'd imagined, but at least I sat in the back behind Summer and away from Noble, who came close to totally ignoring me. What was I doing here? I should have left last night after the way he treated me. But then again, maybe he would settle down eventually, and I did want to stay in town to see what developed in a possible relationship with Cam, and also to reconnect with Summer.

I clenched my fists and refrained from saying anything to break the silence. If Summer asked me something, I'd answer, but that was all. And I certainly wasn't going to ask Noble why he had been watching Cam and me from Wild Blueberry Bog, even though I really wanted to know. He probably wouldn't admit to being out there anyway.

We parked down the way from a charming lake house, which was set back from an unpaved side road in a few trees with a scenic view of Cove Lake.

"Here we are," Summer said. "I hope we're not late. Did you see all the cars parked along the road?"

"I did," I said.

I opened the door and stepped out, handing Summer the wrapped present that had been on the seat next to me. A cool breeze blew in off the water, freshening the thick, earthy air that had probably drifted over from the bog on the other side of the music camp.

"I hope Eleanor likes this," Summer said. "I bought her a

pair of crystal candlesticks."

"What a nice gift," I said. "I'm sure she will."

Noble walked ahead of us down the road, continuing to not say anything.

"What do you think, dear?" Summer asked.

"Yeah, whatever," he said, grumpily.

Same old Noble. He never did appreciate the finer things in life, other than the interest in music we all shared. But, even though he'd been extremely irritating when we were a couple, I honestly didn't remember him being this moody unless I counted how he acted when we broke up, which I didn't. Break-ups made everybody crazy, didn't they?

We reached the cottage and, as we stood on the porch while Noble rang the doorbell, I glanced at his shoes. The tops and sides were greenish and mucky, which seemed appropriate for someone who'd been standing in a peat bog even if that was hours ago. When he abruptly turned in my direction, I raised my head, guiltily. He glared at me and wiped his shoes on the mat before facing the door again.

How was I supposed to mingle at a party with him sporting such a dour expression nearby? He'd probably scare people away from me. And that could be his intention if he thought I was a murderer. Did he really think that? I tapped my foot impatiently while we waited for someone to answer the door.

I'd hurt him once, but that was a long time ago. Didn't time heal all wounds? Maybe the saying only applied to certain people and not him. Or maybe that only applied to people who hadn't been essentially left at the altar by a jittery fiancée who changed her mind the night before the wedding and then married someone else a few months later. I plead guilty as charged.

Noble rang the doorbell again at Summer's request.

My only excuse for what I did is that I didn't know my future first husband felt the same way about me that I felt about him until the last minute, and I had to make a choice. I chose Daniel over Noble, who didn't take it well at all. But Daniel was dead now, anyway. And I'm not going to think about that right now.

I wish Daniel had turned out to love me as much as I loved him. But, like I said, in most relationships, one person is usually more in love than the other. With Daniel and me, I was that one person. With Noble and me, Noble was.

The door finally opened, and Cameron stood in the entranceway amidst a thrumming of upbeat music and the hum of a garrulous crowd. A little white dog ran out, wagging its tail.

"C'mere, Bobo," he said.

The dog ran back in again.

"Hello. Come on in," Cam said, heartily in greeting. "Sorry to make you wait. I was tending to our guests. Faron, you made it."

I felt myself blushing at the shoutout. I hadn't expected him to be so effusive when he saw me.

"Yes. I wouldn't miss it," I responded as I stepped over the threshold behind the Dixons.

Cam looked casually posh in gray chinos and a blue shirt, and my heart fluttered. Meanwhile, Noble turned and sneered at me again. What the heck? I ignored him this time. Turnabout is fair play.

"Oh, do you two know each other?" Summer asked, raising her eyebrows slightly.

I remembered I'd told her yesterday that we didn't."

"Yes. I picked her up on the beach," Cam said, laughing.

Summer's eyebrows stayed in their upward position.

"That didn't happen quite the way he makes it sound," I said, laughing, as well. "More like we ran into each other, and I couldn't say no. Well, no, that's not quite what I meant either."

Cam and I grinned at each other while Summer looked back and forth between us. "Okay. Whatever you say. Where's Eleanor? I want to say 'Happy Birthday.'"

"Over by the table with the appetizers," Cam said.

"Come on, Noble, let's go say 'hi, '" Summer said. She tilted her head and gave him a half nod.

He didn't seem pleased, but he went with her, leaving Cam and me alone together.

"I'm glad you're here. I'm kind of out of my element with all these music people here," he said.

He could have fooled me. In my opinion, his presence and charm made him a shoo-in to fit in anywhere.

"Actually, I'm a music person, too," I said. "But I feel a little out of place myself."

I didn't mention that I often felt like an outsider looking in at social gatherings and in groups. The detached feeling was something that was probably ingrained in me growing up. I never considered myself a true family member but only an extra child. At least that's the way I saw things.

"Well, we'll have to orbit this crowd together then," he said, lightly. "Are you a singer or something?"

"Not really. I play the flute."

"Oh, that's great," he said, nodding slowly. His beautiful, blue eyes began to glaze over.

"We don't have to talk about music, though," I said quickly. "We could talk about fishing if you want."

He perked up. "Okay. Like what?"

It was my turn to lose my concentration. "Um. I'm not sure

exactly." Darn. I wished I could have come up with something to hold his attention. But what did I know about fish?

"I'll tell you what, let me introduce you to my daughter."

He raised his hand and gestured. A few seconds later, a young girl with a braided, blonde ponytail and oversized, round glasses walked up to stand next to him.

"Did you want something, Dad?" she asked.

Her voice sounded very mature.

"I want to introduce you to someone. Kasey, this is Faron. Faron, Kasey."

"Very nice to meet you, I said.

"You, too," she said, matter-of-factly.

"Faron plays the flute, too," Cam said to her.

"Oh, you play?" I asked, surprised.

She nodded. "I take lessons from Mr. Kestin at the music camp. That's him over there. Mr. Kestin," she said loudly enough to be heard over the music.

A lanky, bespectacled man turned and waved at Kasey before excusing himself from the group he was in and coming over.

"Hi, Kasey, Cam," he said.

"I'm going to let you guys talk while I check on the cake and candles," Cam said. He looked at me. "See you later?"

I nodded. I hoped he'd come back soon. Kasey turned to Mr. Kestin.

"This is Faron. She plays the flute," she said.

"Do you? Are you pretty good? I could use someone to help tutor the kids at the camp," he said.

"Oh, well, I don't know if I'm that good. You can ask Summer Dixon. I'm staying with her for the rest of the summer." I hoped what I said was true. If things became unbearable at the

B&B, I might not stay. "I plan to, anyway," I added.

"Mr. Dixon is my music theory teacher," Kasey said. "He's really nice."

"Is he?" I asked. I was glad she thought so.

"Yes. And he composes songs on the piano."

"That's nice," I said. "I used to play with him and his wife, Summer, in a trio."

"How about that? They're such nice people. Are you still doing gigs?" Mr. Kestin asked.

"No, I'm free for a while."

"Well, then I won't take 'no' for an answer," he said. "You'll love teaching. Trust me. I'll run this by Eleanor, but since you know the Dixons, I'm sure this will be fine."

Did small towns operate so casually as a rule? Here I was in town for two days, and I already had a job offer, which was fine with me. Helping out at the music camp would be the perfect way to fill my free time during my stay in Cove Pointe.

"Alright then. We have a deal," I said.

"Good," Mr. Kestin said, smiling. "I'll call you at the B&B, if you'd like, and let you know when to start."

"Great."

"You'll be my teacher then, too," Kasey said.

"That will be fun," I answered.

The music stopped abruptly. A sudden chill ran up my arm, and I looked around. Noble was staring at me from the other side of the room by the stereo, which he seemed to have just turned off. Or was he staring at Mr. Kestin? It was hard to tell. I hoped he wouldn't put in a bad word for me if Eleanor asked for a reference. Somehow, I had a feeling he would, but Cam and Summer could probably counter that.

I put on what I imagined was a tough face and stared

back, hoping he would drop his eyes and lose our impromptu staring contest, but he didn't. Eventually, I looked away. Was my disgruntled ex-fiancé going to end up being even more of a problem than I thought? I'd have to wait and see.

"Hey, everybody. Can I have your attention, please?"

Cam stood next to a long table laden with food, tapping a crystal goblet with a fork to cause rhythmic chimes. The crowd slowly quieted.

"As you know, my mother, Eleanor, turned sixty this week, and I hope you'll all join in singing 'Happy Birthday' to her. Noble, would you do the honors?" Cam gave a slight wave.

A sprightly rendition of 'Happy Birthday' resonated throughout the room, and I looked over to see Noble playing the piano and smiling as though nothing was wrong, even though he only frowned when I was around him. The crowd joined in singing the tune to an attractive older woman with graying, short, brown hair and glasses on a chain around her neck. Eleanor, I presumed. She certainly had a lot of friends. When the song ended, everyone clapped and called for a speech.

"Well, I don't have a speech prepared," Eleanor said. "But I do want to thank you all for coming, and I hope everyone will line up for a slice of this wonderful-looking cake. And thank you, Cam and Kasey, for putting this all together."

Everyone clapped again, and a few people lined up in front of the table where she handed out plastic forks and paper plates, holding pieces of cake. One of the men in line handed his plate with cake to a beautiful, blonde woman standing behind him, and then glanced over at me. His eyes flickered as though in recognition before he looked quickly away. Did he know me? Did I know him? I think I would have remembered seeing someone with a long mustache like he had, but I didn't. Maybe he'd seen the publicity photos about Gill's murder. I decided to keep my distance from him just in case.

Cam walked over to me.

"How are you doing? You look like you're having fun," he said.

"Yes, I actually agreed to teach flute at the music camp," I said. "Mr. Kestin asked me to."

"Wow. That's wonderful. Sounds like you're fitting in around here," he said.

"I hope so. This seems like a nice town."

Luckily, no one else, other than possibly the man in line, seemed to have recognized me from the publicity photos—not yet, anyway. Maybe I could establish myself in this town and let my presence and brave attempts at sociable interactions squelch any possible rumors about me. I'd love to be part of a community, especially one that Cam belonged to.

"You know, they're having a campout at the music camp for the flute students next week," Cam said. "They sleep outside under the stars around a campfire. Kasey's excited about it because she likes anything to do with the outdoors and nature. She mentioned Summer was chaperoning, but they needed another chaperone. If you're interested, I'll let Eleanor know."

"Sure, I guess," I answered.

I might as well try going on a campout, although I couldn't help thinking of the local people who had disappeared in the past. But I supposed sleeping outside must be safe if the teachers at the music camp approved. Like fishing, I'd never been camping before, but as long as I was up north, I'd do as the others did.

I talked with Cam for a while until he was whisked away by his daughter, at which time Summer pulled me into a group. She introduced me to a few of her friends, so at least she had some, even though she'd said otherwise. We chatted until the outside light began to dim and the inside lamps were switched on.

"Oh, look at the time. We should go," Summer said. "I need to be home in case anyone stops by looking for a last-minute vacancy."

"Okay, sure," I said.

"Let me find my husband, and I'll be right back," she said.

As she walked away, I noticed Kasey pointing at me from her position behind the appetizer table. She stood next to Eleanor, who waved, having obviously been apprised of who I was. I smiled and waved back. Maybe this short interaction with her served as my reference for the flute teaching job since she was in charge of the music camp. I wouldn't be surprised, given the personable way people related around here.

I scanned the room for Cam, and when I saw him, I raised my hand to catch his eye. After he noticed me, I gestured toward the front door. Then I made my hand into a pretend phone and raised it next to my ear. "Call me," I mouthed, knowing he could look up the number of the B&B. He grinned and nodded. I hoped he would, and soon. I really wanted to get to know him better.

Kasey came back over while I was waiting, and we talked about her interests in biology and nature. She told me more about the bog and the forest than I'd ever imagined in a very short period of time. I wondered if Cam knew he had a burgeoning scholar on his hands, or at least a very smart girl.

The little, white dog who'd run in and out of the house when we first arrived scampered up to her, and she reached down to scratch his ears.

"This is my dog, Bobo," Kasey said.

"He's so cute," I said, petting his head.

"Yeah. He likes to go wherever I go," she said.

Summer returned with Noble, and I said goodbye to Kasey and told her I was looking forward to giving her flute tips, which I really was. I imagined she would pick up on things quickly. She said she was excited, too, and headed back toward her grandmother.

Summer, Noble, and I made a beeline out the door and out to the road. The clear night sky overhead sparkled as though sprinkled with the facets of a million stars. And a comet suddenly streaked across the sky, releasing its brilliant tail of shimmering dust. I gasped in amazement at the unexpected show. Living in the northern wilderness certainly had its perks.

Summer waited for me to catch up to her, and we walked down the road toward the car, staying behind Noble.

"Well, that was fun," Summer said. "I'm glad we came."

"I am, too. Did Eleanor like the candlesticks?" I asked.

"Oh, she said she'd open the presents later and call or write everyone. There were too many to open all at once. She seemed to enjoy herself. What a nice thing for Cam and Kasey to do."

"Yes, I agree," I said.

Cam seemed like a wonderful son, and his daughter followed in his footsteps in the courteous way she treated people. I enjoyed being around them. I slapped a mosquito on my arm and then another. Summer followed suit.

"Maybe we should make a run for it," she said, picking up the pace. "Mosquitos are out with a vengeance tonight."

We nearly raced each other to the car, which was parked near the forest, now that I took note of it, then hopped in as fast as possible. Noble started the engine. When he turned on the headlights, Summer unexpectedly screamed.

"What? What is it?" I asked, leaning forward quickly.

"A face. I saw a face in the woods staring at us. Did you see that, Noble? I think it was someone wearing a black hood."

"I didn't see anything," he answered. "Where?"

"Over there, between the two spruces. I don't see anyone now, though. Oh, my goodness. How startling," she continued, placing her hand on her heart. "Must have been someone from the music camp walking home and getting caught in the headlights or something. I'm sorry I overreacted."

"What scared you so much?" I asked.

"I'm not sure. The eyes, I think. They were black and deeply set in a pale, wizened face, and the expression was pure evil."

"Evil?" I asked, trembling. If Summer was scared, I was, too.

She glanced over her shoulder at me, and her eyes widened. "Oh, don't pay any attention to me. You look ashen. I'm sure there's no one evil at the music camp. I've been listening to too many ghost stories." She turned to Noble. "Let's go home."

He pressed the accelerator and pulled out onto the unpaved side road, which took us to the dirt road that led us out to the main road. I looked behind me out the back window, searching the dark woods for something, anything. I didn't know what. But nothing appeared in the forest that I could see.

I turned back around and took a deep breath. I glanced at Noble, who was driving silently. Could he be ignoring me again, or was my imagination running away with me? I sighed heavily before convincing myself that, if he was, I didn't care. But whatever Summer saw in the woods, better not follow us home. With my antagonizing ex-fiancé around, I was already dealing with more than I could handle, and one more thing might send me over the breaking point. Believe me, no one wanted that to happen, least of all me.

CHAPTER 5

I woke up groggy in the middle of the night, wondering where I was. You wouldn't think that would be the case, considering I usually had a pretty good sense of place and time, but I did. The glass of wine I accepted when we returned from the birthday party probably knocked me out, given that I don't often drink anything stronger than Coke.

What woke me, though? A sound? I leaned over on my elbow and glanced around the dark room, which was illuminated only slightly by the moonlight shining through the window. What was that noise? I listened for a moment. The doorknob jiggled. Someone was trying to get in.

"Who is it? Who's there?" I cried out, shakily.

Silence. The doorknob remained still.

"I said, 'Who's there?'"

No answer.

I sat up and turned the lamp on the nightstand on. My heart raced, and I took a deep breath. Could Noble have been trying the door? While I was sleeping? Summer would have had no reason to disturb my slumber. Kudos to me for locking myself in. I hadn't really expected to find my caution tested. I glanced nervously toward the window where a spidery tree branch swayed and scratched a pane in the wind. The branch wasn't what I'd heard. I looked back at the door.

What was I dealing with here? A jilted lover or an angry, albeit misdirected, justice seeker for my dead husband's murder?

I couldn't imagine Noble still had romantic intentions toward me. No. Something else drove him. Power over me, maybe? I didn't know exactly.

I slid out of bed and padded to the door. Not having the courage to open it, I knelt down and peered under the crack at the bottom. The hallway was dark and impenetrable. No shadow or anything else met my gaze. Whoever was there must be gone. I let out a breath before standing and walking to the bathroom, where I splashed cool water on my face.

I looked in the mirror after patting my skin dry. The pupils of my eyes were huge and dark. I looked terrified, which made sense because I was. Should I run after all and leave my hopes for moving on with my life and teaching flute at the music camp, as well as my romantic aspirations with Cam behind?

I mean, how bad could rattling around my lonely house at home really be? At least no one would try to get into my bedroom. Or would they? My husband's murderer was still at large, and someone could be coming after me. I sighed. I was trapped one way or the other. Maybe I should stay. At least I had Summer here on my side. The world might look rosier in the morning.

I shuffled back to the bed, climbed in, and sat there for a moment. Then I laid my head on the pillow and stared at the ceiling. The last time I'd felt this scared was when I'd found the yellowed newspaper clipping in the outside pocket of the purse of one of my foster mothers. My first name was written in pen at the top. The article was about a woman who shot her husband to death and then tried to kill her daughter and herself. But the police arrived in time to prevent a further tragedy. I wiped my clammy forehead with a corner of the sheet.

The same foster mother who had the article had told me once that I was cursed. Maybe she was right. What if the daughter in the article was me? If so, was the woman who killed her husband, a.k.a. my father, coming after me? And could my father's murder be the reason they put me in foster care in the first place? I always wondered. I still do. Maybe no one ever planned to adopt me because of my family history. Who would want someone with such a gruesome background? The story haunts me on nights when I can't sleep—nights like tonight was turning out to be.

But of course, Noble wasn't coming after me. I mean, we had been close once. Love doesn't completely disappear because of a fiery breakup, does it? Hmm. Maybe.

I remembered how devastated he had been when I gave him his engagement ring back and how he'd told Daniel I was only after his money and he'd live to regret marrying me. But he didn't. Daniel didn't live long enough to regret anything about me, least of all our marriage. Noble was wrong. I yawned. Time to stop thinking. I reached over, turned off the lamp, and decided to try to get some sleep.

I went downstairs late the next morning, determined to keep the incident the night before a secret until I could confront Noble alone and find out what was going on. I didn't want to cause a problem between him and Summer if I could avoid doing so, and basically accusing him of trying to break into my room last night might cause a problem. Summer was in the kitchen, which smelled like bacon, washing a frying pan.

"Good morning," she said when she saw me. "Wade Kestin called a little while ago. You've got the teaching job at the music camp. How did you manage that already?" She smiled at me.

"Oh, good," I said. "I don't know how I got the job so soon, but I'm looking forward to working there."

"He said to show up Monday afternoon at 1:00."

"I will," I said. "But now I have the whole weekend in front of me. I don't know what I'm going to do first."

"You could go into town and look around. Cove Pointe is very friendly and has some nice shops."

"Good idea," I said. "I might grab breakfast or brunch at a local restaurant and get a feel for the place."

"The Covewater Restaurant is a nice spot," Summer said. "They're known for their wonderful breakfast menu, although they're open all day." She picked up a dish towel and began drying off the pan.

"Sounds good," I said.

"Oh, and by the way, a nice, older couple showed up after you went to bed last night. They're staying here for a few days. I wanted you to know."

"Thanks for telling me," I said. "See you later."

I turned and headed for the front door. This was an interesting turn of events. Maybe Noble hadn't been the one to turn the doorknob last night. Perhaps someone else had tried to enter my room in error. I hoped so. I sighed with relief at the new possibility. Now I didn't have to confront him. But I would still keep an eye out. Where was he, anyway? I glanced around cautiously. For my own sense of safety, I'd rather have him around than not know where he was. I think. I hurried out the door.

My car still sat in the driveway. A white splat or two on the roof reminded me of the hazards of the otherwise lovely, silver-tinged seagulls squawking nearby. When I returned, I'd move the Lexus to the designated gravel area in the shade closer to the road, where another car, which probably belonged to the new guests, was parked. Maybe I'd attempt an impromptu car wash by hand, as well. I hopped in, backed out, and headed for town.

The sky was a clear, cerulean blue reminiscent of a painting by Monet, days up north by the lake were known for. I rolled the window down and breathed deeply of the crisp, cool morning air. Freedom. For the first time since Gill's death, I suddenly felt free of the oppressive memory of his murder, which had troubled my mind for months. Tooling down the road with the wind in my hair probably contributed to the unfettered feeling.

I passed the sign for Cove Pointe Music Camp and thought about my new job. I couldn't wait. Maybe later in the day, I'd clean my flute and practice a little bit to get ready to teach. I hoped teaching the flute wouldn't be that much harder than playing the instrument, but regardless, I was looking forward to meeting my new students and seeing how things went. For now, though, I needed to find out what Cove Pointe was really like.

Eventually, I reached the turn-off into town. After driving slowly down the main road past the busy establishments for a while, I noticed the sign for the Covewater Restaurant across from the harbor and pulled into the parking lot. The view of the harbor was beautiful, and I stood on the sidewalk in front of the restaurant and took in the sight for a moment before going inside.

Blue water, blue sky, and fluffy white clouds filled the scene along with a slew of activity as fishing boats and cabin cruisers headed in and out of their slips. The peaceful view soothed my jittery nerves, still frayed from last night's episode and also from Summer's earlier revelation at dinner my first night here about Cove Pointe's missing persons. What could have happened to them? A ferry pulled in and moored, and children got off and ran down the dock in front of their parents, waving to me. I smiled and waved back.

How could this lovely, small town encompass such a serene

and pleasant backdrop and yet hold such frightening secrets? What other untold things lurked behind the gilded frame of this seemingly innocent and picturesque community? A squawking seagull suddenly swooped down, startling me, and then soared away over the harbor. I turned and went inside.

The restaurant's interior decor was similar to a soda shop from the fifties. I walked past red vinyl seated booths and small tables and took a seat on a barstool in front of a long counter.

"What'll it be?" a man behind the counter wearing a mostly clean, white apron asked.

"I'd like a breakfast menu, please," I said.

"Sure," he replied. "But if you want my advice, I'd get the early bird platter we serve until noon—sausage, bacon, eggs, and choice of toast."

"My," I said, surprised at the offering. "I'm looking for something a bit lighter. Yogurt and a fruit cup with pancakes, maybe?"

"Best cakes in town. Blueberry okay? We're famous for those around here."

"Sure."

"Be right up," he replied. "We have some on the grill already. Coffee?"

"Tea, please. Oh, and a glass of orange juice."

"You got it."

He poured hot water into a cup and added a tea bag to the saucer before setting it in front of me.

"Thanks," I said.

I dipped the teabag in water and glanced around while waiting for my order. A man at a barstool down the way stared at me. I looked away quickly. But apparently not quickly enough. Someone tapped my shoulder moments later.

"Hey, aren't you that lady? The rich lady whose husband got murdered?"

I glanced over to see the grizzled-looking, older man who'd been staring at me leaning in right next to me.

"Could you please move away a little?" I asked. "You're crowding me."

"Huh? Yeah." He didn't move. "Do they know who stabbed him yet? Do they know who did it?" he asked.

"No, I'm afraid not," I replied as politely as I could. My worst fears had come true. Someone recognized me, and now I didn't know what to do.

"Oh, well, they'll find him. Don't worry, lady. They always get their man."

"Who does?" I asked. He sounded like he was narrating a television show.

"The coppers. They always get their man. Yessir."

"Okay, thank you. I'll remember that," I said. I hoped he'd go away if I was pleasant to him.

"Hey, Lenny, leave this nice lady alone and go sit down."

I breathed a sigh of relief when the man behind the counter showed up with my food.

"Yeah, alright, Rick." He turned back to me. "They'll catch him. You'll see," he added before walking back to his seat at the counter.

"Thank you," I said to Rick. "I didn't feel like chatting."

"Sure. Here's your stack of cakes, your juice, and your fruit and yogurt. Anything else I can get you?"

"No, thanks," I said.

He smiled and walked over to a customer sitting at the other end of the counter.

The fluffy pancakes with pure maple syrup were

marvelous, and I scarfed them down in between sips of cold, fresh-squeezed orange juice. If anything, they knew how to eat well in this town.

A folded newspaper on a stool next to me caught my eye, and I gingerly picked it up. *Cove Pointe Gazette,* the banner read. Tidbits of local news were sprinkled among columns written by the newspaper's editors. I was surprised to read quotes from Noble Dixon, a member of the local Chamber of Commerce, about future economic development as well as conservation plans in Cove Pointe and surrounding communities. Summer's husband appeared to be quite a prominent individual in the area, something I wasn't aware of. I hesitated before setting the paper back down on the stool. Why did this new information about Noble give me such a chill? I shivered and pulled the sides of my light cardigan closer together.

"Excuse me," a male voice said.

I turned, intending to make clear to the bothersome, staring man that I didn't wish to talk at the moment.

"Is this seat taken?" Cam asked, picking up the newspaper I'd just put down.

"What are you doing here?" I asked, surprised.

"I just stopped in for a cup of coffee before taking a charter boat out fishing. We're running a little late, so I had some time."

"Please sit down," I said.

"Thanks. Black coffee to go," he added to Rick, who nodded and grabbed a coffee pot.

"I had so much fun last night," I said. "Eleanor and Kasey both seem like wonderful people."

"They are," Cam said. "My mom mentioned that you're teaching flute next week at the music camp. Kasey's really excited about the prospect, as well."

"Oh, good," I said.

"And if you're interested in chaperoning the overnight next week, you're in. Wade Kestin and I are chaperoning the boys on their end of the camp, and Summer Dixon and you would be chaperoning the girls."

"Say no more. I'm more than happy to fill in," I said, smiling.

"Good. We'll have fun." Cam accepted the coffee from Rick and took a sip. He glanced at the newspaper he'd set on the counter. "Hmm. The county fair is coming up in a week or so. Ferris wheel, food trucks, oh, and a best pie contest. They have that every year," he said. "My mom won once. She's an excellent baker."

"How nice," I said. "Sounds like fun."

"It is," he said. "If you'd like to go, I'd be happy to take you."

I jumped at the chance. "That'd be wonderful," I said. "I've never been to a county fair."

"Well, there's a first time for everything," he said, grinning.

"Yes, of course," I said, smiling back. "Oh, before you go, I hope I might ask your advice about something."

"Sure. What about?" he asked.

"I hesitate to mention this, but since you're a lawyer, I wondered if you knew what to do when a will is contested. A house I own could be in jeopardy."

"Oh, man, I'm sorry to hear that," Cam said. "I'll tell you what. If you want me to represent you, I'd be more than happy to do so."

"I have a lawyer," I stammered. "I guess I just wanted a second opinion." Spending time alone with Cam was uppermost in my mind, but his legal expertise could come in handy, as well.

"Oh yeah? Well, a lot of variables could be involved, but I'll talk to him if you want."

"Would you? I hate to ask."

"No problem. No one as pretty as you should be harassed by the legal system."

I smiled and tried not to be obvious about how much his flattery meant to me. After all, I didn't want to seem too eager to connect with him and, in the process, scare him away.

"Whose will?" he asked.

"My deceased husband."

"Sorry to hear that. I didn't know."

"Yeah, thanks. His kids want the money and the house in Florida."

"Isn't that always the way?" Cam said. "I'm on your side, okay? And if you need a shoulder, I'm here. You have my number."

"Thank you for the thought," I said. He was so compassionate and didn't seem phased by my situation at all. I'd add these to my growing list of his attractive traits. "But I'm in pretty good shape right now." A boat horn honked. I turned and glanced out the front window. "Is your fishing boat leaving?"

"What? Oh, yeah, probably," Cam said. "I guess I better go. We'll talk later, okay? After I catch a monster trout."

I laughed. "Okay."

He raised his cup in salutation before walking through the restaurant and out the door. I was glad I'd talked to him. His generous offer of assistance in handling Gill's kids relieved my mind. And the fact that he'd offered at all gave me a warm feeling of acceptance and welcome in this town, which was quite different from the way Noble had made me feel.

I tried a few bites of the fruit cup before getting up,

walking to the register, and settling my bill with Rick. He wished me a good day as I turned to go. The gray-haired man who had come up to me turned around on his barstool and stared at me. I averted my gaze. I suppose I'd have to get used to running into people who knew who I was.

As I walked toward the door, I overheard two women in a booth whispering.

"That's her, alright," one of them said. "She looks just like her picture."

"That can't be her. She should be locked up. She obviously killed him. No one else was there."

Did they want me to hear them? If they didn't, they should have lowered their voices. I trembled in spite of myself. I'd thought I was above malicious gossip, but evidently not. Their vicious words hurt. Maybe my hopes of finding a safe place in this town were just wishful thinking. I gritted my teeth and continued on past them.

As I left the restaurant, I pulled my sunglasses out of my purse and slipped them on. With any luck, the tinted lenses would disguise my appearance and hopefully protect me from the sinister undercurrents that obviously flowed through this otherwise pleasant lake town. But when I got in my car, I decided against shopping and headed instead back to Hidden Glen B&B, where I could burrow in and keep out of sight for a while.

CHAPTER 6

I stepped over a moss-covered log obstructing the path in Wild Blueberry Bog on Monday afternoon on my way to Cove Pointe Music Camp. Summer had mentioned I could walk and not drive to the camp if I carefully followed the path marked with tiny yellow flags through the forest, then through and around the bog, and through the forest on the other side. I preferred to walk on such a beautiful, sunny day, not only for the exercise but to see what the bog was like. Plus, I had washed and chamoised my car yesterday, and I wanted to avoid driving on dirt roads and driveways and keep it clean for a while, if only to admire my handiwork.

"Twenty minutes tops," she said when I asked how long a trek I was in for. "And don't fall in or get stuck in the quagmire," she added, which I had no intention of doing.

The amount of time required to get there sounded reasonable, so I borrowed a pair of Summer's boots, of which she had several, shouldered my flute in its case in a crossbody tote, and headed off to teach.

I'd had a pretty relaxing weekend reading and hiding out at the Hidden Glen B&B to stay away from the gossipers in Cove Pointe. And Noble had kept his distance after finding out I would be teaching at the music camp. I couldn't help but think my new job was the reason he steered clear of me, because after Summer mentioned the fact to him at dinner Saturday night, he'd closed his eyes and sighed heavily. When he opened his eyes and looked in my direction, I nearly fainted from the glint of pure hatred in them. He obviously didn't want me working at the same place he did. I was still fazed from the incident even though he hadn't said or done anything upsetting since.

A small, grayish snake slithered by my foot after I cleared the log, and I stifled a scream, sidestepping quickly. We didn't have many snakes where I was from. But I stepped too far, and my foot plunged into the squishy mire. I sank forward, then threw myself back and grabbed the log, which expanded over the soggy area, for support. Luckily, the wood didn't crack, and the log stayed put.

I hung on desperately as I struggled to free my foot. But it wouldn't budge. I tried again while realigning my tote to keep my flute safe. My foot moved a little, but the muck wouldn't release its grip. What was this stuff?

Taking a deep breath and holding firmly onto the log, I garnered my strength, braced myself, and yanked my thigh up with my other hand. My foot popped free. But the boot was gone. I looked more closely at the spot, hoping to secure the boot, but it seemed to have completely disappeared.

After a moment, I crawled a few feet to the path and sat there taking stock of my situation. The shaded area I was in was under one of several copses of trees sprinkled around the area, some of which appeared shadier and more menacing than where I was. The ground and grasses around me were greener than other areas of the bog, which probably meant this area was wetter and perhaps more prone to sinking into. I wished I'd noticed the color change before, but then again, taking more precautions wouldn't have prevented the snake from winding around near my foot and scaring me off the path.

I brushed sweat off my forehead with the back of my hand

before realizing my fingers were muddy. I must be quite a sight. My only future option seemed to be to negotiate the rest of the way with one boot on and one boot off as best I could. I stood in resignation and headed awkwardly for the forest on the other side of the bog. Summer was right to warn me about getting stuck in the quagmire. Luckily, I seemed to have escaped unharmed.

I scanned the wide expanse of wetlands, which seemed to extend partially into the woods as well, before starting on my way again. Wild Blueberry Bog, I had found out from Kasey, was made up of peat moss, mostly lying underwater, which had developed from decayed plant material, and sphagnum moss, a kind of spongy, greenish matter on the surface that bounced if stepped on. Obviously, the possibility of being sucked into the muck and morass if I stepped off the path also existed, considering what I had just been through. But I wasn't going to dwell in negativity. Like I said, stewing about something I couldn't do anything about wasn't my forte. I forged ahead.

A chubby snowshoe hare whose nest I seemed to have disturbed when I passed by a bush hopped across the path in front of me, followed by an agitated dragonfly that hung suspended and iridescently splendid in mid-air for a moment before darting off again. The spasmodic movements reminded me of my life. I was hanging in the air in the same way while waiting for the right moment to dart away.

The bog was more humid than the cooler shade of the forest, and whiny mosquitoes skimmed my ears and arms. I determined I probably wouldn't walk through here again except to return home, although the pink orchids and water lilies that dotted the landscape, along with a few bushes and trees, were lovely. I hurried forward toward the beckoning, shaded depths of the woods in front of me. I wanted to cool off, and I also didn't want to be late for my first day of work.

After finally reaching the more solid ground and protective canopy of the forest, I slowed my pace and continued following the yellow flags until I eventually reached the outskirts of the music camp. My socked foot was soaked and muddy, and I hoped to borrow a dry pair of socks from someone and maybe a pair of shoes, too. I wish I'd thought to be more prepared, but at least I had my flute with me.

A large building reminiscent of a long, log cabin loomed ahead of me. I stomped and shuffled forward until I reached the door, which I pulled open. I stepped inside. Argh. Noble stood in front of me, blocking my entrance.

"Well, well. Look what the cat dragged in, literally," he said, sneering.

"Oh my gosh. Can we not do this?" I asked, shuffling past him. At least he didn't stop me.

"Not do what?" he asked.

Before he could continue, Wade Kestin walked around the corner and raised his hand in greeting. I had seldom been so happy to see someone.

"What happened to you?" he asked, walking over to me. "You didn't come through the bog, did you?"

I nodded bashfully.

"Oh my goodness. You fell in, didn't you?"

"Something like that," I answered. "You wouldn't have a dry pair of socks lying around, would you?" I ignored Noble, who was snorting with laughter and acting like a juvenile.

"I'm sure we can get you fixed up," Wade said, solicitously. "Come with me. Our first class doesn't start for another fifteen minutes, so we have some time to make you presentable."

How bad did I look? I was about to ask him out loud, but

the pitying look he gave me said volumes. I followed him through the front room, which was filled with tables and benches. They'd obviously just finished lunch because the room smelled like pizza, and aproned teenagers were washing dishes in the kitchen behind an open area in the wall.

Wade led me to a hallway in the back where he pointed to the restrooms and said he'd be back with socks and an extra pair of majorette boots, which the baton twirlers wore when practicing for marching band. I hoped they'd fit someone who'd been out of high school for longer than I cared to mention. But beggars can't be choosers, as they say.

After washing up and removing the streak of mud from my forehead, I headed back out and found Wade sitting at a table in the front room. Noble wasn't anywhere around, much to my relief.

"You look better," Wade said, handing me the boots.

"Thanks. I feel that way," I replied as I set my tote down on the table.

"Is that your flute?" he asked.

I nodded. "Luckily, I didn't lose it in the bog."

"What make?"

"I have a Pearl."

"Oh, they have some nice ones. I'm looking forward to hearing you play."

I sat across from him and pulled on the white, embroidered boots that sported leather fringe at the top. They fit, albeit snugly. But they looked kind of silly with my jeans. Summer had mentioned that everyone at the camp wore jeans, which, from what I'd seen so far, seemed to be the case.

"What do you think?" I asked Wade, standing and showing him my new footwear.

"Perfect. The kids will love them," he said, smiling. "Would you like to meet your students?"

"Sure."

We walked down the hallway to the back, where we entered the middle room in a line of rooms with windowed doors. About ten students of varying ages sat around in wooden chairs behind music stands, practicing scales and talking. They looked over when we walked in.

"Hi kids," Wade said. "I'd like you to meet your new tutor, Mrs. Chevalier."

"Hello," I said to the class when he paused and turned to me.

A group "hello" resonated back to me. Kasey, who sat in a chair on the far end of the row, waved and smiled, which prompted me to smile in return. Seeing a student I recognized made the class seem less daunting.

"Mrs. Chevalier will be helping out in the class and working individually with those who would like extra attention on the more difficult passages. I know we've taken on some challenging music this year. Shall we get started?"

Everyone nodded and agreed.

"Take out the first score in your folders, and we'll work on the arpeggios in the coda."

I walked over to a nearby desk while they played and set my things down. Surprisingly, the butterflies I'd had in my stomach the night before while thinking about teaching didn't return, probably because of the welcoming atmosphere. After removing my flute from the tote and case and putting it together, I stood and faced the students. I was ready to go. Just then, they finished the piece.

"Would you like to play something for us?" Wade asked.

"How about an Irish tune?" I asked.

When he nodded, I played "Danny Boy" for them to a rousing round of applause when I finished.

"Well, I guess we know a good flute player and teacher when we hear one. Right, kids?"

They all agreed and shouted compliments.

"That's one of my wife's favorite songs," Wade said, "and you play the tune beautifully."

"Thank you all very much," I said.

My cheeks warmed at the all-around praise. Although I had practiced on and off, I hadn't played in front of people since I was in the trio in college with Summer and Noble. I was glad to see I hadn't lost my touch. And tutoring didn't seem so implausible after the way the students reacted to my rendition. Maybe I'd found my calling. I couldn't wait to start teaching.

We spent the next few hours working on various pieces, and I helped individual students with different parts they had trouble with. Kasey picked up very quickly on a pointer I gave her, which I had imagined she would, given how bright she was. By the end of the class, I felt like I'd accomplished something significant, and I was also feeling more at home than I had in a long time. I actually felt like I fit in.

"Okay, everyone. Class is over. You did well," Wade told everyone. "See you tomorrow." He looked at me. "Tomorrow. Same time."

I nodded, then walked to the desk and packed up my flute while the kids did the same. Wade came over and handed me a key to the lodge in case I was late sometime or ever locked out, that I had to return at the end of the summer. He also mentioned that if I needed to get in sometime without my key, one was under the mat at the back kitchen door, but to keep that to myself. I said

I would, and I'm glad that he trusted me enough to tell me that. As I was turning to leave, Kasey came up to me.

"That was so fun," she said. "I'm glad you're my new tutor."

"I am, too," I said.

We walked out together after waving goodbye to Wade, who gave me a thumbs up and headed toward the front. I planned to call Summer after I walked Kasey to the door to see if she'd pick me up. Kids with a variety of instruments in cases milled about in the front room, talking as they waited for their parents to pick them up. I glanced around warily, searching for Noble, but luckily, he was nowhere in sight. Cam walked in just as we neared the door.

"Hi, Faron. Did you start teaching today already?" he asked.

I nodded.

"How did things go?"

"Great," I replied. "You have quite a good student here." I smiled at Kasey.

"That's nice to know," he said. "I came to pick her up."

I noticed him eyeing my majorette boots.

"Oh, I had a mishap in the bog while walking over here and had to borrow clean boots. I'm wearing these to keep from going barefoot."

"Well, those are quite a fashionable look for you," he said, grinning.

Amusement flickered in his gorgeous, blue eyes, and I warmed to the teasing tone in his voice.

"Yes, I'm quite stylish, aren't I?" I replied, in kind. I put my hand on my hip and struck a cover girl pose.

"Perfect," he said.

We both laughed along with Kasey.

"Can I give you a ride home?"

His handsome face, bronzed by the sun, crinkled into a charming grin. How could I say no?

"That would be fantastic," I said. "I was going to call Summer to come and get me because the last thing I want to do right now is walk home through the bog. I'd have to go barefoot to keep these nice boots from getting dirty."

"Oh, you definitely can't walk barefoot through there," Cam said, shaking his head. His expression became more serious. "C'mon. I'm parked at the curb. Let's go, Kasey."

We all walked out together and got in Cam's black pickup truck. Noble was talking to a man in a car parked behind Cam's truck, and for a moment, I thought he was going to come over, but luckily, he stayed put. I'd see him at dinner tonight anyway, whether I wanted to or not.

After Cam pulled away from the curb and headed down the driveway, I slipped off the boots, which had become quite snug, and leaned back. I'd have to remember to bring them back tomorrow when I drove to the music camp. Kasey had jumped in the back seat, so I was sitting next to Cam in the front.

"By the way, the campout is Friday night. Are you still planning to chaperone?" Cam asked, after we'd driven down the road for a while.

"Yes, and Summer is, too."

"Yay," Kasey said. "This will be fun. Did you find your sleeping bag, Dad?"

"Yes. I'm all set. I put yours with mine near the back door, so we're ready to go when we need to. How about you, Faron? Do you have one?"

"Yes. Summer has an extra one I'm borrowing. That is, if

she'll trust me to borrow something else. I lost one of her boots in the bog."

"Oh, no."

"Yeah. The muck swallowed it whole."

"You do have to be careful in the bog," Cam said, solemnly. "If you lose your footing in some of the deeper areas, getting out can be a problem."

"So I noticed," I said.

"Really? Were you trapped in the quagmire?" he asked quickly.

"Not trapped so much as stuck," I said. "I pulled my foot out eventually."

"Well. I'm glad you're okay," he said, sounding concerned.

I glanced over at him. He was looking at the road, but his jaw was clenched in such a way that I realized that he really was concerned. The bog was obviously more dangerous than I'd thought. I made a note to avoid it when I could from now on. What if I got sucked under and couldn't pull myself back out? But I didn't mind the fact that Cam seemed worried about me. Maybe his solicitude meant he liked me. I scoffed to myself. Now I really sounded like I was back in high school.

After a few more minutes, Cam pulled into the gravel driveway at the B&B.

"We're here," he announced.

"Great. Thanks," I said, picking up the boots and exiting the truck.

Kasey hopped out and hopped back in in the front seat, closing the door behind her.

"Bye, Cam. See you tomorrow, Kasey."

I waved and walked around the front of the truck to the porch steps. I turned and waved again when Cam honked on his way out. Then I walked up the steps thinking about how nice Cam was and Kasey, too, and what a wonderful day I'd had at the music camp despite running into Noble. And I began to feel hopeful again that with a few tweaks and adjustments to whom I spent time with, the places I lived in, and the establishments I frequented, I may have found a safe haven in Cove Pointe.

CHAPTER 7

The first thing I thought of when I headed out to my car on Friday was that my first week of teaching at the music camp had gone pretty well. I was as surprised as anyone that the end of the week had crept up on us so soon. I couldn't remember the last time I'd had so much fun and felt so much a part of a community.

Chaperoning for the campout, which was beginning shortly with a cookout for dinner, was next on my list after I retrieved my overnight gear from my car.

After strolling through the gravel parking area and reaching the Lexus, I placed my case with the flute in the trunk. Then I grabbed the sleeping bag and overnight bag I had brought with me when I drove over this afternoon to teach and walked back toward the lodge.

I was actually quite relieved that I didn't have to spend the night at Hidden Glen B&B. Noble was staying there to take care of the new guests, who were a nice couple from Ohio in town on vacation, while Summer chaperoned the overnight with me. The couple hadn't appeared to know who I was, and I didn't want to press my luck by being around them much. I only saw them at dinner during the week, along with Noble, who I tried to avoid at other times and at the music camp.

When I got back to the lodge, I dropped my bags with other gear near the door and headed out back to a cookout area overlooking the lake. Cam was flipping hamburgers on a grill while campers, along with Summer and Wade, played volleyball in a sandy area set up with a net nearby. Volleyball seemed to be the sport of choice in the area, given that Cam had mentioned playing beach volleyball when I first met him.

Cam looked good in his faded jeans and navy polo shirt that stretched tight over his broad back and shoulders. He wore scuffed docksiders with no socks, which made him seem like he was about to jump into a sailboat. I'd hop in with him if he asked, but I settled for walking over to talk to him.

"You look like quite the chef," I said, sidling up next to him but careful not to get too close. I didn't want to interfere with his grilling.

"Thanks. I try," he said, smiling. "What'll it be? As long as you're here, I can cook yours to order."

"Oh, you mean how do I like my hamburger done?" I asked.

"Yeah. I'd peg you for a medium well."

"Not exactly," I replied. "Medium rare."

"Oh, well, I'm glad I asked. I have one ready for you right now, then. Grab a plate."

"Okay, sure. I'll be right back."

"Anyone else for medium rare? They're ready," Cam called out.

A few kids sitting nearby stood and followed me to a picnic table set up with plates and silverware, where we grabbed plates and headed back to the grill.

I ate with the campers at another picnic table, surprised at how wonderful the freshly grilled hamburger tasted. Cam was definitely a good cook. Kasey and several more campers joined us eventually, including those who'd played volleyball, followed by Noble, Wade, and Summer, who all seemed to like their burgers done medium well. We talked and laughed and finished the meal with a delectable blueberry cobbler made by the camp cook and left on the stovetop in the lodge's kitchen for us to scavenge.

After dinner, everyone grabbed their campout gear by the front door and walked down to their respective campsites. The boys were on one end of the music camp property with Cam and Wade as chaperones, and the girls were on the other side with Summer and me chaperoning.

Building a campfire was a new experience for me, and I searched for sticks and downed branches in the cool woods along with the campers until we had gathered quite a pile of kindling and small logs. We placed the wood in the center of a circle of stones and unrolled our sleeping bags around it a few yards away.

I went back into the woods by myself to grab a few more sticks to make sure we had enough for the night. I thought of the boot I lost, which Summer had been gracious about when I told her of the incident, and decided to try to find it. After all, she'd let me borrow her sleeping bag, despite my losing her boot, and I wanted to repay her kindness and prove my trustworthiness.

I walked for a while to the other edge of the forest and stepped into the bog, which was still as wet as it had been before. Daylight was dimming but still bright enough for my purposes, and I found the path I'd been on before and walked down it. After several yards, I realized I'd made a mistake when I was attacked by a swarm of black flies. Screeching and waving my arms, I ran back toward the forest, but my shoes got stuck in the spongy moss. I had to slip them off and yank them out a few times, all the while slapping flies.

A beaver unexpectedly ran in front of me, and I fell back a bit in surprise. But I regained my footing quickly and ran the rest of the way. Luckily, I could still see in the dimming twilight and was able to stay on the path. Reaching the forest was a welcome relief, and, as the black flies didn't follow me out of the bog, I slowed my pace on my way back to the campout.

Summer and the campers didn't seem to have missed me, and I added the few sticks I'd picked up on my way out of the woods to the pile of wood in the center of the fire pit. Then I put on my jacket and sprayed myself with mosquito repellent. I sat in a circle around the fire pit with Summer and the campers. For the next half hour, we talked and sang songs.

When the light had faded into dark, we lit the fire, and when the flames were high enough, toasted marshmallows on sticks until they were brown and gooey. The fire was so warm I took my jacket off again.

We placed the marshmallows between graham crackers with milk chocolate squares and made them into s'mores, which we all ate messily in between bouts of laughter. I couldn't remember the last time I'd had so much fun.

The air became chillier as the night progressed, and eventually, most of the campers climbed into their sleeping bags and stared at the flames. I sat on a log with Summer away from the fire.

The deepening night was alive with the somnolent music of the wetlands and the forest. Crickets trilled rhythmically to the light rustling of leaves in the trees, keeping time with the soft percussion of katydids and the occasional croak of a frog. I listened, enchanted.

"Tell us a story," Kasey said after a while. "Campouts are the best with ghost stories."

"Hmm. I don't remember any ghost stories," I said. I was sure I must have heard one or two sometime, but they didn't come to mind.

"Maybe I could think of one," Summer said. "Let me see."

She placed her elbow on her knee and leaned forward to put her chin in her upturned hand. She maintained the pose and closed her eyes, appearing to be lost in thought. I imagined she was thinking of a story. Suddenly, she sat up straight.

"Shh. I heard something," she said. Summer looked behind her at the dark woods.

"I don't hear anything," I whispered. I peered behind me at the forest, as well.

"Look," she said, pointing.

A murky shadow edged along the tree line.

"What is that?" I asked.

A twig snapped.

"The bog people," she said, in a loud whisper.

"What?" I leaned toward her.

"The bog people," she said again. "The bog is right on the other side of these trees."

"What are those?" asked a voice near the campfire.

The girls remained huddled in their sleeping bags around the flickering flames.

"Dead people who rise out of the bog at night and search for unsuspecting victims."

"Dead people?" the voice continued.

"Victims?" another voice rasped.

"Yes. Many bog people are thought to have been murdered or left for dead in the bog long ago, never to be seen again. Their bodies are perfectly preserved in the acidic quagmire. They arise when the moon is full to seek retribution on those who killed them or left them there."

"How terrifying," I said. "Is this for real?"

Of course, she must be only telling a story. Ghost stories

and the like were known for being told around campfires. But she sounded serious. And I was quite mystical and prone to believing stories from the other side, even though I tried to be sensible and logical most of the time.

"So I hear," Summer answered.

"Well then, what should we do? Should we run or fight them or something?" I peered into the woods again, but I didn't see anything.

"No. The campfire will keep them at bay."

"Are you sure?"

"Yes. They're afraid of fire."

Something scurried behind me through the underbrush. I screamed and twisted around to look. Nothing.

"You're okay," Summer said, patting my arm. "We have the campfire. They're hiding from the flames in the woods."

"That doesn't make me feel much safer," I said.

"What do they do when they find them?" the first voice asked.

"Who?" Summer asked.

"The victims."

"No one knows. Take them with them, maybe, to die in the bog and turn into bog people themselves."

A collective gasp rose from the group.

"And when the bog people roam, the howling begins," Summer continued, mysteriously. "Or so they say."

"The howling?"

"Yes. Some believe wolves come out and howl at the full moon at night, but some think the bog people do."

"Are there wolves around here?" I asked, horrified by the thought of both wolves and bog people hovering about.

"Wolves do live in the forest, but they won't come close to

the fire or the music camp."

"If you say so," I said.

I glanced around again and then up at the moon glowing hazily behind wisps of clouds in the night sky. Another unnerving possibility entered my racing mind, probably because of what I'd been through in the past and my ongoing fear that whoever killed my father would someday hunt me down and kill me, too.

What if a murderer lurked in the woods waiting for me? You never knew if someone, perhaps someone you least expected, could turn on you. The newspaper article I'd found as a child, which was probably about my father's murder, had convinced me of that. I scooched closer to the fire.

"How do the bog people know who their killers are?" a thin voice asked.

"They don't. They could think it's anybody."

"Oh my gosh," I said. "Are you saying they could come after us?"

"I hope not," Summer said.

I shivered and tried to come up with another explanation for the shadow we'd seen. Maybe Noble had returned in the middle of the night to play a prank. He could do something like that. An owl hooted dolefully in the distance, and I jerked sideways in spite of myself at the unexpected noise. I was even more on edge than I thought.

"Are you sure you're seeing the bog people tonight and not nocturnal animals?" I asked, diplomatically leaving out any reference to her husband.

"No. But if there's a chance I'm right, I want you and everyone else to know the story."

"Okay. Go on."

"Remember, I told you that people in Cove Pointe have

disappeared?"

I nodded.

"They disappear especially around the time of the Thunder Moon, which is the full moon we see tonight."

She looked up, and I followed her gaze. The wisps of clouds floated sideways, revealing more of the moon than had been previously visible. The Thunder Moon threw a silvery glow across the sky and onto the tips of the tree boughs, casting a soft light into the eerie darkness of the forest. But still, no moving presence was visible.

"The missing persons are rumored to have become lost in the bog and perhaps buried there by the bog people."

I gasped.

Summer paused, but no one said anything. They were probably shocked into silence like I was. I shivered again and grabbed my jacket, which was tacky and smelled strongly of the mosquito repellent I'd been liberal with earlier in the evening. Unfortunately, I hadn't worn my jacket when I went into the bog, which several itchy bites on my arm attested to. The campfire crackled and snapped, breaking the still hush of the night.

"What do they look like?" I asked as I pulled up the jacket zipper.

"The bog people?"

"Yes."

"Local lore has it their skin is stained brown from the tannin in the bog, and their hair is stringy and red. They smell dank and rancid, and bits of mud and peat drip from their leathery, wrinkled bodies."

Somebody groaned.

"How awful," I said. "But you've never actually seen them up close?"

"No. Thank goodness. The bog is very large with many places to hide or become lost, especially in the dark. However…"

"'However' what?" I asked, quickly. What if the story was true and not folklore?

Summer looked over her shoulder, then back. "I've glimpsed a strange, hunched-over figure in the bog a few times, but I've never met her. She could be a living bog person. Others who've sighted her call her the bog witch.'"

"Do you think the bog witch is here now?" a frightened voice asked.

"I don't know," she answered.

I rubbed my arms to smooth out the goosebumps that had popped up in spite of the jacket I'd donned, then leaned toward Summer.

"Can we keep the rest of this conversation to ourselves?" I asked.

"Alright. Why?" she asked, lowering her voice.

"I don't want everyone to hear this."

I not only wanted to keep what I told her next a secret, but I also didn't want the kids to be scared any further. She leaned in next to me.

"Remember when you saw someone staring at us from the woods at Eleanor Talbert's birthday?" I whispered. "Could that have been the bog witch?"

I waited for her answer with bated breath. I hoped she hadn't actually seen the possible murderer my mind had conjured up.

Summer looked at me. "I hadn't thought of that. Maybe."

I trembled, unsure if her seeing a bog witch was better than seeing a murderer. Both were scary. Then I remembered the frightening creature I'd almost run over when I first got here.

"I wonder if the bog witch ran across the road in front of me in the rain when I first drove up here. Remember, I told you I almost hit an odd-looking creature? Maybe she was wearing a black, rain cape or poncho that disguised her appearance."

"I hadn't thought of that either. Could be," Summer said.

We sat together, pondering, while the flames danced and glimmered in the night. As time wore on and no more sounds emanated from the woods, the campers drifted off to sleep one by one. I was still frightened, but Summer appeared calm. Eventually, she said goodnight and walked over and climbed into her sleeping bag. I sat up alone listening to the far-off croak of a bullfrog and the resumed trilling of crickets whose presence gave me hope that the bog people were gone.

When my eyelids began to get heavy, I stoked the fire one more time with a stick before unzipping my sleeping bag and slipping inside with my jacket still on. I placed a spare stick by my side to use as a weapon if I needed to. Then I zipped up my sleeping bag, laid my head on my pillow, and closed my eyes to try to get some sleep.

Later, I jolted awake in the thick darkness. I heard something. What was it? I poked my head out of my sleeping bag and grabbed my stick. Then I sat up straight, wielding my makeshift weapon in front of me.

"Who's there?"

The campfire had turned to glowing embers. Where were the leaping flames that kept the bog people and wolves away? I whipped around at another noise.

"Faron, don't worry, it's me."

Cam stood on the outskirts of the fire circle with a flashlight. His face was barely visible in the low light, but something about his taut body language bothered me.

"What's going on?" I asked.

"Wade's gone," he said. "He disappeared after the cookout and never returned."

"What's wrong?" Summer called out in a whisper from her sleeping bag.

"Wade's missing," I said.

"What?"

Cam continued. "He got a call from his wife after dinner and left our group at the boys' campfire, and when he didn't return by sunset, I figured he went home for some reason. I'm okay with chaperoning alone, but I just went to the lodge to use the facilities and noticed his car is still in the parking lot, which means he's still here somewhere. And did you hear the wolves just now?"

"Wolves?"

"They're howling in the distance, and I'm concerned about Wade now."

"Oh, my gosh," I said.

I gripped my stick tightly despite the fact that now it didn't seem to be enough to protect me or anyone else.

"I only made a detour over here to let you know. I have to get back to my campers," he said.

"Maybe we should all move into the lodge," Summer said. "Just to be safe."

"Good idea," I said.

"I agree," Cam said. "I'll see you in there with my campers. I may go out and search for Wade later if he doesn't show up."

He turned and walked away quickly.

I stood and called out to the campers to wake them, then told them what was going on. We all rolled up our sleeping bags and headed back to the lodge after Summer poured water on the fire. The boys showed up in the lodge with Cam soon after we did.

The campers slept on the floor in the lodge for the rest of the night. Cam, Summer, and I stayed awake, but since none of us knew Wade's cell phone number or home number, we couldn't call him or his wife. Cam left to make a cursory check of the grounds with his flashlight. Summer and I drank hot tea and ate crackers we found in the kitchen pantry until Cam returned, having had no luck. We decided to call the police.

As the first rays of the sun shone through the lodge windows, we told the police Wade Kestin was missing. Little did I know how that simple statement would change the future trajectory of my life.

CHAPTER 8

Mason Snyder sat in a parallel parking spot in his dark blue sedan, stuffing a sandwich from the local deli in his mouth and watching fishing boats in the harbor at Cove Pointe. He'd spent most of Monday afternoon driving north after being alerted by an informant, who was in reality a P.I. friend of his with a cottage on Cove Lake, to a missing person's report filed in the town over the weekend. The info had punched him straight in the gut. Faron Chevalier had messed up big time if she thought she'd get away with another murder by changing venues. Cove Pointe wasn't that far away from his home base in Fenton City, where she was from, and he was hot on her trail.

She'd killed them, alright. There was no doubt in his mind that the men she hooked up with didn't stand a chance of staying alive. He didn't know what the statistics were for having three husbands in a row tragically die, but he was for darn sure the probability was pretty low. And who knew how many other men she'd knocked off. Gill Chevalier, her third husband, probably never saw it coming.

Mason turned on the car and the radio to listen to music while he ate, but he couldn't get a good signal. He finally found the local news and listened to hog futures and a weather report that predicted highs in the seventies and eighties for the rest of the week. A county fair was coming to the area soon, as well. When the station went to ads, he turned the dial again but couldn't get a signal except for a die-hard country music station. So he shut the radio and the car back off.

Faron's second husband, Bryce Landon, whom she'd married only months after her first husband died, had barely lasted through the honeymoon. He'd been found unresponsive in bed two days after they returned home, probably smothered with a pillow, and died soon after.

Friends of her second husband, who had also been a wealthy chump, said he complained that she talked about her first husband, Daniel, all the time and didn't love him. They said she was cold. Mason would add 'and calculating' to that description. How was it possible that such an obvious gold digger had escaped justice then and now? Looks, maybe. But her lucky streak wasn't going to last—not if he had anything to say.

Mason sucked his Coke hard through a straw to wash his bite of the sandwich down and flinched when the cold drink sprayed out the side and doused his shirt. Shoot. It would probably leave a stain. At least his ex-wife, Sandy, wasn't around anymore to scold him about making more work for the laundry. He could spill as much stuff as he wanted to now.

He dabbed at the expanding spot above his significant paunch with a napkin to no avail. Luckily, he wouldn't have to fend off comments from Sandy about how he should be working out more, either. Or about how he should comb his hair and change his clothes once in a while, so he didn't always look like he just got out of bed. Who could put up with a wife who said things like that? So what if his hair was messy and longer than she liked. At least it was still brown and not graying at the temples like Joey's. He had that going for him, anyway.

The expanding, wet circle of the soft drink stain reminded him of a photo he'd seen of the crime scene in Gill Chevalier's mansion. He'd been stabbed numerous times with a butcher knife as the targeted victim of a murderous crime of passion, according to the police report. Gill's death wasn't the result of a random burglary or some other concurrent crime. Someone wanted to kill him in the most hurtful way possible. Mason shook his head. Faron didn't look the part, but she didn't fool him. The murder weapon was never found. But a butcher knife was missing from a set in the Chevaliers' kitchen. That was too much of a coincidence for Mason to accept.

He gave up on the stain. Fortunately, he'd packed plenty of other shirts under the assumption he would be in town for a while, and he could change at his destination. He quit thinking about Sandy and continued thinking about his deadly quarry.

Faron was also a musician. And the bloody, penciled, one-line music score found next to her first husband, who'd been shot in the head, was almost definitely composed by her, probably as the final love offering of a deviant mind.

She'd vehemently protested her innocence then and each time since and was continuously allowed to return home after questioning. In the first murder, no murder weapon was found, no prints were discovered, and the writing analysis on the music notation from the first murder was inconclusive, so she hadn't been detained. But still, why did everyone believe her? Mason didn't. No other suspects existed. In his mind, Faron was the only one who could have done it.

A ferry cruised into the harbor and honked when pulling up to the dock. Mason was surprised at the number of people who disembarked. Cove Pointe must be more of a tourist town than he'd imagined, although the quaint shops and eateries across the street from the harbor should have been a tipoff. Maybe he'd come back later and poke around. You never knew what you might find out talking to the town's residents.

Anyway, to get back to his musings, anyone who'd dated as many men as Faron had, criminal and otherwise, was obviously on the prowl. He couldn't prove any of this yet, but give him time. She'd even gone out with Jaymie Macksworth, a saxophone-playing grifter who'd plied her with hot jewelry and diamonds. Jaymie was a probable wise guy from a family out east who was well known by the street cops back home, many of whom he'd been friends with when he was still on the force and with whom he continued to keep in touch. Mason could prove her relationship with Jaymie if he had to.

Finding out another man in Faron's proximity had disappeared so soon after her arrival in this small town was too much of a coincidence for Mason to stomach. This drop-dead gorgeous femme fatale, using her looks for profit, was going to the slammer. And he was going to make that happen, not only to see justice served and keep her grubby little hands off the will and life insurance money but also to satisfy his grieving client, Paul Chevalier, Gill Chevalier's oldest son, and collect his reward.

He chewed another big bite of ham and cheese with dijon mustard and contemplated his next move. Staying out of sight might be hard to do in a small town, but he'd do his best to keep Faron from knowing he was snooping around. He'd already been to the police station, but they didn't even know she was here. At least that's what they said.

He knew her location because he'd talked to Gill's son, Paul, after losing her from his purview and surveillance when she left Fenton City. Since the gardener trimming bushes at the Chevaliers' fancy estate hadn't been any help in determining where she'd taken off to, and the place was locked up tight, he'd had to call Paul. Paul got Faron's address in Cove Pointe from Gill's lawyer, with whom she'd left contact information, and

Mason had relayed her whereabouts to the same informant up north who had recently contacted him about the missing person's report.

Mason shook his head. Wasn't this not so new black widow aware that the lawyer was playing both sides of this thing to the hilt? Who cared? He sure didn't. She'd be behind bars before the distribution of the will was settled, anyway, if he had anything to say about it.

A couple of seagulls flew across the harbor in the clear, blue sky, and he watched as they soared out over the big lake. Free as a bird. That's what she was, but not for long.

He'd already done a deep dive into Faron's early background. She was a nobody from nowhere who'd cleverly married herself into a boatload of money. And her family history was suspect, too. Mason had it on good authority that her birth family, before she entered foster care at age three, had a long history of domestic violence, although he didn't have all the details. Somehow, the news hadn't picked up on that. What would she do if her past became public? Good question. With any luck, he could make that happen, and her charade as a sophisticated member of the upper crust would be over.

He leaned his elbow out the open window and took a deep breath of fresh, lake air. The summer breeze was nice, but it smelled a little fishy, too, just like the details in the Chevalier case. He turned on the car, along with the air conditioning, and rolled up the window before jamming the last bite of sandwich in his mouth.

The recent missing person in Cove Pointe had been identified as a local teacher named Wade Kestin, and the police were more than happy to have a former detective and current P.I. to assist in investigating the situation, although they declined to discuss Faron. Kestin was married and hadn't appeared to possess much money according to the investigation so far, but who knew?

In Mason's experience, people stashed money in investments all over the place, and a woman like Faron wouldn't care if her target was currently married or not. He knew the type, having once been married to a conniving female. His cheating ex-wife had taken all their money in the divorce settlement. He was still trying to figure out a way to get his fair share back. When he came up with something, she'd better watch out.

His phone rang on the seat next to him, and he glanced over to see a call from his friend on Cove Lake. He'd be there shortly, so he didn't answer. He took another sip of Coke instead.

Anyway, according to his informant friend, after the disappearance of the teacher and possibly even before, Faron had moved in on another man named Cameron Talbert, who was definitely from a wealthy family background. But still, the cops had bowed out on listing Faron as a person of interest, citing the facts that his suspicions about her were sketchy at best and that there was no evidence yet of foul play. What would they say when this Talbert guy disappeared? He'd bet on that happening if Faron had set her sights on him, too.

Mason sighed, and a bit of Coke dribbled down his solid chin. He swiped at it with his damp napkin. Locals. What're you gonna do? He knew better than they did, and he carried the truth on his side. And when he was after someone or something, he usually got what he wanted, no matter what.

So maybe he'd messed up a little in Fenton City, and maybe he'd gone to jail once for overstepping in a gambling situation to get his money back. But that's the way he was. Vigilante justice, they'd called it when they kicked him off the force. But now he knew both sides of the fence as far as prison was concerned, which upped his proficiency in solving cases. And he made a lot more money now, too, than he had as a police officer by working privately for wealthy people with major problems who wanted retribution but didn't want their names in the paper. And he was good at what he did.

Anyway, once he proved his theory about Faron's guilt in the murders, wrote her up, and handed over his report to Paul Chevalier, he would undoubtedly be rewarded handsomely. Gill's son had promised substantial compensation if he came through for him when contracting his services. And because of his contentious divorce settlement, Mason could definitely use the extra cash, which is why he had put his other cases on hold and driven north to Cove Pointe.

Mason crumpled the napkin and tossed it on the floor mat next to the sandwich wrapper. Then he pulled away from the curb into light traffic. He almost got rear-ended when he stopped suddenly at a crosswalk. A white dog had abruptly leaped in front of his car, followed by a frantic young girl with glasses and a blonde braid. Mason rolled down the window.

"Hey, get out of the way, kid. You'll get yourself killed running in front of cars," he yelled. "You and your little dog, too."

"Sorry, mister," she said. She picked up the dog and ran the rest of the way across the street.

He scoffed and rolled up the window. Didn't parents teach their kids how to cross the street anymore? He made sure the crosswalk was clear before continuing to drive down Main Street and on through town. He had more investigating to do. But first, he wanted to check in with his informant friend at his cottage on Cove Lake because that's where he was going to stay.

Mason drove until he saw a sign with an arrow reading Cove Pointe Music Camp and turned on the dirt road the arrow pointed to. The missing person had been a teacher at the camp, and he wanted to check it out personally before driving around the lake to the other side, where his friend lived.

Several cars were parked in the gravel parking area, and he drove in and parked next to one. But as he was getting out of his car, a uniformed police officer got out of a cruiser parked under a tree in the back and came over to him.

"You can't park here," the officer said.

"What's going on?" Mason asked.

"You don't need to know. Just head on out of here," he said, gruffly.

"Alright," Mason responded quickly.

He stayed standing while leaning on the car so he could stretch his legs for a minute. He didn't want any trouble. Staying on the right side of the law in this tightly knit community might give him an edge in finding out what Faron was up to, and he could use all the help he could get.

The guys at the station in town were pretty close-mouthed about her. Could their reticence have something to do with her cozying up to that lawyer, given that Talbert was a long-time resident of Cove Pointe and therefore one of their own? Maybe they were actually aware of Faron's existence here and didn't let on. Faron could have more power around here than he thought if that were the case. He'd take that possibility into account.

The cop finished scratching something on his notepad and then turned and headed back to his cruiser.

"Have a good day," Mason said, brightly.

No answer. Whatever. Mason had other things to do. He sat back down in his car, drove to the road, and continued on around the lake. A wetlands area ran for about a mile on his right before the scenery reverted to lengths of forest affording intermittent glimpses of the lake, interspersed with the occasional cottage or home. This stretch of land and water was pretty remote. Talk about wilderness. After about ten minutes, he reached the address his friend had given him and pulled into the driveway of a good-sized lake house. His friend Joey had done well for himself if he owned this place.

Mason walked up and rang the doorbell. A stout, middle-aged man with a streaky brown, walrus-type mustache opened the door.

"Hey, Mason. You're here," he said, loudly.

He grabbed Mason's hand in a firm handshake.

"You bet I am. Nice place ya got here."

"Think so? It'll do, I guess. Come on in."

He followed Joey into a wide, great room with high ceilings and floor to ceiling windows that overlooked the lake.

"Wow. What a view. You can see across the lake."

"Pretty much. That's why I like living here. Hey Tina. This is Mason, my friend I told you about."

A beautiful, statuesque blonde in white shorts and a pale pink tank top walked into the room and said hello. Mason's eyes nearly popped out of his head. She was a real looker. She reminded him of Sandy. He and Joey seemed to lean toward marrying gorgeous women who were years younger than they were. But then he remembered he wasn't married anymore. His initial euphoria was replaced with a wave of bitterness. Mason sighed and relegated Sandy's memory to a far corner of his mind.

"Hello," he replied, donning a fake smile to cover his sudden wistfulness about his ex-wife.

He turned and patted Joey on the back.

"So, have you cleaned up at the tables lately?" he asked.

Joey had always been a pretty good gambler.

"I do okay," Joey said. "Don't I, Tina?"

"More than okay. You're the best baby."

"You know it," Joey said, winking at her.

"Good. Good," Mason said.

He wrested his gaze away from Tina and looked around the room. Oh yeah. Joey Benson had done real well for himself. If Faron liked the high life, which she did, Joey would be in a good position to hobnob with her friends and help undermine her and bring her to justice. Joey had already run into her at a lakeside party, so maybe he could run into her again and bring Mason with him. He walked toward the sliding door to the deck and looked out over the lake.

"Do you have a sailboat out there?" Mason asked, squinting to see better.

"Yeah," Joey said. "And a motorboat. Feel free to use them anytime. The key's in the boat."

"Great. Thanks," Mason said.

"Here. Go on out. You'll get a better view," Joey said.

He walked over and opened the sliding glass door for him. Mason stepped outside and was instantly hit with a cool slap of fresh, pine-scented air. He took a deep breath and patted his stomach as he took in the view. Oh yeah. This was definitely the place to be. A deep blue lake rolling with low, white capped waves and dotted with an occasional sailboat or two spread out far and wide in front of him.

The brilliant shades of blue in the water were matched only by the vibrant greens of the surrounding pines. A pair of geese flew overhead, honking, and a brown hawk dipped and rose agily in the distance, then circled slowly in the sky.

"Like the view?" Joey asked, stepping up beside him and smiling.

"Unbelievable," Mason answered. "You've got it made here."

"We like living here. By the way, Hidden Glen Bed and Breakfast, where Faron Chevalier is staying, is across the lake there," he said, pointing.

Mason's mood instantly tanked again at the reminder that he was here in this stunning, secluded wilderness on business and not on a vacation. A cunning and lethal maneater resided nearby, and he had to prove that before she struck again.

"Do you want a beer?" Joey asked.

"Sure."

Mason shook his head and put Faron out of his thoughts.

"Let's go back in," Joey said.

They stepped back into the great room and headed for the bar. Mason glanced surreptitiously at Tina again, who was sitting on the sofa, filing her nails. She was a real looker, alright. Maybe she had a friend she could introduce him to. In his experience, beautiful women tended to run in packs other than Faron, of course, who subsisted solo. Tina might know someone he'd like. You never knew.

"Here. Try this," Joey said, handing him a cold bottle of ale.

Mason took a swig, then swallowed and sighed contentedly. He imagined a pleasurable future here in Cove Pointe and a quick resolution to the Chevalier case.

CHAPTER 9

I didn't know the authorities would close down Cove Pointe Music Camp because Wade Kestin went missing. After the police showed up in response to our call the morning after the campout, I assumed they would find him, and everything would go back to normal. I was wrong. They didn't find him, and things certainly didn't go back to normal.

Evidently, people in the area, including the police, remained extremely frightened and upset that members of their community had suspiciously disappeared over the past few years. And Wade going missing was the last straw, so to say.

We sent the campers home with their parents on Saturday morning, but many of the parents, upon hearing the news, returned to the music camp later in the day to help search for Wade. Along with local law enforcement, we searched the boundaries of the camp, and after having no luck, searched the woods and entered the bog.

We linked arms and walked in a row on the firmer ground, which was still quite mushy and difficult to navigate as we looked through the wetter areas and under groups of trees for footprints or clues to Wade's whereabouts. But nothing appeared.

When we checked the path I'd walked on before, I looked again for the boot I'd lost, but I only ended up with my arm dripping with peat. One of the group members lost his footing and ended up waist-deep in a goopy morass of moss and glop. We all had to struggle to pull him out and almost fell in ourselves.

At that point, law enforcement called off the search and told us they were calling in the fire department and other professionals to do the job instead of us laypeople. I felt bad that we couldn't find him.

A search party went out on Sunday and yesterday, which was Monday, but no one found Wade. They were planning to go out again on Tuesday, which was today, and probably bring dogs with them on the search, which they may or may not have done before. I hoped they'd have better luck this time, but I couldn't help but wonder if the bog people had gotten him. I shivered. What a horrible thought.

I was sitting on the porch steps of the B&B on the Tuesday after Wade's disappearance when Cam pulled into the driveway in his pickup. Kasey hopped out along with her little dog, Bobo, and I stood and swung my purse over my shoulder. Cam was taking me out to lunch while Kasey helped Summer in the kitchen.

I said 'hi' to Kasey and petted Bobo before walking over to the truck. The front door opened as I did so. Noble, who was a permanent fixture now at the B&B since he didn't have to teach at the music camp anymore, stepped out after letting Kasey and Bobo in. He walked down the steps and over to Cam while I got in the truck on the passenger side. He seemed to be carrying something.

"Hey, man. Good to see you," he said, shaking Cam's hand when he reached him. He handed him a pie with the other. "Summer wanted you to give this to Wade's wife, Dottie. Eleanor evidently called her and said she was sending her a pie with you, and Summer wanted to do the same."

I was amazed again at what a good actor Noble was when he was around other people. He seemed like a normal person, and I felt like I was the only one who knew otherwise, except for maybe Summer on and off. But she seemed to prefer to pretend that everything with Noble was fine.

"Yeah. I have one in the back seat. I'll put this with it," Cam said, taking the pie from him.

He handed the pie to me.

"Could you put this in the picnic basket in the back with the other one?"

"Sure." I nodded as I took it from him and did as he asked. I was impressed that people around here were so nice and neighborly.

"Sorry to hear about your colleague. Hope they find him soon," Cam said.

"Yeah, thanks. Say, Summer wants to know if you can come back for dinner later. She's making her special lasagna," Noble said.

Cam shook his head. "I appreciate the invitation, but I'm swamped at work, and I have to stay late to catch up on paperwork. So I think I'll pass. I'll pick Kasey up, though, when I bring Faron back."

"Okay, sure," Noble said. "You two have fun."

Noble's expression was hard to read, but the tone of his voice was slightly mocking. He appeared to smile and grimace at the same time.

"This is a business lunch," Cam said sharply, correcting him. "Faron and I are discussing legal issues."

"Oh, sorry, man. You, too, Faron. I had no idea you were in legal trouble. Cam's your man, though. He knows his stuff."

This time, he really did smile, and I got a sick feeling in the pit of my stomach. I didn't know what Noble thought my legal issues were, but I didn't like the fact that he seemed happy about them. At least he didn't mention anything about Gill's murder to

Cam. But I supposed I would have to tell him something about that soon anyway.

Cam nodded, seeming bemused at Noble's interaction.

"Yeah, well, we'll see you later," Cam said, putting the truck in gear.

"Yeah, sure," Noble said as he stepped back.

Cam gave a curt wave and pulled out of the driveway.

"Wonder what that was all about," he said as we drove down the road.

"I have no idea," I replied, evasively.

I had no way of explaining what was going on with Noble to anyone in a way that made sense, and I wasn't exactly sure I comprehended him myself. He couldn't be jealous, could he? At this late date? No. Probably not. I kept my mouth shut.

"We need to make a stop before lunch to deliver the pies to Dottie Kestin. I hope you don't mind," Cam said.

"Of course not," I said. "I'd love to help with that." I thought for a moment. "Didn't you say Wade had talked to his wife on the phone before he went missing?"

"Yes. Now that you mention it, I did."

"Well, I don't want to be too intrusive, but maybe we could ask her a few questions and uncover a clue or two as to where he went."

"Maybe," Cam said. "But I'm sure the police already questioned her."

"Oh. You're probably right," I said, somewhat disappointed that I couldn't play amateur detective.

Cam looked over at me.

"We'll see how things go," he said.

We drove down the dirt road, which ran along Cove Lake for a while and then on past the turn for Main Street. We turned left on a road about a mile after that. The big lake, which was larger than Cove Lake by far, shimmered through the trees in the distance. Cam turned left again, after seeming to note a mailbox number, onto a gravel driveway next to a small ranch house.

"Here we are," he said.

He shut off the truck and reached back to grab the pies out of the picnic basket. Then we both got out and walked up to the door. A petite, young woman with dark brown, shoulder-length hair curled up at the ends answered Cam's knock right away. I remembered seeing her talking to Wade at Eleanor's birthday party. She was obviously Dottie.

"Thank you," she said, as he introduced himself and handed her a pie. "Oh yes. We met briefly at Eleanor's party."

"I remember. The apple pie is from Eleanor," he said. Then he pointed to the one in his hand. "And this is a blueberry pie from Summer Dixon at Hidden Glen B&B. Faron, here is a friend of hers."

"How nice. Why don't you both come into the kitchen, and we'll set these on the counter? They look so good."

We followed her down a short hallway.

"Any more news in town about Wade?" she asked as she and Cam set the pies down.

"I'm afraid not," Cam said. "I hope we'll hear something shortly."

"I don't know what could have happened to him," Dottie said, shaking her head. "I talked to him on the phone after the cookout, and everything was fine. I told the police that. Wade said he'd be home Saturday morning, and then this happened." She wrung her hands. "Oh, where could he be?" She sounded frustrated and frantic at the same time.

"Did you call him or did he call you Friday night during

the music camp overnight?" I asked. Maybe I could uncover a clue as to what happened and make her feel better.

"What? Oh. Well, I called him. I had just found out the best pie contest was an event again this year at the country fair, and registration had opened. I called to tell him I was thinking of entering."

"Yeah, I know about that. My mom won a blue ribbon once, I think," Cam said.

"Yes, she did. Well, I didn't win last year or the year before. I haven't actually won a ribbon yet at all, but I was going to try again this year. I wanted to enter a blueberry pie this time, like Summer's. She always makes such nice pies. But now I don't know." She looked down and shook her head. "That doesn't matter anymore."

"They're doing everything they can to find him," I said softly, hoping to relieve some of her obvious distress.

"I know," she said, looking back up.

"So Wade didn't mention what he was doing or what he was going to do next?" Cam asked.

"Well, he did say the campers were going to build a campfire and toast marshmallows, but that's all."

"Huh. He didn't help us with gathering sticks or anything," Cam said. "I wonder if he went off on his own to do that."

"Do you think so? Do you think maybe he got lost in the forest?" Dottie asked.

"If he did, they'll find him," Cam said. "They have quite a search going on at the music camp."

"I hope so," she said.

"Maybe he was in the kitchen at the lodge looking for something to make s'mores with. When I left the campfire to use the facilities in the middle of the night, I noticed a few pots and pans strewn on a counter in the kitchen," Cam said.

"Do you think so?" I asked. "Could he have left to get something at the store? Oh, but that doesn't explain his car in the parking lot, does it?"

"No, it doesn't. I don't know what happened to him," Cam said, sounding resigned. "I hope you hear something soon."

"Thank you for your concern," Dottie said.

"Sure. I guess we'd better go. Faron and I have a business lunch scheduled."

"Oh. Well, I'll show you out." She led us to the door and opened it. "Thanks so much for coming over," she said as we walked down the steps. "And tell Eleanor and Summer thanks for the pies."

"We will," Cam said.

We walked to the truck and got in, then waved as we backed out and drove away.

"She seems like such a nice person," I said as Cam drove toward town. "It's so sad that this happened."

"Yes. We can only wish for the best," Cam said.

He continued driving until, upon mutual agreement, we ended up in town in front of a deli across from the harbor. We headed inside to order. The day was shaping up to be a nice one, and the scenery was so beautiful I didn't want to eat inside at one of the few tables. After all, I'd spent most of the weekend and yesterday cooped up at the B&B, even though I did go down to the shore on Cove Lake a few times. But I'd caught a glimpse of the searchers in the bog from the dock and felt so melancholy that I went back to my room again.

"How about we go on a picnic?" I asked while we stood in a short line. "We could take our lunch to the beach on the big lake."

"I'm game if you are," he replied.

We ordered our Reuben sandwiches, which it turned out we both liked, and root beers to go, and, after getting back in the truck, drove to a picnic area that Cam knew of.

Cam parked in the shade near a breathtaking lake overlook that showcased several small sailboats gliding over calm, blue water in the summer sun. I grabbed our bag of sandwiches while he took the root beers, and we trudged down a sandy incline to the beach. We found a nice spot near the water, and Cam unfolded a blanket he'd kept in the truck and spread it out on the warm sand for us to sit on.

I sat with my legs crossed under my white, gauze skirt and gazed out over the water. The brilliant beauty of the lake embraced me and imparted a calm solace I hadn't known I needed. I stayed still for a while, taking in the view, grateful that Cam seemed to feel the same way about the lake as he remained silent throughout my reverie.

A beach ball abruptly bounced over the sand in the light breeze and into a sand castle a few children were constructing nearby using plastic buckets of sand and water. They squealed when the ball hit a parapet and set about quickly repairing their masterpiece after kicking the ball back to its owners.

I smiled. What fun they were having. They seemed so safe and happy. I would have liked to join them if I weren't already grown up. Their joy made me feel young again, although I didn't remember going to the beach as a child. I shook my head to clear away my musings and looked over at Cam. He smiled.

"Beautiful, isn't it?" he asked.

"Yes," I said, softly.

"Like you," he added, handing me my sandwich.

I smiled as I took it from him.

"Thanks."

My sandwich was perfectly stacked and tangy, and I savored it as I ate, along with sips of icy root beer.

"So tell me about your deceased husband's will and this house you're in danger of losing," Cam said when he was about halfway through his sandwich. "You piqued my interest the other day when you mentioned it."

"Oh, yes," I said. "I'm so glad you agreed to help me."

"But first, could you tell me when he passed on and if he was sick or in an accident. I don't have many details."

I let out a breath, relieved that Cam hadn't heard about me from someone or from the publicity about Gill's death. That meant I had a chance to relay the circumstances to him gently in a way that would portray me and my situation in the best possible light.

"Alright. I'll tell you," I said.

I waited for him to swallow before continuing.

"There's no easy way to say this," I said.

"Go on," he prompted.

"My husband was murdered."

"What?"

"Yes. He was stabbed to death in our bedroom a few months ago. I found him. It was awful."

Cam stared at me, apparently dumbfounded.

"I had no idea. You must be quite a survivor to have recovered from such a traumatic experience already."

"Yes," I said, quietly, for lack of anything else to say.

"Do you want to tell me any more about the crime scene and the state he was in when you found him?"

I shook my head.

He continued to stare at me as though looking for

something. Emotion, I suppose. People often tried to find that in me or to maybe pry it out of me. I don't know which.

"Do you know who did it?" he asked, holding my gaze.

"No. I haven't got a clue, and neither do the police. You're right, though. The whole ordeal was very traumatic."

"I'm sure it was," he said softly. He shook his head.

I sighed. I hoped he wouldn't ask me any more questions. But there wasn't much chance of that if he looked into my legal issues. He probably wondered if I was in denial. I'd heard that term before when someone tried to explain my blandness about the murder. But I'm not. I just don't feel emotional, not right now anyway.

"Before we go any further, do you think you need to hire protection for yourself? Was your husband in a dangerous line of work or anything?"

Cam's mention of hiring protection struck me as oddly prescient because I'd been advised to do that once before when I broke up with a saxophone player with mafia ties. I hadn't hired a bodyguard then, when the danger to my life seemed even more real due to the obvious threat of being pursued by a jilted criminal, and I didn't see the need to hire one now—at least, not yet. I turned my attention back to Cam.

"No. Not really, but he was well known, and he had a great deal of money," I replied, honestly. "I don't want to hire a bodyguard. I just want to hide out in Cove Pointe for a while, not so much because of being in danger, but to come to terms with everything that happened."

I didn't mention the P.I. I was trying to escape anything about my two previous husbands. Maybe I'd tell Cam more about them later. Relating my past a little bit at a time seemed the best route to go for now.

"I understand," he said. "But what's the deal with his children then?"

"They want the house in Florida because I wasn't married to my husband, Gill, for very long. And they're contesting the will. For the same reason, the short marriage, that is, they don't feel I'm entitled to the money he left me."

"Well, they're wrong," Cam said. "I can help you with this. His kids don't seem to have your best interests at heart, but I do." He gave me an earnest look and then smiled at what I supposed was my relieved expression.

"Thank you," I said, sincerely.

I was so lucky to have met someone like him. He seemed to trust me implicitly, which was a trait I'd had trouble finding in people lately.

"Shall we get going? I'll take you back to the B&B and pick up Kasey. Then I have to go back to my office for a while."

"Sure," I said, standing up.

I didn't want to leave, but I had no choice. I didn't bring my car for one thing, and I didn't want to stay there alone for another. A seagull swooped down and pecked at a leftover end of bread near the empty sandwich bag. I shooed him away and watched wistfully as he soared high into the clear, blue sky. Where was he escaping to?

"Okay, then," Cam said. "I'll pick you up on Saturday to go to the county fair. They usually set the Ferris Wheel up on a side street in town on Thursday or Friday, along with a few other rides and food trucks. The fair runs for a couple of weeks."

"Sounds fun," I said.

We shook sand out of the blanket together and folded it up before heading back to the truck.

"So what's your lawyer's name?" Cam asked as we

trudged up the sandy incline to the truck.

"Jay Morrison in Fenton City."

"I'll get in touch with him with your permission. I've got a form in the truck you can sign."

"Yes. Great," I casually replied, distracted.

Thinking about seeing Cam again on Saturday and anticipating the fun and maybe even romance we would have made me giddy. The date could put me on the road to securing another husband, and a rich one at that, which I desperately needed. Living alone wasn't how I envisioned my future.

Because of my preoccupation, though, I don't think I grasped the importance of what I agreed to when I basically gave Cam carte blanche to handle my legal affairs.

I did know I didn't want Jay Morrison to mention my past to Cam, which he might do, but I didn't have any other options but to put them in touch with each other, as far as I could tell, if I wanted a fair shake with the will and the house in Florida. I either took the chance that Cam could handle Jay and whatever he told him, or took the risk of letting Gill's kids get everything.

If the kids took all of Gill's money and assets, I'd be close to destitute except for Daniel's money and Bryce's money, which wasn't all that much. Again, I had no choice. That is, I had no choice if I wanted to continue to live in the manner to which I had become accustomed. And I wanted to do that.

I mean, money can't buy happiness. I, of all people, am aware of that. But money does buy a feeling of peace and security, something that was missing for most of my parentless life and something I need on a gut level to survive emotionally. It's a welcome panacea that brings solace, if only for a while, from the deep, aching loneliness of tremendous loss that ravages the soul and clutches the heart.

And maybe I didn't end up getting along with my husbands all that well, and maybe there were times when we had fights that didn't always end well. But that's just the way marriage is, right? Marriages come and go, and moving on is essential in finding the one true love of your life. And I believe in true love because I thought I found it with Daniel. But for now, I am again the autonomous, needy widow of a man who was the unexpected victim of violence, and I want out. I want love and security, and I need to move forward with my life to achieve those things.

So anyway, the way I see it, right then and there on the side of the lake, I naively handed my lonely, tattered heart over to Cameron Talbert, the possible future love of my life, and trusted that he would handle it with care.

CHAPTER 10

When Cam picked me up Saturday afternoon, he seemed as excited about our date as I was. I only say that because he showed up at the door with flowers. Like I said, he was a charmer, and I was falling for the whole seduction act big time, if that's what it was. I was usually right about these things.

Before we left for the county fair, I put the daisies in a vase with water and set them on the kitchen table for Noble and Summer to enjoy when they returned. Summer had gone to the fair this morning to register her famous blueberry pie for the best pie contest. The contest was to be judged the following weekend, and she planned to bake the pie next week and enter it then. Luckily, Noble had left with her before Cam came over, so I didn't have to worry about another awkward, unreadable situation with him in relation to us.

Patty and Lloyd Martin, the new guests at the B&B, came in from the lake, bringing fresh air with them after kicking sand off their sandals outside as they opened the kitchen door. They said 'hi' on the way up to their room. Lloyd said they planned to go to the fair tomorrow and told us to have fun for them today. We happily agreed.

Patty mentioned seeing someone walking through the bog—a woman, she thought—but she couldn't make out any details in regard to her appearance from her distant vantage point on the beach. Someone was probably searching for the missing person on their own, she said. Probably. I couldn't help thinking about the bog witch and wondering if she could have seen her. But I was only speculating.

The only damper on what I hoped would turn out to be a lovely afternoon was the stark reality that Wade Kestin was still missing, and no end to his ongoing disappearance seemed imminent. I hoped Dottie was okay. The music camp remained closed, too, as an eerie reminder that all was not right in Cove Pointe.

When I finished fussing with the flowers, as I wanted to arrange them to their best advantage, Cam walked with me out to the truck, and we headed into town.

"Where's Kasey today?" I asked, when we were on our way.

"She went to the fair with my mom this morning to register my mom's pies in the best pie contest. The judging takes place next weekend."

"How wonderful. Summer is registering her famous blueberry pie, too. She left for the fair this morning and is probably still there with her husband." I didn't want to mention Noble's name if I didn't have to. "What kind of pie is Eleanor entering?"

"Let's see. One each of apple, blueberry, and strawberry rhubarb."

"I never heard of the last kind."

"Well, trust me. They're all good if my mom made them. And she did."

I chuckled. "I'm sure you're right," I said. "But I bet Summer will give her a run for the money. She's quite a good baker, too."

"So I've heard." He paused. "Care to make this interesting?"

"Make what interesting?" I asked, befuddled.

"You know. Bet on the winner. If my mom's pie wins next

weekend, you make me dinner at the B&B. If Summer's pie wins, I'll make dinner for you at my house.

"Are you kidding?" I asked.

"Not at all."

I thought for a moment. "Alright, you're on," I said. "But I don't know if you want to win or not. I'm not that great of a cook."

"I'll take my chances," he said, laughing.

I smiled, knowing I'd win either way as long as I saw Cam again.

When we got to town, Cam parked near the harbor, and we walked to the fair, which was on a side street blocked off on each end with orange-striped construction gates. Carnival music added a festive flair to the rides and games set up near a large Ferris Wheel, which turned slowly to the sound of shouts and laughter from its patrons. The spicy scent of cinnamon filled the air.

"Oh, look. Elephant ears," I said.

I recognized the aroma of the large, flat pastry I loved. I'd had one once a long time ago on a school outing and still remembered the flavor. The dough was usually fried, sprinkled with cinnamon sugar, and served warm to eat by hand. I pointed to the food truck where a man in a white apron handed them out through a window.

"Would you like one?" Cam asked. "I'm buying."

"Sure," I replied.

We walked over together and stood in line. Kasey ran up to Cam with Eleanor close behind her.

"Hey, Dad, can you get me one, too?" she asked.

"Of course. Do you want one, Mom?" he asked Eleanor.

"I'd love one," she answered.

They both fell into line behind us.

"I'm so sorry the music camp closed," Eleanor said, loud enough for me to hear. "And just when you started to teach flute, too. Like I told Kasey and Cam, I'm sure Wade will turn up any minute with a good explanation of where he's been, and everything will turn out fine."

I turned to look at her. "I hope so," I said, before turning back around.

She sounded so sure of herself and comforting, but also as though she couldn't grasp the possibility of anything other than a good outcome to Wade's disappearance. I hoped she wasn't wrong. After what happened with my husbands, I knew what it was like to end up on the wrong side of a bad situation, and I didn't wish that for her or anyone, for that matter.

We reached the front of the line, and Cam ordered for us. Before long, we were all eating Elephant Ears and licking cinnamon sugar off our fingers. The unique treat tasted even better than I remembered.

"Let's sit on the bench over here, so we can watch the Ferris Wheel go round," Cam said.

"Okay."

I followed him and sat next to him with Eleanor and Kasey on my other side. I sighed. Seeing the way he cared about his family and the way they cared about him was heartwarming. Maybe I'd have a similar experience someday with a family of my own. I hoped so.

The rich scent of caramel corn wafted through the warm, afternoon air from a nearby concessions stand, and a child walked by, jamming wads of pink cotton candy into her mouth. We obviously weren't the only ones indulging in sweet treats for the day.

Eleanor leaned forward to talk over me to Cam.

"You know, when I registered my pies, I saw Beth Parker's name on the blueberry pie list. She's Millie Parker's daughter. Remember Millie?"

Cam nodded.

"She went missing a few years ago around this time," Eleanor said to me. "It was so sad. She disappeared one afternoon and never showed up again. I guess Beth is carrying on for her and baking a pie to enter in the contest. Oh, forgive me." Eleanor dabbed at her nose with a tissue. "Her loss still affects me."

"Of course it does," I said, patting her arm. I suddenly thought of something. "Were any of the others who disappeared in Cove Pointe bakers?"

"Hmm?" Eleanor glanced over at me. "Now that you mention it, Deb Lundy was quite good at baking. She used to enter her pies in the fair, too. She went missing two years ago. Why do you ask?"

"Oh, no reason," I said. "What kind?"

"What?"

"What kind of pies did she enter in the fair?"

"Oh. Blueberry, I think. That's a popular type of recipe around here. Why?"

"I just wondered," I answered.

The thought that had occurred to me was probably a long shot, so I didn't want to mention it until I came up with more information. Cam stood and walked over to throw his napkin in a nearby trash can. I stuffed mine in my pocket.

"Anyone want to ride the Ferris Wheel?" he asked when he returned.

"Yes," Kasey replied. "C'mon, Gramma. You can ride with me."

"Alright, dear."

Eleanor stood and followed Kasey toward the Ferris Wheel.

"And you can ride with me," Cam said, extending his hand and smiling.

"Okay."

I stood and accepted his gentle grip. We walked together over to the line for the ride. The giddy feeling I'd had the last time I'd seen him returned. I was hand in hand with someone who I was sure was the most handsome man at the fair. And I felt extremely lucky to be with him.

"So when's the last time you were on a Ferris Wheel?" Cam asked.

"Never," I said.

"Really?"

"Really."

"I think you'll like the ride. Looks like we'll have quite a view over the big lake from the top," he said.

"Oh, how nice," I said.

The Ferris Wheel slowed and began to let the riders off, stopping its rotation intermittently to do so. We handed our tickets to the ride operator and waited until everyone disembarked to take our seats. Kasey and Eleanor were in a passenger car behind ours. When our car arrived, I sat down next to Cam and held onto the bar in front of me, shivering with anticipation or trepidation or maybe both. The car moved backwards and up, and the next one came down in front of us to accept riders. When everyone was on the ride and seemingly secured, the wheel began to move faster. I grabbed Cam's arm.

"We haven't even really started going yet," he said, chuckling. "But I don't mind if you want to hold onto me."

"Good," I said. "Because I think I have to."

As the Ferris Wheel rotated, we climbed higher and higher into the air until eventually we were at the top, about to come down the other side in front of the wheel. I gasped. The view of the big lake was incredible. Blue, white-capped waves shimmered under a golden sun, and the wide expanse of water reached to the horizon.

"Oh, my gosh. The view is just breathtaking," I gushed, tightening my grasp on Cam's arm. We really were quite high up in the air. "I had no idea the lake was so large, and what incredible shades of blue in the water."

"You're right," Cam said. "And your enthusiasm is contagious. I'm glad to be here with you on your first Ferris Wheel ride, terrifying as it is."

I glanced over at him. His blue eyes were vibrant and shining with amusement.

"Oh, you're just teasing me, aren't you?" I asked.

"Not at all," Cam said. "I meant every word. And I'll hold you as tight as you want." He grinned.

"Oh. Get out of here," I said, leaning into him.

"I would, but I can't go anywhere," he said, sounding dry.

"Well, your nearness does help relieve my jitters."

"That's what I'm here for."

He gave me a devastatingly charming smile. His sandy hair blew about his chiseled face, and I sat there stunned by his male charisma before smiling back. He was fun to be with and the perfect date. As we descended while hanging perilously in thin air, I took deep breaths to calm myself. Cam's murmurs of comfort also helped, and eventually, I began to relax a bit.

I looked around at the fair far below us. A grandstand was set up near the harbor with what looked like a set of drums on the dais, with a dance area nearby. A spinning teacup ride and a fake rifle range with giant panda bears on an outside shelf, which were probably prizes, promised future entertainment. I didn't know if Cam would be interested in winning something to take home or not. I'd ask him when we were back on solid terra firma. As we neared the ground, I sighed deeply and released my death grip on Cam.

"We made it," I said, relieved.

"Yeah. But we're taking another spin," he said. He looked over at me. "Sorry."

I guess my face showed my concern.

I glanced at the ride operator as we began to go around again and sucked in a sharp breath. Standing next to him was the private investigator who'd followed me around in Fenton City. I was sure of it. Wasn't I? I took another look. I was right. What was he doing here? He was standing with a couple I recognized from Eleanor's birthday party. Kasey had mentioned they were neighbors on Cove Lake, but I hadn't met them. I looked quickly at Cam, but he didn't seem to have recognized the neighbors. I looked back.

Just then, the P.I. turned toward me, and our eyes met. His sly eyes widened. He definitely pegged me. What should I do? I looked around desperately. I couldn't do anything. Like Cam had said earlier, I couldn't go anywhere. I grabbed Cam's arm again instead.

"What's wrong? Don't tell me you're afraid to go up to the top again. We were already there, and nothing happened."

"It's not that," I said, breathlessly.

"What then? You're shaking." He patted my hand.

I looked down but didn't see the private investigator anywhere.

"I thought I saw someone I recognized, that's all," I said, glossing over my fright. "But I was wrong. Must have been a body double or something."

"Body double? Where'd you hear a term like that?" Cam asked. He looked at me quizzically.

"Thriller novel," I said, as nonchalantly as I could.

I needed to change the subject quickly so he didn't know how much time I'd spent talking to cops and following news about true crime incidents in my sordid past. I wanted him to see me as more innocent and protected, sophisticated even, in the way a future wife of his might be. "Like the ones you like to read."

"Oh yeah, that's right," he said. "We were both reading thrillers when we met in the bookstore."

"I was reading a mystery," I said, "but who's keeping track? I like thrillers, too, which is something else we have in common."

"Along with what?" he asked.

"Umm. Good looks," I said, jokingly.

He laughed.

I laughed, too, but then reverted to shaking. We were at the top of the Ferris Wheel rotation again, and our passenger car began its descent. But that wasn't the only cause of my fear. Seeing the P.I. had seriously unnerved me and also made me think of Gill's kids. I closed my eyes for a moment to steady my thoughts, but I couldn't stop thinking about the will and the life insurance.

"By the way, did you get a chance to call my lawyer?" I asked, keeping my eyes closed so I couldn't register our height above the ground. I continued to hold onto Cam for safety and because I didn't want to break the romantic momentum of the date. But I did need to know if he'd talked to Jay Morrison.

"I did," Cam said, suddenly sounding serious. "We had quite a conversation." He paused. "You might want to consider other options as far as a lawyer is concerned."

"What? Why?" I opened my eyes and looked at him.

"I'll tell you later," he said, patting my hand again. "Don't let anything worry you right now, though. We're here to have fun, okay?"

"Of course," I said. What could he mean about finding another lawyer? Did Cam want to take over as counsel? I might consider the possibility. "Thanks for talking to Jay and letting me know."

"Sure."

I held my breath and looked around as we neared the ground, but thankfully, I didn't see the P.I. anywhere. The Ferris Wheel slowed and then stopped to let us off. We walked over to the gate in the fence and left. Kasey and Eleanor exited right behind us.

"That was so fun," Kasey said, running up next to us. "I'm going to ride again if we come back to the fair next week."

"Are you leaving?" I asked.

"Yes," Eleanor replied. "Kasey's helping Summer in the kitchen at Hidden Glen again this afternoon. She's working on becoming an apprentice baker someday."

"Really?"

"Yes. Summer's quite impressed with her."

"Good for you," I said to Kasey.

"Thanks," she said. "And when we're done in the kitchen, I'm going to gather leaves from the forest and press them between sheets of wax paper with an iron on a towel. That way, I can keep them and identify them in a notebook."

"Wow. That sounds scientific," I said.

She nodded.

"Yes. Since the music camp is closed, it's nice that Kasey has found another way to spend her time this summer," Cam said.

"I wish the camp would open again, though," Kasey said.

"I do, too," I said.

"Well, we'd better get going. See you two later," Eleanor said.

They walked away, leaving us alone together. We spent the rest of the afternoon playing games and listening to piped-in music. Cam wasn't a very good shot, so he didn't win a panda bear at the fake rifle range. But that was okay with me, because I didn't want to carry something that big around with me anyway.

We had our photo taken in a booth with our faces poking into a historical royalty scene. We laughed at the sheet of photos portraying us as a king and queen on horseback and wondered who we'd show them to.

As Cam slipped the photos into his wallet, I felt a sudden chill and looked around. I had a feeling someone was watching us. Was that horrible private investigator still hovering about? I glanced quickly behind me and to the side. I didn't see him, but that didn't mean he wasn't here somewhere. His probable presence made me feel guilty for some reason. But I shook off the feeling. Maybe he only happened to be in Cove Pointe for the fair, and seeing him was a coincidence. I tried to believe that, but I didn't have much luck. Oh well. I wasn't going to let that furtive little man ruin my date. I put him out of my mind and continued walking around the fair with Cam.

As the sun waned lower in the sky, we picked up corn dogs at a food truck and ate them as we admired landscapes and jewelry in an arts and crafts tent. I recognized some good prints of a few famous pictures, but decided to forgo purchasing any of them. I was having the most wonderful time with Cam, just browsing.

When we finished our corn dogs, we strolled down the street toward the harbor, where the grandstand was set up with a dance area nearby. A five-piece band tuned up on stage as people from the fair made their way over to the waterfront.

A purple twilight slowly descended, and amber lamplights clicked on along the harbor road, adding a warm glow to the evening. Strings of tiny white lights strung along the rails added an elegant touch to the grandstand and dance area.

"This is lovely," I said, taking in the romantic scene.

The band began to play an old song. Moon River, the announcer said, which seemed appropriate given the silvery cast of the moon over the water.

"Would you care to dance?" Cam asked.

I looked up at him and nodded. He took my hand and led me to the makeshift dance floor set up on the lawn in front of the grandstand. We swayed together to the nostalgic tune as a gentle breeze blew in off the lake. A boat horn honked in the distance, and waves lapped quietly against the wooden docks in the harbor. I couldn't remember the last time I'd felt so happy and secure.

Before long, other couples joined us, and the cool, night air filled with music and quiet conversation. Cam nuzzled my neck. I predictably shivered.

"This has been the most wonderful day," I said, softly. "I'm so glad I spent this time with you."

"I feel the same way," Cam said. "I haven't had this much fun in a long time."

I put my arms around his shoulders and laid my head against his muscular chest, moving in time with him to a new, slow tune from the band. We seemed to exist in our own little world, if only for a moment. Just as I thought of that, he leaned down and kissed me. His lips were warm and soft, and I trembled in response, pressing my lips to his. After a moment, the tune ended, and he pulled back, gazing at me in the dim light. I didn't know what to say, so I just gazed back. Sometimes words aren't necessary.

"I hope this can be the beginning of a beautiful moment in our lives together," he said. "We may have other things going on in Cove Pointe that make the timing imperfect, like Wade going missing for one thing, but I'd like to think we could see each other again. I had a good time."

"I'd like that," I said. "I had a good time, too."

The band began to play another song. This one was a faster jazz tune.

"Well, our date isn't over yet," Cam said. "Shall we keep dancing?"

"Great idea," I said. "We can dance the night away."

And as a myriad of stars twinkled in the night sky over Cove Pointe, we did just that.

CHAPTER 11

I sat at the breakfast table the next morning, along with everyone who stayed at the B&B last night. This included Patty and Lloyd Martin, who were the nice couple from Ohio, Summer, Noble, me, and Kasey, who had slept overnight in one of the rooms along with her dog, Bobo, after helping Summer in the kitchen on Saturday. Bobo had been running around the B&B all morning getting petted by everyone.

Kasey and Summer were baking pies again this afternoon, this time using a new recipe for a blueberry pie that Summer was entering in the fair. The pie might have Kasey's name on it, too, if they ended up submitting one of those they made together to the contest.

"If you need more blueberries, I'll pick some," Kasey said to Summer, who was talking about the pie contest.

"Thank you. I was thinking we could use wild blueberries from the bushes in the backyard. The flavor of the berries is so much more pungent when they're wild, and with the right ingredients, we could come up with a real winner of a pie."

"Do you think so?" Kasey asked, exuberantly.

"I do," Summer said, nodding.

"I'll find some real good ones then," Kasey promised.

I suddenly recalled the thought that had popped into my mind when I was talking to Eleanor at the fair. We were discussing the pie contest and the people in Cove Pointe who had disappeared around the time they would have registered or entered.

"Where do people usually get blueberries around here?" I asked Summer.

"The grocery store, I guess. Why?"

I paused, contemplating. "I just wondered if anyone else had used wild blueberries before for pies they entered in the contest."

"Probably," Summer said. "I'm sure I'm not the first person to think wild blueberries would make a difference in the flavor of the pie."

"Where would they get wild blueberries?"

"Everywhere around here, I guess."

"Like in the bog?" I asked. I remembered seeing quite a few blueberry bushes when I walked through there.

"Oh, no, not in the bog, although I suppose with a name like Wild Blueberry Bog, that would seem self-evident."

"Yes," I said, thinking, as I crunched on a salty piece of bacon.

"It's too mucky and gross for most people to pick the blueberries there, even though there are a lot of them. Dangerous, too. People stay away from the bog."

"Hmm," I said. I wasn't sure she was right.

Everyone was silent for a moment, seeming to concentrate on their breakfasts, or maybe they were thinking, as I was, about Wade Kestin's disappearance and the people searching in Wild Blueberry Bog for him.

I remembered, too, that Wade's wife, Dottie, had told Cam and me that she planned to enter a blueberry pie in the contest this year. And she also said she had relayed her intention to Wade when he called her during the music camp overnight. Could that be a clue as to what had happened to him? Maybe. If

Dottie intended to use wild blueberries in her recipe, she might have mentioned her plans to Wade. That could be a relevant path to pursue. I'd ask Cam what he thought when I saw him again.

"We're planning to go to the fair today," Patty said, after a while. "Did you have fun yesterday?"

Kasey nodded.

"Yes. Gramma and I rode the Ferris Wheel with my dad and Faron."

Noble looked up abruptly from spreading strawberry jam on a homemade biscuit and stared at me, a foible about him that was definitely beginning to annoy me.

"Y-Yes," I stammered. "We had quite a good time, didn't we, Kasey?"

"It was great. I want to ride again."

Noble set his biscuit down and picked up a piece of bacon. Then he set that down, too, and stood up.

"I'm going to get another cup of coffee," he said. "Anyone else want some?"

Everyone passed on the idea, and he left the dining room, but not before shooting me a wicked glance. Evidently, Noble wasn't aware I'd been out with Cam. He really did seem jealous, but I couldn't do anything about that, nor did I want to.

"I'm glad you had fun," Patty said. "Maybe we'll go on a ride on the Ferris Wheel while we're at the fair. What do you think, honey?"

"Worth a try," Lloyd said, offhandedly.

He took a sip of orange juice. He wasn't very talkative, but he fit well with Patty, who seemed to enjoy having conversations and talked enough for both of them.

"I hope the weather holds out for you," Summer said. "The light rain this morning seems to have let up a bit."

"The weather report only shows a low likelihood of rain this afternoon. I'm sure we'll be fine," Patty said.

I hoped she was right for their sake. Being caught at the top of a Ferris Wheel in the rain if the weather report didn't hold out didn't sound like much fun to me.

Rain seemed to come and go quickly in the area, giving little forewarning of storms, which reminded me of an incident last night. I'd had to shut the window in my bedroom in the very early morning when a sudden deluge awakened me from my slumber. Cam had brought me back to the B&B after our date only hours before, and I was in a deep sleep.

During the incident, I jumped out of bed and hurried to pull down the sash. As I did so, a figure, obscured by the rain, ran through the backyard. I squinted and looked more closely. The small, hunched-over person dressed in black then ran into the woods. Was it the same figure I'd almost run over when I first got here? Could have been.

I stabbed a forkful of scrambled eggs and angled them into my mouth as last night played through my mind.

The odd thing about the incident was that, before I closed the window, I could have sworn Noble called out to bring more next week. I didn't know what that meant. Supplies being delivered so early in the morning and through the back door didn't seem probable. Something strange was going on, but I didn't know what. I shut the window and went back to bed to sleep.

Now, in the morning, I wasn't as frightened as I'd been last night, maybe because other people were around. I was still uncomfortable with Noble there, though. Just then, he walked back into the dining room carrying his coffee. The coffee steamed from the cup and sent the chocolatey aroma of roasted hazelnut around the room. I took a bite of buttery wheat toast and watched him.

"We'll have your room refreshed and ready for you when you return this evening," Noble said to the Martins as he walked to his seat. "Dinner is at 7:00 as usual if you return by then." He sat down without looking at me.

"Thank you. We'll see how things go at the fair," Patty said. "But we'll probably be back by then."

"Good."

We all carried on a light conversation while finishing breakfast, then helped with the dishes and went our separate ways. I went up to my room to practice my flute because even though I wasn't teaching at the moment, I hoped things would turn around soon, and I wanted to be ready.

When I went back downstairs later, hoping to scrounge up some lunch which wasn't typically served, the unusual silence in the B&B made me think I was the only one home. But that changed quickly. Piano music emanated from the parlor room, which was really just a small room in the back by the kitchen.

I tiptoed over and peeked through the doorway. Noble sat on a bench behind the piano, pecking keys and scribbling notes on a pad on the sheet music stand. He was obviously hard at work, probably composing one of the love songs he used to be known for. We'd played some of them when he and Summer and I were in the trio together. But those were happier times long ago, and this was now. I stepped back and walked away before he saw me.

I went to the kitchen and grabbed some crackers and iced tea before heading to the front porch to sit in one of the Adirondack chairs. Summer was already there, sitting in a chair and drinking iced tea herself.

"Oh, hi. Your flute playing sounds good. I've been listening," Summer said when she saw me.

"Thanks."

"Is Kasey back yet?"

"I don't know. I haven't seen her," I said, sitting in a chair next to her.

"She must have gone into the forest to look for more leaves to press. She was working on her notebook this morning. I hope she'll come back soon. If she doesn't, I may pick blueberries myself for the pies and get started."

"Hmm. Missing baking with you doesn't seem like something Kasy would do. She's usually so excited about it."

"Yes. I thought so, too," Summer said, sounding puzzled. "But I'm afraid the rain will start again, and I want the blueberries picked and inside before that."

I nodded. I decided to mention what I saw last night.

"By the way, someone was in the backyard last night. Whoever it was ran into the woods before I got a good look at them. Is there any reason someone would come by in the middle of the night?"

"What? Really? I have no idea who that would have been. Are you sure you saw someone?"

"Yes, or something," I said. I didn't mention hearing Noble because I wasn't sure the voice I heard was his, and because I thought of another possibility for what I saw. "You don't think the bog people could be roaming around Hidden Glen, do you?" The story Summer told around the campfire still haunted my dreams.

"Did it look like a bog person?"

"I don't know. I've never seen one and only slightly recall the description. Or could I have seen the bog witch?"

"I've never seen the bog witch outside of the bog. But, I suppose the possibility exists," Summer said, seeming perplexed. "Oh dear. With all this talk about the bog people and the bog witch, I'm really getting worried about Kasey. I wonder if she could have gone farther into the forest than she was supposed to, and even into Wild Blueberry Bog. She did hear us talking about the blueberries there this morning."

"That's right," I said. "But you told her to pick the ones in the backyard."

"That doesn't mean she didn't go exploring," Summer said. "And after what you've just told me about seeing someone in the backyard and with Wade missing, too, I can't help but wonder if something has happened to her." She started wringing her hands.

"She'll probably turn up any minute," I said, hoping to comfort her.

I didn't see the need to worry yet, given that Kasey couldn't have been gone that long, and she was pretty smart and able to take care of herself. But then again, Wade was the same way, and he had disappeared. Maybe Summer was right to be concerned.

Drops of water abruptly pattered on the porch roof and dripped off the leaves of the trees in front of us.

"Oh, dear, and now it's raining. She should have been back by now. I'm going to call Cam." Summer pulled her phone out of her pocket.

"Why?"

"Because his daughter's missing, and so is Wade. And the Thunder Moon was high in the night sky only a week or two ago. Something's wrong. I can feel it."

I nodded. I wasn't going to mess with intuition. I'd trusted my own many times. While she was talking, I stood and went back into the B&B, where I put my glass in the sink and headed out back to call for Kasey. I shouted her name a few times, but to no avail. The rain intensified and soaked my top and capris as I ran to the path. I pushed wet hair off my face and peered into the forest. Where was she?

"Kasey," I called again.

No answer. A bird or a squirrel, maybe, rustled through trees. I stepped back warily.

"Kasey?" I asked, tentatively.

I stood deathly still, aware as I'd seldom been before of how alone I was. The haunting coo of a mourning dove echoed through the dark forest. The bog, which was the home of the bog witch and the bog people, was just on the other side of the trees. Could Kasey have ventured there by herself? My drenched clothes clung to me in the cool rain, and I shivered. Suddenly, through the pelts of water, a white shape appeared and ran toward me.

"Bobo?"

The little dog barked and jumped around me. I was so happy to see him, I picked him up and hugged him, but he squirmed frantically until I let him down again.

"What's wrong, Bobo? Why are you acting like this?"

He circled me, barking loudly and running back and forth.

"Are you trying to tell me you know where Kasey is?"

He ran a few yards into the forest and then back toward me again, barking.

"You do, don't you?" I asked. "You know where she is."

He barked again and ran into the woods.

"Okay then. Take me to her," I said, stepping into the wet underbrush and following him.

I hurried after Bobo, struggling to keep him in sight as sheets of rain poured down. He scampered down the yellow-flagged, dirt path straight toward Wild Blueberry Bog. That had to be where Kasey was. I swallowed hard and struggled to calm my rising fears about her safety as I forged ahead. She must be alright. But if by chance she was in trouble, I had to reach her in time. Bobo barked again, and I picked up my pace. Puddles formed on the path, and I desperately splashed through them.

As we approached the outer limits of the forest, Bobo turned and barked again. He was definitely leading me to something. I ran forward and into the bog. The ground was even soggier than I remembered, obviously soaking up the new rain. I tried to remain on the path, but the yellow flags were barely visible. Bobo suddenly veered to the left toward a thick copse of trees. I took my chances that the mushy, quaking ground would support me and followed him.

When I reached the red maple trees, which were underlaid with brambles and encircled inside and out with a plethora of wild blueberry bushes, I stepped forward under their thick canopy. The light diminished considerably there. And the clamor of rain suddenly stopped, leaving a dreadful silence. A rich, fertile odor permeated the damp huddle of trees, suffused with the rotten smell of decay. I scrunched up my nose and inched forward past tall, spindly trunks in the deep shade, painfully aware of the thick, black, quagmire of danger around me.

"Kasey?" I called out.

No answer.

"Bobo?"

A clipped bark broke through the quietness. Her dog must be here, but I couldn't see him. Several drops of rain dribbled through the leaves above and dripped to the ground, adding shine to the glistening muck percolating ominously under logs and mosses.

"Kasey, are you there?" I tried again.

"Faron?"

I almost fell to my knees with relief when I heard Kasey's thin voice.

"Yes, it's me. Where are you?" I called out.

"Over here. I'm stuck."

"I'm coming. Hold on."

"Hurry. I'm sinking."

I ran forward toward her voice, trying desperately to stay on solid ground. But the ground was wet and mushy. A log spanned a short distance in front of me, and I sat on top to swing my legs over. But as I was about to drop to the other side, I realized a pool of sludge lay below me. I pulled my feet back up and looked around for a stick. After a moment, I found one that might work without having to jump off to do so.

"The water on the bottom is really cold," Kasey called out.

"I'll be right there," I called back.

"And I'm stuck in the peat, too."

I grabbed the stick and stabbed the ground. The stick disappeared. Obviously, the bog was deep here. I didn't want to take a chance on how deep.

"Faron?" Kasey sounded frantic.

"I'm here. I'm coming."

I jumped off behind the log and frantically searched for another stick. I grabbed a thick one that was more like a branch before reevaluating my surroundings and heading to the side of the mire. The muddy side of the quagmire was sloped and slick with moss. I nearly fell in.

"I can't hold on," she yelled. The bog is pulling me down."

"I'm on my way."

Upon finding a firmer area, I sprinted toward where I'd

heard Kasey's voice. I tripped over a rock. As I righted myself, I saw her clinging to a fallen tree branch extending over the quagmire. But she didn't seem to have a good grip and was struggling to stay above water.

Bobo ran frenetically back and forth on the branch. When he saw me, he barked and dashed back to land and toward me. We raced together to a spot on the firmer ground parallel to Kasey's location.

"Here. Grab a hold of this," I shouted.

I extended the stick toward her, but she couldn't reach it. I tried again. She let go of the branch to grab the stick, but missed. She started going under, flailing her arms.

"No," I yelled.

I extended the stick again, almost straight to her. She reached forward and this time succeeded in grabbing it.

"Hang on tight," I said. "I'll pull the stick toward me."

The suction pulling on Kasey was greater than I had imagined as I struggled to pull her out, and my arms began to tire. She took in a mouthful of peat.

"Keep your mouth closed," I shouted.

She did so. I clutched the stick and pulled slowly, using all my strength. Eventually, she began to slide toward me.

"Don't let go," I said. She looked exhausted. "This is working."

I continued to pull until I had her close enough to grab her shirt. I pulled her sleeve toward me and grasped her arm and then the other one and pulled her onto solid ground. I fell back, sweating. Bobo ran over and nudged her neck. Kasey started crying.

"You saved me, Faron," she said between sobs. "I could have died."

"Let's not think about that," I said when I caught my breath. "I've got you now. But we have to find a way out of the bog and home. The rain seems to have let up, which is good." I looked around to get my bearings. "Did you lose your shoe?" I asked.

Something floated on top of the mire a few yards away. It looked like a tennis shoe. Maybe the rain had saturated the peat and loosened the bog's grip on the item.

"No. I lost my sandals, though."

"That's okay."

I looked more closely. The floating item was a tennis shoe.

"Stay here," I said.

I stood and moved along the side of the quagmire until I was parallel with the shoe. I braced my feet and leaned forward. I screamed.

"What's wrong?" Kasey shouted.

I took a deep breath and tried to put what I saw out of my mind. I had to take care of Kasey.

"Nothing. I almost lost my footing, that's all," I said. "Let's go. This isn't important." I hurried back to her as quickly as was safely possible. "We have to get you home and safe."

I helped Kasey stand. But she dropped to the ground when she put her weight on her left side.

"What's the matter?" I asked, looking down. "Oh my gosh. How did you get that gash on your leg? It's bleeding."

"I think I slashed it on a branch before I fell into the bog," Kasey said. "There were a lot of brambles around."

"That's true. There are. Can you stand?"

We tried again. This time, Kasey took a shaky step forward.

"Yes. I can walk, too. Let's just get out of here."

"I'm with you on that," I said. "Put your arm around my

waist, and I'll help keep you steady."

We walked together with Kasey limping and Bobo close behind around the quagmire and eventually out of the bog and into the forest. I breathed a sigh of relief as we headed down the path through the woods together, grateful that Kasey was safe and thankful that the rain had let up.

"What were you doing in there anyway?" I asked, after we seemed to be out of danger.

"Looking for wild blueberries," Kasey said. "Until I slipped down the slope and fell into the bog. There were so many bushes there. Didn't you see them?"

I nodded. "Yes, I did. And you're right. You found the mother lode of blueberry bushes."

"And I would have had the best ones, too. They were tart and plumper than the tiny ones on bushes in other parts of the bog. They would have made a perfect pie."

I wondered how many other people had seen and investigated the plethora of bushes and thought the same thing when looking for blueberries in the bog. I thought of Wade in particular.

"I wish you hadn't done that. You could have been badly hurt," I said.

"I know," she said, sounding chagrined. "I'm sorry."

She limped along next to me.

"That's okay. I'm just glad you're safe," I said, sincerely.

Kasey was covered with black sludge and bits of moss, but despite that and the fact that she was also soaking wet and shivering, she seemed fine.

We reached the other edge of the forest and stepped into the backyard of the B&B. Bobo barked, and soon after, Summer and Cam ran out the back door, obviously having seen us from the kitchen window. Cam ran over and hugged Kasey, seemingly unbothered by the fact that she was covered in mud.

"My gosh. What happened?" he asked. "Summer called me, and I came right over. Where were you?" His eyes glistened.

"I got lost. Faron found me," Kasey said, simply.

"Thank God," he said. "Thanks, Faron."

"Yes. Thanks, Faron," Summer said.

I nodded.

She turned to Kasey and gasped. "What happened to your leg?"

"I cut it on a branch when I fell into the bog."

"You fell into the bog?" Cam asked, sounding worried.

"Yes, but Faron got me out," Kasey said. "She saved me."

Cam turned to me.

"I can't thank you enough," he said.

"I'm just glad I found her," I said.

"Your leg is bleeding," Summer said to Kasey. "We'll have to get you fixed up. Come with me." She took Kasey by the arm and helped her forward.

I walked behind them toward the bed and breakfast with Cam by my side. I'd wait to tell Cam and Summer what I saw in the bog. I didn't want Kasey to hear me when I told them I'd found Wade Kestin immersed in the quagmire and that he definitely wasn't alive.

CHAPTER 12

Mason Snyder shook his head when his friend Joey told him the news about Wade Kestin first thing Monday morning. He was surprised to find out that Cove Pointe's missing person was discovered so soon, but not surprised to hear that Faron Chevalier was the one who found him. That made perfect sense. What better way for her to disguise her guilty tracks than to unwittingly trip over the body.

Faron hadn't literally tripped, but she'd still discovered Kestin's lifeless form floating in the bog yesterday. Or so she'd said. But her statement wouldn't stand. Mason knew that because he planned to prevail upon Joey to contact his neighbor on Cove Lake, who had an untoward connection to Faron, and arrange a meeting with him. Mason planned to enlist his help in proving Faron was a liar for pretending she didn't know Wade was already dead in the bog and in proving she was a murderer as well.

Mason sipped his strong coffee and looked out over the steaming lake from his seat at the patio table on the back deck of Joey's cottage. The cool air refreshed him as he struggled to become fully awake and process the new reality of Wade's death. Joey, who was sitting across from him, looked in the same direction, which made Mason bet he had suspicions of his own about Faron.

Hidden Glen B&B, where he'd been advised Faron was staying, was diagonal across the lake from them but hidden behind a misted forest of trees and far enough away to make seeing someone on shore difficult even when the usual morning mist cleared. Still, he was pretty sure he'd seen Faron once, standing at the end of the dock. He continued to glance over there as he thought about his plans.

Joey's neighbor was a wealthy lawyer named Cameron Talbert, who Joey had mentioned was Faron's next conquest after Kestin disappeared and maybe even before that. Joey had seen her drooling over Cameron at a recent birthday party at the Talberts' cottage on Cove Lake and had heard she'd been seen with him around town.

Mason himself had seen Faron at the county fair riding the Ferris Wheel with Talbert when he'd gone over there after receiving a tip from Joey about where she was and who she was with. She sure didn't take long to pick up and move on after her husband's death. Her ongoing ruse as a grieving widow was up, at least with Mason.

Several geese flew overhead, honking noisily before quieting and landing on the lake near a pair of white swans. They floated together silently and occasionally dipped their beaks in the water, sending out small ripples across the smooth surface. Mason sighed, enjoying the peacefulness of his new refuge, and took another sip of coffee.

Mason had things to say to Cameron Talbert, too, not the least of which was that he was playing with fire as far as Faron Chevalier was concerned. No two ways about it. Talbert needed to be warned that he ran the risk of being Faron's next victim if he continued to allow her to play up to him. A lawyer should be more astute in regard to gold diggers. But Faron was drop-dead gorgeous, and she'd turned savvier heads before. So maybe the young counselor's naïveté was understandable. Mason would set him straight.

A rowboat floated on the clear mirror of the lake, and a fisherman cast his line from it far out into the water. Then he sat still, waiting, in the quiet serenity of the morning. After a while, he reeled his line in and cast again. A slow game, perhaps, but an honest one. Mason could appreciate that.

The main reason Mason wanted to talk to Cameron Talbert was to ask for his help in trapping Faron into confessing to the murders of her late husbands, as well as Wade Kestin, and any others she cared to name, and giving herself up to the law. He'd settle for a confession to any of the murders as long as he could get enough out of her to put her behind bars.

Once Talbert realized what he was up against in his new relationship with Faron, he would come around. Mason was sure of it. A lawyer who'd grown up in this small, close-knit community would want to protect his hometown at all costs from a murderous interloper. Mason set his coffee mug down on the table and looked at Joey.

"So, what do you say we head into Cove Pointe later and talk to that lawyer neighbor of yours. I understand he has an office in the Chamber of Commerce building," Mason said.

"Yeah. What do you want to talk to him for?"

"I want to get him in on my investigation. I want his help."

"His help? With what?"

"My investigation of Faron Chevalier."

"What are you, crazy? He doesn't think she's the culprit. He's going out with her for criminy's sake," Joey said. Joey set his mug on the table as well and patted his substantial mustache with a napkin.

"Culprit? Oh, so you do think Faron's involved in Wade Kestin's disappearance," Mason said.

"I didn't say that."

"Sounds like it."

"Well, you came all the way here, didn't you? And you had me trailing her before that. Something's going on. Why don't you tell me what it is? You think she murdered him?"

"Who? Wade?"

"Yeah. Wade. Who else?"

Mason shrugged, then looked away. Joey obviously wasn't having it. He was smarter than Mason thought. He looked back. Joey's eyes flickered.

"Her husband? You think she murdered Gill Chevalier?"

Joey's bushy eyebrows shot up, and his eyes widened. He looked completely flabbergasted. Mason paused a moment before answering. He didn't want to overplay his hand with his friend. But then he decided to tell him what he thought anyway. Joey was either with him or against him on this.

"Yeah. Yeah, I do. I think she murdered both of them and maybe more."

"A serial killer? In Cove Pointe?"

"That's what I think. And I want to catch her and put her behind bars. Are you in?"

Joey sat still and didn't say anything. Mason didn't recall telling him about Faron's other two husbands, and from the looks of things, Joey hadn't found out about them himself either. He didn't appear to be buying Mason's game plan.

"Look. You're either in this thing with me or you're not. I want this lady locked up," Mason said.

Joey leaned over the table toward Mason. "Yeah? Why? What's in it for you? Money or something? Don't tell me you're altruistic all of a sudden."

"Yeah, maybe. Maybe not. But Faron's getting on my

nerves bad. Worse even than Sandy did."

"Sandy? Your ex-wife? Is this a vendetta about Sandy?"

"No. This is a vendetta about a lady who murders all the men in her life. I want it to stop."

Joey's mouth dropped open. "Murders all the men in her life? How do you know that?"

"I haven't proven it yet, but I will. I wanna nail her with something concrete and have her arrested, and I need your help. Are you in or not?"

Joey pushed his chair away from the table and began to stand. Then he sat back down again. He looked over the lake and then back at Mason before leaning forward to say something.

"Look. Other people have disappeared in Cove Pointe in the past. Wade Kestin is just one in a long string of missing persons around here," he said.

"Yeah, well, he's also one of a long string of hapless guys in Faron's past. I don't know what happened to the other people in Cove Pointe, but I'm not lumping Wade in with them. I'd put my money on Faron having something to do with his disappearance."

"Hmm. Maybe."

Joey rubbed his face. Then he sat back and took a sip of coffee. He looked over the lake toward the B&B again and then toward the cottage he'd mentioned Cameron Talbert lived in. Eventually, he set his mug back on the table and looked at Mason.

"Are you sure about this?"

"Positive."

"Why?"

"Because I saw her at her husband's funeral. Cold as ice. That's what she was. I never saw a woman so unemotional."

"That doesn't mean she killed him."

"It doesn't mean she didn't. She married the old guy for his money two years ago. Then she waited around for the right moment to off him. Now he's dead, and she gets the money instead of his kids. But not if I have anything to say about it." Mason pounded his fist on the table. She was just like Sandy in that regard. Take the money and run, honey. Wrong.

Joey sat still, staring at him for a moment. Then he clenched and unclenched his jaw before seeming to make a decision.

"Alright. I'm in. Her finding Wade dead is too much of a coincidence for me, too, and I don't want a serial killer wreaking havoc in Cove Pointe. I'll call Talbert and set up a meeting."

"Good," Mason said. "He may know more about Faron than we do."

"We'll see what he has to say," Joey said. He pulled out his cell phone and began pressing numbers.

"Thanks. You won't regret this."

"I hope not."

Mason waited while Joey made the call. He talked for a while before hanging up and standing.

"The receptionist said to come right over, and Talbert would fit us in," Joey said. "Nice to know neighbors around here treat each other right. I told her who I was and that you were a private investigator visiting me on Cove Lake."

"Great. Let's go," Mason said, standing as well and heading for the sliding door.

He ditched his coffee mug in the sink along with Joey's, and they headed out. A doe and two fawns stepped gracefully out of the forest as he followed Joey outside to the car. Mason was constantly amazed at how truly wild the area was. A bear had ambled past the deck the evening before. Disappearing around here didn't seem so unlikely given the remoteness of the location.

In fact, it seemed almost probable, especially if a bloodthirsty serial killer lurked in the untamed wilderness. He looked quickly over his shoulder to banish the thought. Then he hopped in the car with Joey, and they drove into town.

Noble Dixon walked out of the Chamber of Commerce building when they walked in. He greeted them cordially before continuing on his way. Oh, that's right, Mason thought. Noble was on the board of the Chamber of Commerce, if he remembered correctly from a newspaper article he'd read. He must be quite a prominent individual around here. What would he do if he found out a serial killer was living under his own roof?

When they walked into the reception area at Talbert's office, he and Joey were ushered into a large, corner office that smelled faintly of fresh paint. The man Mason had seen on the Ferris Wheel with Faron stood and walked around a large, wooden desk to greet them. He waved them into chairs in front of the desk and took a seat behind it.

"What can I do for you gentlemen?" he asked, formally.

Talbert appeared formal as well in his tailored suit. Mason wished he'd thought to wear something other than wrinkled khakis, but he was living out of a suitcase. So what the heck. He'd make do despite the power difference in appearance. Mason was sure he himself had the upper hand.

The lawyer obviously didn't know Joey as well as Mason had thought he did, given how aloof he was. But that wouldn't matter once he told him what they were there to see him about. This was strictly business as far as Mason was concerned.

"Thank you for seeing us on such short notice," Mason began.

Cameron nodded.

Mason continued. "I'm sure you're aware that Cove

Point's latest missing person turned up dead in a bog yesterday, and I wanted to talk to you about that. I want to find out what happened."

"Really? I'm not sure I can help you with that. Have you tried the police?"

"No. Not yet."

Mason glanced at Joey, who was looking straight ahead and appeared to be uninterested in adding to the conversation.

"The reason I wanted to talk to you is because I'm investigating Faron Chevalier, and I understand you know her."

"Do I? Where do you get your information?"

Mason laughed uncomfortably. "Joey here," he said.

"Huh. I didn't know I was under surveillance," Cameron said.

"You're not," Joey said, shaking his head. "Mason, let's go. This was a bad idea."

"No. Wait a minute," Cameron said. "Tell me what this is about."

Mason answered. "Well, I hate to be the bearer of bad news, but your girlfriend isn't everything she pretends to be. Were you aware her husband was murdered earlier this year?"

"She's not my girlfriend. And yes, I'm aware of her husband's tragic passing. Now what do you mean by your snide comment about Faron?"

"I mean, she isn't completely cleared of her husband's murder. She can't leave the state. Did you know that?"

Cameron stared at him for a moment. Did Mason detect a flicker of surprise? He read poker faces pretty well, and this guy didn't have a good one.

"Regardless of whether I know that or not, how do you know that?"

"Hey. It's my line of work," Mason said, shrugging. "And this is the second time in less than six months she's found a dead body. I find that suspicious."

"You do, do you?"

"Yeah. I do," Mason said, firmly.

"Well, I don't," Cameron said. "Maybe your friend is right. Maybe you should leave."

Mason stood. "Yeah, okay. I'll go if you want. But before I do, I think you should know you're not completely safe yourself."

"What do you mean by that?"

"I mean, the possibility exists that you could be her next target."

"Target for what?"

Mason turned and headed for the door. Joey stood and followed him.

"Target for what?" Cameron called out.

Mason turned back around and looked at him. "Alright, I'll tell you, but only because your safety and that of Cove Pointe is at stake. Your girlfriend had two other husbands before Gill Chevalier was knocked off. Why don't you ask her what happened to them? C'mon, Joey."

"Why? What happened to them?" Cameron asked, loudly.

"I'm getting a bad vibe here," Mason said, as he opened the door. "That's all I'm gonna say."

He walked out the door and into the reception area. Joey remained behind, and Mason heard him tell Talbert he hoped he wouldn't take the meeting personally and that he could borrow fishing gear from him anytime. Then Joey followed him out, closing the door behind him. Mason headed down the stairs and out to the car.

"We shouldn't have done that," Joey said, after they got

in. "Now you just have Talbert ticked at you for no reason. He won't tell you anything about Faron after this."

"Maybe. Maybe not," Mason said. "I had to tell him about her."

"Your loss," Joey said.

Joey drove them back to his cottage in silence. As they walked up the front path, Tina passed them on her way out and said she'd be home from the office early and make dinner for all of them. Joey stole a quick kiss and told her to be good. She laughed and said she never was before hopping into her Mercedes and driving away.

"She's something," Mason said as he followed Joey into the house. "How'd an old guy like you end up with a dish like her?"

"Luck and timing," he said. "I was flush in a casino once, and she'd just quit her job as a dealer. I had to spend my money on something. So I spent it on her. And we ended up together even though they hired her back later."

"You're right. Luck of the draw for a crummy gambler like you."

Joey scoffed. "What about Sandy? What happened with her?" he asked Mason.

"Oh, same old story. I found her with another guy in our own home, and they weren't just holding hands, if you know what I mean. I kicked her out right then."

"Geez. That's rough."

"Yeah. She's gonna marry the bozo soon after our divorce goes through. I'm not planning on crashing the wedding, though. I'll probably stay home and drink myself blind."

"Sorry that happened to you." Joey shook his head.

"Me, too," Mason said. "But at least I got her pegged as

another conniving woman. She's bad news."

"Yeah," Joey said.

He walked over to a sideboard in the great room and poured two whiskeys. He handed Mason one.

"Before lunch?"

"Sounds like you could use a drink."

"Yeah. You're right." Mason took the glass from him.

"So anyway, like I said, I'm not thinking the meeting went too well with Talbert," Joey said, taking a seat on a sofa.

"Could have gone better," Mason said. "But at least he knows to watch his back, whether he believes me right now or not."

Mason walked over and sat down on a sofa across from Joey. He leaned back and sipped his whiskey.

"Yeah. I suppose," Joey said. "What did you mean when you told him Faron had two other husbands? Is that for real? You never mentioned she was married before."

"Oh, it's for real, alright."

"Okay." Joey paused for a moment. "So what happened to them?"

"They're both dead."

"Dead?" He leaned forward and set his whiskey glass on the coffee table.

"Yeah. One was shot in the head. The other one was probably smothered."

"Holy crap." Joey's face paled. "You weren't kidding when you said she'd murdered all the men in her life, were you? You really think that."

"I'm dead serious."

"Wow. But we still don't know if Faron was involved in Wade Kestin's death."

"Not yet, we don't," Mason said. "But we'll see how this plays out. I think Talbert will call me when he has a chance to think about what I said. Once he finds out Faron has two other deceased husbands, and I'm sure he'll do some checking, I think he'll come around. I think he'll help us put her away."

"We'll see," Joey said. He grabbed his glass off the table and guzzled the rest of his drink.

"Yeah," Mason said. He took a long sip of whiskey and let the strong, warm liquid trickle down his throat and relax him. Then he smacked his lips and smiled. "We'll just see."

CHAPTER 13

I made sure Kasey was comfortable and tucked in for a nap in one of the twin beds in a guest room at the B&B on Monday afternoon after the doctor saw her. Bobo stayed with her, curled up at the end of the bed with his head between his paws. He was fluffy and sparkling white after his bath yesterday and seemed quite content as long as he was with her. I petted his head.

"Good dog. You saved Kasey's life," I said.

The doctor had come over at the behest of Eleanor, who had shown up after Kasey and I returned from the bog yesterday and insisted that she have a check-up and have her leg looked at. But Kasey had crawled into bed and fallen asleep after she'd gotten cleaned up and showered, so Eleanor had arranged for a house call today instead.

The doctor had just left after giving Kasey a clean bill of health, to the immense relief of everyone. I closed the curtains to dim the light in the room she'd shared with Eleanor last night and told her to get some rest before leaving and closing the door behind me.

I went downstairs to join the others who had stayed overnight at the B&B after Kasey was found safe, and, after I, as delicately as possible, had relayed my shocking discovery of Wade Kestin's dead body immersed in the quagmire.

Kasey hadn't taken the news of her flute teacher's death well, but she seemed in better spirits today, although she was still exhausted from her harrowing experience in the bog.

Cam and Eleanor sat in the living room with Summer, Noble, and the Martins. They all were still probably discussing the fact that the authorities had removed Wade's body from Wild Blueberry Bog and had remained there to search, it seemed, for something. Everyone looked up when I walked in.

"Kasey's resting," I said, quietly.

"Good, good," Eleanor said, sounding distracted.

She'd been traumatized by her granddaughter's disappearance and her subsequent account of the frightening event.

Cam gave me an odd look I couldn't quite interpret. He'd risen early and gone into Cove Pointe to help coordinate the search and rescue efforts, along with the resulting publicity over the gruesome discovery, from his office in town. He'd obviously gone home to change first because he had on a suit and tie when he returned this afternoon, which made him look completely different from the laid-back person I knew him to be. I wasn't sure I liked his new, authoritative look, but if he could help us deal with the new reality of Wade's death and the accompanying fallout from his discovery, I'd adjust.

Cam didn't want Kasey or me to face a slew of questions about Wade from the police or reporters at the B&B, which is why he'd run defense in town, and I welcomed his chivalrous protection. But upon seeing his drawn face and haggard expression when he walked in the door earlier, I couldn't help but wonder if something more had happened at his office, although he was probably worrying about Kasey. After all, he seemed to have made it a point to come back in time to hear what the doctor had to say about her health. But now, I didn't know what to make of his strange demeanor.

"Dottie called while you were upstairs," Summer said

to me. "She's devastated, of course. The police called her last night after they confirmed the body was Wade's and that he was deceased."

"Oh dear. Maybe she shouldn't be alone," I said. I hoped his nice wife would be okay.

"I asked if she wanted to come over, but she declined," Summer said. "She probably doesn't want to see people yet."

I nodded.

"Or maybe she doesn't want to be in the same room with the woman who found her dead husband," Noble said, nastily.

I froze and stared at him. A cold chill ran down my back.

"Why would you say that?" Summer burst out, turning to him. "Of course, that's not true."

Noble remained silent, staring back at me with his wicked, dark eyes while maintaining a cold, blank expression. No one else said anything, and I stood still, aghast, through an awkward silence. Lloyd Martin's cell phone rang, and his resulting conversation kept us all respectfully quiet.

"Yeah, okay. Got it," he said eventually and hung up. He paused for a moment before looking around at our expectant faces. "I hate to tell you all this, but they found another body."

"What?" I blurted out.

"Yeah. She's been identified as a Cove Pointe resident who disappeared two years ago."

"Millie?" Eleanor shrieked.

"I'm sorry. Did you know her?" Lloyd asked. "The resident's name was Millie Parker."

"Oh no," Eleanor said. She buried her face in her hands and began to sob.

I walked over and patted her arm. Summer got up and walked toward her after grabbing a box of tissues off an end table. She swayed slightly when she passed me, and I grabbed her elbow to steady her.

"Are you okay?" I asked.

She nodded and handed the tissues to Eleanor. I turned to Lloyd.

"How did you know they found another body already?" I asked him, feeling confused.

"Oh, I'm sorry we didn't tell you, but Lloyd's a police detective," Patty said. "Semi-retired. He's helping with the investigation."

"What? What investigation?"

"That's not important," Lloyd said. "Suffice it to say that I'll be apprised of developments in the situation in a timely manner."

"Oh, well, that's good," I said.

I felt dizzy. Something was going on behind the scenes that I didn't know about, and I was getting a bad feeling about whatever it was.

"Yes. The location where the bodies were found will be cordoned off and fenced after a thorough search is conducted to make sure no other bodies are in the area," Lloyd said.

"You mean, you're not from Ohio?" I asked, slowly, still dazed.

Patty shrugged.

Lloyd turned to Noble. "I trust the environmental group and a local business are taking care of the fencing."

Noble nodded. Cam nodded, too. Had they coordinated on the effort? I shivered, feeling another chill. I'd had a similar feeling before, after my husbands' deaths. I looked around the room. No one looked at me. This couldn't be happening again. I'd done a good thing by finding Wade's body, hadn't I? Why didn't anyone look at me?

"Can I get anyone anything?" I asked, hoping to break the eerie silence. "I was going to pour some iced tea."

Cam shook his head. No one else answered.

"Okay, then," I said, adding a bright lilt to my voice that I didn't feel.

I pivoted and walked into the kitchen. I placed my hands palms down on the counter and bent over, breathing fast and deep. Was I hyperventilating? What was happening? I needed to leave this place, and I needed to leave now.

"Can I help you with something?" Cam asked.

I turned to see him walking up behind me.

"No. I was just taking a break. I wanted to get some iced tea," I reiterated quickly. I straightened.

"Look. Don't worry about them," he said. He tipped his head sideways in a gesture toward the living room. "Everyone's having trouble adjusting to Wade's untimely death and now Millie's apparent death, as well. Don't take anyone's rudeness personally."

I sighed. Maybe he was talking about Noble, or maybe about everyone. He was probably right. We'd all had a shock. Of course, Cam wasn't suspicious of me, and maybe the others weren't either. I mean, I wasn't even around Cove Pointe when Millie disappeared, not that I should be a suspect in Wade's death just because I moved here right before he went missing. I don't know why I felt like everyone suspected me of something again.

"Really?" I asked, feeling immensely relieved that Cam seemed to be on my side.

"Yeah. This will all work out eventually, especially now that Millie's body was found near Wade's. A pattern could be established that leads away from the possibility of murder."

"Do you think so?" I asked.

"I do. But this new reality of their deaths is still hard to come to terms with," he said.

"I agree," I said.

"Do you want to go for a walk?" he asked.

"Do you? Dressed in a suit?"

"Yes. That's why I asked. We could go down to the beach and talk. That'll get us out of here."

"Okay, sure," I said.

Cam kicked his shoes off by the door and rolled up his pants legs and shirt sleeves after taking off his socks and suit coat.

"You look more like your casual self now," I said, smiling.

"Good. Let's go," he said.

I took my shoes off, too, and followed him out the door. We walked across the warm grass to the path where we carefully navigated the rougher ground until we reached the steps and descended to the beach. The sand was gritty and cool in the shade of trees, but warmed up as we continued forward into the sunnier area of the beach. Cam took my hand, and we strolled down the beach together toward the dock.

"So, how have you been holding up?" he asked. "I've been concentrating on Kasey's recovery, but you've had quite a time, too, finding her and then Wade. Are you okay?"

"Yeah, I am, thanks," I said, surprised that he was so thoughtful. "Finding Wade was quite a shock, but I'm back to normal. I recover quickly."

Cam nodded. "I remember you told me that." He looked away and then back. "Maybe this isn't the best time to bring this up, but is there anything else you want to tell me about your past? I need to know about you if I'm going to represent your interests with the will and everything you're dealing with after the death of your husband."

I stopped and looked at him. "You talked to Jay Morrison again, didn't you?" I asked.

He nodded. "Along with a few other people. I guess I just need to hear directly from you."

"Hear what?" I asked.

"That's up to you," he said. "I don't want to press, but I do need to know more about your background."

I gazed out at the lake and thought for a moment before deciding to tell him what I was pretty sure he already knew based on the strange looks he'd given me earlier.

"Alright. I was married before. Two times. Once, to a man I loved dearly, but he passed on. I didn't think I'd ever get over it."

"I'm sorry," Cam said, softly. "He must have been a very special person."

He sounded as though he really cared about my feelings and about how grief-stricken I'd been.

"He was," I said, venturing to share more. "I fell so hard for him."

I fell silent as I thought about Daniel. I thought I'd put my feelings for him in the past, but maybe not. Cam's caring nature seemed to bring out the emotional side of me.

We started walking across the sand again. Eventually, we reached the dock and stepped onto the rustic wood. When we got to the end, we stood there gazing at the scenic wilderness together. The fresh, lake breeze ruffled Cam's sandy hair, and I wanted to smooth it for him again in the same way I'd wanted to when I first met him. But I didn't.

"What was it about Daniel that you loved so much?" Cam

asked.

I thought for a moment. No one had ever asked me that question before.

"Daniel understood what it was like to be lonely," I said, after a while. "And he understood that loneliness was possible even when other people were around. We were soul mates in that regard."

"That's true about loneliness," Cam said, nodding.

I turned my head sharply and stared at him. "You understand that, too?"

"Absolutely," he said. "I felt that way a lot after losing my wife."

I leaned into him, feeling his comforting warmth. His statement made me feel a deep connection with him, similar to what I'd felt with Daniel. I didn't know other people besides my first husband could feel that way about loneliness. Noble never had, or at least he didn't understand me talking about it, probably because he was so into himself to the exclusion of other people that he kept himself company. But because of his self-centeredness, he also couldn't accept the fact that I rejected him and married Daniel instead, even though I had tried to let him down easily.

"I remember you told me about losing your wife and baby," I said. "What a terrible thing to have happen."

"Yes. But we're all scarred by life," Cam said. "We can only do our best to deal with what comes our way."

"You're right," I said. "That's a very astute statement."

He squeezed my hand, and I continued.

"After Daniel died, I felt as though the world went on, and I didn't. But I had to. So I married my second husband, Bryce, on the rebound from Daniel, but then he passed away, too." I swallowed hard and looked away. "Is that what you wanted to know?"

"Yes. Is there more you wanted to tell me?"

I looked at him, raising my armor back up at the probing question.

"Oh, so you want to know the whole thing, huh? Okay. They were both murdered, and I was under suspicion both times in the same way I was after Gill's death, my recent husband. But I was cleared both times. Okay?"

"What about this time?" Cam asked.

"What about this time?" I asked.

"Were you cleared this time?"

"Well, of course, I must have been. I wasn't arrested."

"Hmm," Cam said.

"What does that mean?" I asked, a little more shrilly than I had intended.

"Nothing," he said. "It doesn't mean anything. I'm glad you told me about Daniel and Bryce. I have to tell you, though, this information gives Gill's kids more leverage in contesting the will. But I'll do my best to get you treated fairly."

"That's all I can ask for," I said.

Cam released my hand and sat on the edge of the dock. He dipped his feet in the water. I sat next to him and did the same, but I suddenly felt as though I was being watched. I looked around quickly but didn't see anyone. Did Noble follow us here? I glanced behind me. No one was on the beach or in the woods. Maybe I was imagining things.

"Did I thank you for rescuing Kasey?" Cam asked, after a moment.

"Yes. I'm just glad I found her and she's okay," I said.

I took a deep breath to calm myself and to banish my

previous trepidation.

"I hope things settle down around here soon, and we can get to properly know each other," Cam said. "All the things that have been happening kind of put a damper on a budding relationship."

I looked up at him quickly, and he grinned.

"Is that what we have?" I asked. "A budding relationship, I mean?"

"I'd say so," he said. His eyes twinkled. "What do you think?"

"Oh, well, I don't know," I said.

"Well. Let's see if I can clarify things for you a little bit," he said, softly. He gently touched my cheek as he leaned closer and looked deeply into my eyes. "Is that okay with you?" His voice cracked.

I nodded.

His warm lips met mine, and I melted into him. He kissed me with a quiet passion that ignited a fire in my soul that I thought was long gone. I kissed him back with all the feelings I thought I had lost as he pulled me to him. We melded together in a deep embrace until the time and space of encumbrance disappeared. There was only us, and we were free. We were together, and yet we were free. My emotions soared higher and higher the longer we held each other.

Eventually, he released me. He looked into my eyes again.

"I've been waiting for the right time to do that," he said.

"I'm glad you did," I answered, smiling. "You picked the right time."

"Good," he said, smiling back.

I looked down and then across the way at the cattails waving in the distance near the edge of the bog. The dark, cool shadows at the edge of the forest beckoned nearby. What had brought me to this place and time? Did a force beyond my understanding guide me to this beautiful wilderness? Or was I here by some strange accident of nature? Was I here to meet Cam? Was I here because of Gill's murder and the need to come to terms with his death? How should I make sense of my life going forward after such a senseless tragedy—another senseless tragedy, I should say. I glanced at Cam, who was gazing at me in a way that made me wonder if he was wondering the same thing. Why was I here? A loon called in the distance, and I turned and looked out over the lake instead.

"There's one other thing I think you should know about Wade," Cam said after a while. "The police found a pan near him in the bog that appears to have come from the music camp."

"Really? How do they know?"

"I talked to them in my office this morning and told them about the pots and pans strewn around the kitchen at the music camp the night Wade disappeared."

"Oh. Does that mean something?"

"Sure does. The pan was part of a set they found at the camp. They talked to Dottie, too, after I told them she was planning to enter a blueberry pie in the pie contest. After talking to her, they determined Wade was in the bog gallantly picking blueberries for her to bake in her pie and putting them in the pan when he fell in."

"Oh, how awful," I said. "But very astute of the police to deduce."

"Yeah. They think he had an accident, so far anyway, and have pretty much ruled out anything nefarious being involved."

"Oh, good," I said. "That's something, anyway. It's still too bad that happened to him, though. I wonder if the same thing happened to Millie."

"Could be. We'll wait to hear. There's just one other thing, though," he said.

"What?"

"Well, Lloyd Martin talked to Summer earlier about the music camp overnight when Wade went missing."

"Yes?"

"He asked her if you were with her at the campout on the girls' side the whole time."

"Why would he do that?" I asked.

"To determine if you had an alibi, maybe," Cam said.

"What?"

"Yeah. I thought you should know. Summer told him you were gone for about forty-five minutes, and no one knew where you were."

"I was in the forest looking for sticks for the campfire," I said, suddenly feeling guilty again. "I went into the bog for a little bit to look for a boot I lost there, but the insects were so bad, I gave up and went back to the campfire. That's all."

"I figured it was something like that," Cam said, nodding.

"So you believe me."

"I do. And I think the police will, too."

"But I thought you said they determined Wade had an accident."

"So far," Cam said. "But I'm only assuming they're telling me everything. Plus, I talked to the local police. Lloyd's from the State Police."

"Does that make a difference?" I asked.

"I don't know. But now that Lloyd knows they found Millie's body as well, he may not see you as a person of interest in Wade's death anymore. We'll wait and see," Cam said. "But they're not going to reopen the music camp until they're sure Wade wasn't murdered and the area is safe. That could take a while."

My heart thumped hard in my chest, and I felt like throwing up. That clinched it for me. I was pretty sure I was under suspicion for murder again. But if Lloyd was with the State Police, was I a suspect in Wade's death or Gill's death or both? Things were closing in on me, and I needed a place to hide, like maybe my house in Fenton City. I glanced quickly at Cam. Could I stand to leave him? I hastily looked away and decided to go with my panicked decision anyway. I had to leave Cove Pointe as soon as I possibly could.

CHAPTER 14

Kasey and Eleanor went back to their cottage the next day, along with Cam and Bobo, leaving me alone and trapped with Noble. I had planned to pack my things and go home to Fenton City, but Summer wasn't feeling well. I didn't want to leave her permanently alone with her husband until she felt better. For some reason, I didn't trust him with her well-being and preferred to stay in the vicinity to check on her myself. She said she was fine, but she didn't look good.

She'd stayed in bed this morning to rest, which was probably a good idea given how her face was sweaty and her eyes were glazed over when I looked in on her. I'd dampened a washcloth with cold water and folded it before placing it gently on her forehead. She'd given me a half-hearted smile and said it made her feel better. So I'd told her to close her eyes and get some rest before shutting the door and heading back downstairs to sit on the porch where I was now.

I tried to think of something to do. I wanted to go into town, but I didn't want to go by myself. And Cam was working, so I couldn't call him. He was another reason I had decided not to leave Cove Pointe. I'd felt a strong connection with him when we talked on the dock yesterday afternoon, and I wanted to continue to see him and hopefully develop a deeper relationship. Also, the gossips in town still worried me, and I didn't want to run into the private investigator who had obviously followed me to Cove Pointe from Fenton City. Could he still be snooping around, stirring up trouble? I hoped not. I had enough to deal with the way things were.

Where else could I go? The atmosphere at Hidden Glen since yesterday was stilted and uncomfortable, and I didn't want to stick around the B&B with Lloyd and Patty Martin still in their room and Noble lurking around somewhere. Why hadn't the Martins been honest with me about Lloyd being a policeman and maybe about other things as well? Their presence now gave me a strange feeling of being under surveillance, and I didn't like that.

Knowing Wade and Millie had both died in the bog also weighed heavily on my mind. I couldn't help but wonder if more of the missing persons in Cove Pointe had met a similar fate picking blueberries. The county fair with the pie contest returned every year around the same time they had all disappeared, and Eleanor had said they were mostly bakers. Finding them might take suspicion about Wade's death off of me in the same way Millie's discovery probably had, because I wasn't anywhere near Cove Pointe in previous years. And the pattern of the cause of death for all of them, including Wade, as drowning or suffocating in the bog could then be established as accidental.

Was I grasping at straws to direct suspicion away from me? Maybe. But my thoughts seemed plausible. Should I search the bog myself? Leaving such an important job to those who may not have my best interests at heart seemed foolhardy, especially now that I was essentially trapped in Cove Pointe until Summer got well. I had as much or more invested in the missing persons' safe recovery as the authorities did if I wanted to live here peacefully. I decided to change and head for the bog.

As I opened the screen door and walked inside, Lloyd and Patty came down the stairs with their suitcases.

"Are you leaving?" I asked, surprised.

"Yes," Patty said. "We're going to stay in town. Summer is sick, and we don't want to impose while she's under the weather."

"Oh, I'm sure that's very nice of you," I said, feeling relieved.

With the Martins gone, Summer could rest. And I doubted that other guests would show up anytime soon, given that people had been found dead so close to Hidden Glen B&B.

"We'll settle up with Noble later, but we're going into town to find another place to stay now."

"Well, it was nice to meet you," I said. I wasn't sure I felt that way at all after their subterfuge, but I wanted to be polite.

"You, too."

Lloyd didn't say much as usual, but he did nod on his way out the door. Maybe he was cutting me some slack. Who knew?

I stayed in the foyer for a moment, looking through the screen door to watch them leave. When they pulled out of the driveway and onto the road, I breathed a sigh of relief and went upstairs to change. Now I only had Noble to deal with, although I didn't know where he was at the moment.

After changing into jeans and a sleeveless top, I quickly checked on Summer, who was sleeping, and headed out after donning the boots Summer had left on the mat near the back door.

When I reached the bog, I made a beeline for the copse of trees where I'd discovered Wade's body. Halfway there, I realized the area was swarming with police and other less identifiable people. I couldn't see what they were doing, but rolls of wire fencing lay on the ground nearby. They were either still searching for something or putting up a fence. Either way, I couldn't see a way to get near the blueberry bushes. I turned around and headed back.

But as I did, I looked out over the wetlands toward the road far in the distance and noticed a hunched-over figure limping through the brush. Was it the bog witch? Why hadn't anyone wondered if she was involved in the disappearances rather than suspecting me? She'd been wandering around Cove Pointe, specifically in the bog, longer than I had.

Now that the police had determined the deaths of Wade and probably Millie, too, were accidents, my question was a moot point. But still, I wondered why the presence of the bog witch hadn't come up. Had she been questioned? Or was her existence largely unknown, in which case she probably hadn't been.

I concentrated on finding my footing, then looked up again and caught a glimpse of the figure as it disappeared behind a few feathery, green tamarack trees. I decided to follow whoever I'd seen and tramped toward the road where the wetlands continued on the other side. Maybe I could find out more than the police had if I crossed the road and looked on the other side.

I slogged through the mush and glop while attempting to remain on the firmer ground near the edge of the forest. My breathing became more and more labored as I trudged on. At the rate I was going, I wouldn't reach the road for another ten minutes. But I wasn't in a hurry. I was just purposeful.

The muggy air smelled earthy and stale with an overpowering odor of decay as I struggled to breathe it in. To my left, turtles sunned themselves in a line on a moss-covered log. A few slid off and dove into the watery morass as I plodded by, startling a bullfrog that croaked in obvious annoyance. Tall, swaying grasses and cattails filled the open areas, and brambles and bushes obscured my way forward. I hopped back when a muskrat scurried in front of me and disappeared into the holly nearby. The bog, as I moved within its watery womb, became a living, breathing entity that fluctuated in accommodation to my unexpected presence, and I was overwhelmed by its natural genius.

When I finally reached the road, which was devoid of traffic except for a car parked on the shoulder down the way, I crossed over to the other side, where the wetlands were less open and more shaded by trees. The air remained thick but not as hot in the stunted pine and spruce-dotted peatland.

I continued on through the area, looking for the figure I'd seen, who I assumed was the bog witch. I thought it was high time to meet her in order to put my curiosity to rest. But I didn't have the faintest idea where to find her. That is, I didn't until I saw Noble near a short, twisted tamarack tree talking to a hunched-over figure garbed in black. The figure reminded me of the one I'd seen in the early hours of the morning a few days ago, leaving the backyard of the B&B in the rain and heading for the woods. "Bring more next week," Noble had called out then. I remembered that clearly.

I darted behind a pair of white pine trees and watched them from my hidden vantage point. What was he doing here? When they turned together and headed into the woods, I slipped out of the shade and hurried after them.

When I reached the edge of the woods where Noble had disappeared, I slowed my pace and kept out of sight behind trees as I continued forward. I caught a glimpse of them up ahead and tried to keep up.

Noble was talking animatedly, but I heard no response. The farther into the woods we went, the more curious I became. What was he doing here, and where were they going? After several more minutes, when we were deep in the woods and the shade was dark and unwelcoming, we entered a small clearing where a rickety, gray shack stood under a canopy of leaf-covered tree branches. Noble looked around furtively before following the figure into the shack.

I stayed behind a black spruce tree for a while before losing patience and inching toward the shack to peer through a hazy spot in a cracked, murky window. I couldn't see much, but what I made out shocked me. Noble was gesturing to a wizened, old woman with a braid of white hair wearing a black, hooded cape with the hood down. She was surrounded in the room by terracotta pots of what appeared to be plants and herbs, and she held a glass jar filled with a yellow powder in front of her. Her cheeks were papery, pale, and wrinkled, and her teeth were yellow. And when she laughed heartily at something Noble said, she cackled. But her eyes were what drew me in. The woman's deep-set eyes were dark and evil, like the eyes Summer had said she'd seen in the hooded face in the woods when we were leaving Eleanor's birthday party. I gasped. Noble had to be talking to the bog witch.

As I watched with bated breath, the bog witch handed Noble the jar filled with powder and seemed to be telling him something about it. Directions maybe? Was he obtaining a medicinal herb? She pointed to a spoon on the table and then at the jar. Could she be relaying dosage instructions? Was she more of a garden witch, securing herbs and flowers from the bog for medicines? The more she gestured toward her plethora of greenery as she talked, the more possible the idea seemed.

A thrush suddenly sang a beautiful flute-like song that broke through my absolute concentration, and I glanced away for a moment. As I did so, I lost my footing and threw my hand against the shack to break my fall before regaining my stature. When I raised my eyes again to window level, Noble stared straight at me. I gasped and ducked down, but it was too late. He shouted, and I turned and ran as fast as I could back through the woods toward the road. How could I have been so careless? I wasn't sure if he'd recognized me through the clouded windowpane, but he obviously knew someone was there. I'd find out later if he knew it was me.

When I reached the road after considerable trouble because I took a circuitous route through the woods so I wouldn't be seen if Noble followed me, I trekked down the shoulder toward Hidden Glen. After a while, I passed the parked car I'd seen earlier when I crossed the road and realized it was Noble's. I turned my walk into a full-out run, although the heavy boots kept me from racing at my full potential. Eventually, I reached the B&B and, after stashing the boots behind the trash bin to keep Noble from seeing them and possibly making a connection to me, hurried inside and up to my room to hide.

I went to check on Summer first. I tapped lightly on her door, and she called to come in.

"What happened to you?" she asked when I opened the door.

She was sitting up and leaning back on a pillow placed against the backboard. I must have looked like quite a sight after tramping through the bog and forest in the heat and mire.

"Oh. I went for a hike and slipped a few times, that's all," I said, hoping she believed me. "How are you doing?"

"I'm feeling better," she said. "The nap helped. But I think I'll stay in bed for a little while more. I was just looking out the window at the birds. They're so chirpy in the afternoons."

"Did they wake you up?"

"I think so, but that's okay."

"Can I get you anything?"

"Not right now. I'm going back to sleep."

"Okay. Well. I'm going to take a shower," I said. "I'm glad you're feeling better."

I walked out of the room and hurried down the hall to my room to get cleaned up before Noble got home. When I got to my room, I went over to shut the window and pull the blinds, but before I did, something caught my eye. A man walked out of the woods and into the backyard. I looked closer at him. It was the private investigator from Fenton City. What was he doing here? Had he been in the bog checking out where the bodies were found, or was he here to check on me?

"Hey," I called out.

He looked up, and when he saw me, he scooted sideways and vanished around the corner of the B&B. I ran out of my room and down the stairs in time to see him running down the driveway to the gravel parking area. He jumped in his car and peeled out while I stood in the driveway frantically waving my arms to get his attention. But he didn't stop. I stood still for a moment with my mouth open. Then I remembered Noble could be back any minute, and I turned and ran back into the B&B and up the stairs to take a shower. I'd talk to Summer about the P.I. later.

When I'd finished getting cleaned up, I peeked out my door, and after making sure Noble wasn't in the hallway, I headed downstairs. When I reached the bottom of the stairs, I heard a noise, so I tiptoed slowly toward the kitchen. I peered around the corner.

Noble stood at the island counter, preparing what looked like a tray of food. He must be making supper to take upstairs to Summer. I wasn't sure what to do next, but I was going to have to make my presence known eventually, so I took a deep breath and stepped into the kitchen.

"Where have you been?" I asked brightly. "The Martins left this afternoon and mentioned they would settle their account with you later. I thought I'd let you know."

He regarded me suspiciously.

"Yeah? Okay. Where have you been?"

"Hmm? Oh, just hanging around and enjoying the great outdoors. What a beautiful place you have here," I replied.

He looked at me a moment longer, then shrugged and returned to preparing the food. He must have bought my act and also not been able to place me as being at the bog witch's shack earlier. The filthy window I'd been looking through when he looked back at me was probably harder to see out of than into.

I walked to the sink and drew a glass of water from the tap as a ruse to see what he was making. A turkey sandwich, applesauce, and iced tea were the items on the tray. That seemed normal enough. But upon bending sideways and peering around him, I realized a measuring spoon spanned the top of the glass with the iced tea, which seemed odd, although I couldn't see if anything was in it. Just then, Noble grabbed the spoon off the glass and, after a moment, swiftly stirred the drink. What an unusual thing to do unless he'd poured sugar in the tea. I didn't see a sugar bowl, but he could have.

I sipped my water and continued to watch him move back and forth. He sliced the sandwich with a long knife before arranging the dishes on the tray. He grabbed something off the counter and stuffed it in his pocket before picking up the tray and walking away. But I caught a glimpse of what he grabbed before it disappeared. I gasped when I realized what it was. Noble had put the jar of yellow powder I'd seen the bog witch give him in his pocket.

What kind of powder was in the jar? Had Noble stirred the powder into the iced tea? Was it medicine or something else? I again recalled his enigmatic statement. "Bring more next week," Noble had said to the rain-soaked figure in the backyard a few days ago, who I now knew was the bog witch. Had he been referring to the yellow powder and gone to get some from the bog witch himself?

I remained in the kitchen, shaking, as I listened to the stairs creak as Noble walked up to Summer's room. How could I find out what the powder was made of? I looked at the counter he'd been working at and noticed a drift of yellow sprinkles. He must have spilled some.

I moistened my finger with saliva and dabbed at a few sprinkles before transferring them to the tip of my tongue. Bitter. What could the taste be from? I'd noticed yellow flowers in the bog that looked like lilies and had the same shade of yellow as the powder. But why would someone want that in their tea?

A terrifying thought shot through my mind as a tight knot of fear formed in my stomach. A number of poisonous plants and flowers grew in the bog. Kasey had told me that. Was the powder meant to be a medicinal herb? Or was Noble poisoning Summer with powder from a poisonous bog flower? I didn't have time to find out. If the latter was the case, I had to stop him.

I dashed out of the kitchen and up the stairs to Summer's room. Noble stood next to the bed where he'd set the tray in Summer's lap. She was leaning on a pillow against the backboard again.

"Here. Let me help you," I said, walking over to the bed.

I made a show of adjusting the tray and suddenly losing my balance. I shook the tray, spilling iced tea all over it.

"Look what you did," Noble yelled. "Get out of here."

"She didn't mean to," Summer said.

"Looked like she did," Noble said, picking up the tray. "I'll be back later after I get this cleaned up."

I left the room before he did and went back to my own. I locked the door and stood there vacantly staring at it. I didn't know how I could prove what I was pretty sure Noble was up to, and I didn't know why Noble would poison his wife. And I also didn't know how to stop him. He had access to all the food in the B&B. He could poison everyone. He could poison me if he wanted to. Plus, if I told Summer my suspicions, she wouldn't believe her husband would do something like that, and I could lose her as an ally.

I was again trapped in an impossible situation. Not only was my reputation wavering between good and bad because of being under suspicion for the murder of Wade and probably Gill, too, I was now at risk for being poisoned and seeing my friend poisoned as well. I didn't know what to do, but I had to do something. And I had to play things right to keep Noble from knowing I was on to him.

One thing I did know for sure. Things were going to be very different around here from here on out. Goosebumps prickled my arms, and tiny hairs stood up on the back of my neck. My intuition told me I was only beginning to realize what was really going on.

CHAPTER 15

Mason Snyder hung up with Noble Dixon, wondering if he should call the State Police again about Faron Chevalier. He'd upped the ante in his investigation after another missing person in Cove Pointe was found dead. Faron seemed to be in the clear on this one, but that didn't mean he couldn't nose around and see if anything related to the second missing person could be helpful to him in regard to investigating her about the death of the first missing person, as well as the deaths of her late husbands.

He glanced out the sliding glass door at the beautiful morning from his position on a sofa in the great room. Joey was on the deck with Tina, and Mason didn't want to interrupt their cozy tete-a-tete. So he just stayed where he was and sipped the mimosa Tina had made for him earlier. The sparkling drink tingled pleasantly on his palate and greatly refreshed him—something he needed after the exhaustion that had plagued him after his trek through the bog yesterday. He wasn't as young or in shape as he used to be, and he reminded himself to work on that.

Mason took another sip of the perfectly mixed Prosecco and orange juice combination. Tina was a genius at the bar. She seemed to know exactly what he liked. She didn't really give him a second look, though. Maybe he'd join a gym. He set his drink down and thought about Sandy and her constant nagging for him to work out. Then he leaned back, stretched his legs, and yawned. The gym could wait.

Mason had gone to the site in Wild Blueberry Bog yesterday afternoon, where Wade Kestin and, more recently, Millie Parker had been found deceased, for a reason. He wanted inside information, and he was going to use his chummy status as a former police officer to get it from the State Police he'd heard had shown up there. He'd accessed the bog through a path from Hidden Glen B&B after receiving permission to park at the B&B and directions to the site from Noble that morning.

A wire fence was partially constructed around the area where the bodies had been found, and the State Police there told him it was no longer accessible to the general public. But they had confirmed what he'd already suspected, which was that the site was still considered a crime scene until otherwise designated.

That clinched things for Mason. Faron wasn't getting away with anything if he had something to say. And he did, especially after she'd yelled out the window and later wildly waved her arms at him on his way back to his car through the backyard of the B&B. She was definitely unhinged, as Noble had just now mentioned.

And what was Faron doing running around a dangerous bog with her boyfriend's daughter and his daughter's dog? They said she'd found Wade's body after she saved the girl from sinking into the quagmire. But if you asked Mason, something seemed off about the whole thing. Cameron Talbert ought to be more careful about who he dates, or Faron Chevalier could end up bringing him down with her.

Mason grabbed another powdered sugar donut off the plate on the end table and jammed it into his mouth. No one was watching, so he bit off a third of it and chewed contentedly while brushing powder off his navy shirt. He didn't have to be careful now that Sandy wasn't around to scold him. He closed his eyes and let the powdered sugar melt in his mouth before washing the donut down with the mimosa. This was what living well was all about, and Joey sure knew how to do that. And now he did, too. Mason's thoughts wandered back to his phone conversation just now.

Noble had told him their guest was acting erratically in the same way she had when she first arrived at the bed and breakfast he and his wife owned. He was, in fact, becoming worried about his own safety and that of his wife, Summer, which was more than understandable given the fact that Faron had most certainly murdered her husband and probably Wade Kestin and was still on the loose.

Mason had spoken with Noble before about Faron after Joey had put him in touch with his neighbor on Cove Lake. They had had quite a productive conversation about her husband's recent murder and about her previous husbands as well. Faron's informal status as a murder suspect in Mason's book was backed up by Noble, and he had confirmed many of the personality flaws and tragic history Mason already suspected or knew about this treacherous femme fatale.

The strangest thing, according to Noble, was that she didn't seem to realize what she was doing or how oddly she was behaving. But then people with personality problems often weren't able to see anything wrong with themselves.

The rest of the donut went down as well as the first bite, and Mason smiled as he set his empty glass on the table, leaned back, and belched. There was something to be said for not having a wife around to bug you about what you ate or to insist you use a coaster for your drink. He could do anything he wanted to do. Freedom was highly underrated.

Dixon had also mentioned that he'd been engaged to

Faron at one time before realizing what she was like and getting out just in time. Lucky for him. Her future husbands hadn't fared so well. And the fact that Noble mentioned Faron might leave and go into hiding was something else Mason was glad to know. He could report that back to Paul Chevalier, Gill's son, and see if he wanted to follow up with his lawyer. Her absence might hold up legal procedures with the will and estate, and they wouldn't want that. In fact, maybe he should call Paul right now. He pulled out his cell phone and pressed the contact number. Paul picked up on the first ring.

"Hey, Mason, what's up?" he asked.

"I was just calling to give you an update on Faron Chevalier."

Paul said a few words before the sound faded away and then came back again.

"You there?" Mason asked.

"Yeah, go ahead. I'm on my boat in the middle of the big lake, and sometimes the phone goes out. I'm good, though. What were you saying?" Paul asked.

"Oh. Well, anyway, I have it on good authority that Faron may be planning to go on the lam. I thought you'd want to know."

"No kidding? Where to?"

"Don't know. I just wanted to tell you she could be heading out in case she disappears and you wonder what happened. If she does do that, you might have a more difficult time getting legal papers filed."

"Yeah, great. Thanks for calling. I'll let Jay know. He might want to get her to sign something sooner rather than later, given this new information."

"I was thinking that might be the case," Mason said. "Just wanted to let you know. So anyway, have a good time on your boat."

"Sure thing. Talk to you later."

The phone went dead. Mason sat looking at the screen for a moment. Paul saying he was on his boat was an understatement. He owned a yacht that he kept on the big lake, and it was just one of a few he owned. Must be nice.

Mason felt like he'd done the right thing by informing Gill's son of Faron's impending flight if that was her intention. That way, the kids could tie up the finances before she disappeared and left them hanging. Who knew how long settling the estate would take if she wasn't around to sign the appropriate documents? Anyway, enough thinking. He had to get ready.

He stuffed his phone in his pocket and took his plate and glass to the kitchen, where he set them in the sink. He wanted to be a good guest and maybe make points with Tina. Then he went back to his room and pulled a fresh shirt out of his suitcase to replace the navy one with sugar on it, and tossed it along with his slacks on the bed. He took a leisurely shower and carefully shaved before dressing again and making sure his hair was neatly combed. After checking the time, he went back into the great room and headed for the deck.

Mason opened the sliding door and stepped outside before walking over to where Joey and Tina sat at the patio table nursing their mimosas. She was looking fantastic in a white bikini and a caftan with gold sandals accenting her red toenails. He wondered again how Joey had lucked out with her and tried not to harbor more bitterness over his lost chance with Sandy. But you never knew with women if you'd end up with an ace or a wild card. Sandy had been a wild card. And from the looks of it, Faron was, too. He didn't like wild cards. You never knew where they'd turn up next or what havoc they'd cause.

"Hey Joey, you wanna get going?" Mason asked.

They had to hurry if they wanted to make their lunch appointment in town with Cameron Talbert, Lloyd Martin, and Noble Dixon on time.

"Yeah, sure," his friend answered.

Joey stood and walked around the table to give Tina a kiss before walking over toward Mason, who went back into the cottage.

"Don't do anything I wouldn't do," Joey said to her as he stepped through the door into the great room.

"Not making any promises," Tina called out after him.

Mason shook his head and grinned as he turned and headed for the front door. She was something, alright. Maybe he could get a woman like that someday.

Joey drove them around Cove Lake and into town. Mason leaned his elbow on top of the car door and let the fresh breeze streaming through the open window blow through his hair and dry it the rest of the way.

"You should have told the cops working in the bog to stake out Faron at the B&B or maybe guard the rooms," Joey said, raising his voice a bit in the wind. "That way the guests at Hidden Glen wouldn't be in danger from her."

"No. They wouldn't do that," Mason said. "We have to find another way to keep Cove Pointe and everyone else safe from her."

"If you say so."

"I do. And I'll bet Lloyd Martin called this meeting to make sure we're all on the same page in keeping an eye on her."

Mason had known Lloyd from his own time on the police force in Fenton City, even though Martin was with the State Police then as he was now. When Cameron Talbert called Joey and said Lloyd was putting together a meeting and wanted them both to attend, Mason happily agreed to go.

Joey parked in the parking lot behind the Covewater Restaurant, and Mason got out and followed him around to the front. The harbor view was incredible, as always, and Mason stopped for a moment to take it all in.

Colorful, moored fishing boats floated languidly in their slips, competing for attention with catamarans farther out, fluttering back and forth in a seeming regatta. The blues and aquas of the water shimmered in the sunshine under a cerulean blue sky. A loud horn sounded in the distance. He wished he had time to watch the boats race, but Joey held the door open and called his name. Mason reluctantly gave up on the picturesque scene and headed inside.

The three men they were meeting sat at one of the small tables near a side window in the back, and Mason walked over to shake their hands. They stood and greeted him, shaking hands with both him and Joey. Mason helped push two tables together, which gave them more space and privacy as well, and they all sat down.

"So what did you want to see us about?" Cameron asked.

"Glad you asked," Lloyd said. "Let's get right to it, so we can get this out of the way and order some food."

They all nodded. Then they waited a moment while a server dropped off menus and glasses of water and said she'd be back soon for their orders.

"Okay. Here's the thing," Lloyd continued. "Millie Parker wasn't murdered. She suffocated and drowned after falling into the quagmire where she'd gone to gather berries for a pie, same as Wade Kestin."

"What? How do you know that?" Mason asked.

"The coroner's report on Millie Parker and simple deductions." Lloyd looked around the table at everyone and then proceeded. "Ms. Parker was found wearing a crossbody bag filled with blueberries from bushes nearby in Wild Blueberry Bog, and Wade Kestin was found in the same location near a pan from the music camp kitchen that was half filled with blueberries. They were gathering blueberries for pies, albeit in different years, and they fell into a particularly lethal area of the bog where they were sucked under."

"What? Are you kidding me?" Mason exclaimed, leaning forward.

Joey nudged him, and he sat back.

"What about the other people who've disappeared from Cove Pointe?" Cam asked. "There were more than just these two."

"The area was dragged for other missing persons, and divers were deployed where necessary. But no one was found," Lloyd said. "They could be in other parts of the bog or somewhere else altogether. Regardless, there's nothing sinister here. These were two tragic accidents, nothing more."

"Wait. How do you figure? What about the coroner's report on Wade Kestin?" Mason asked.

"The release on that is currently held up for some reason, but I'd say the outcome is obvious. These deaths were accidental," Lloyd reiterated."

"Wait a minute. I don't know how you can say that," Mason said.

"Well, I just did," Lloyd said.

"But that's just an assumption. We don't know what really happened to Wade yet."

"I'd say the answer is pretty clear. Cove Pointe is a safe,

fishing community, and everyone knows that. The last thing anyone needs around here are rumors of missing persons being purposely killed," Lloyd said.

"Exactly," Noble chimed in. "Rumors like that are killers for the tourist season. And Cove Pointe needs the income tourists provide every summer. We need to put these discoveries to rest."

"Not until a final determination is made as to what happened," Mason said.

Lloyd sat up straight and looked straight at Mason. "Look. This missing persons situation is over. The missing people were found. The case is closed. You can stop following Faron Chevalier around."

"I knew it. I knew she'd be cleared, and I knew you were stalking her," Cam said. "He glared at Mason. "From a legal standpoint, I'd advise you to stop following Faron around, too, if that's what you're doing."

"Is that a threat?" Mason asked.

"If you think it is," Cam said.

"Now hold on," Joey said. "He's just doing his job."

Mason appreciated the collegial support. "That's right," he said, giving a nod to Joey.

Cam scoffed but remained silent.

"Who's cleared? Faron? Is she under suspicion for murder?" Noble asked stridently, emphasizing the last word. His face brightened as he looked around.

"No," Cam said.

"Not anymore," Lloyd added.

Just then, a scruffy-looking, older man stuck his head over Cam's shoulder. "The coppers will get him. Don't worry," he said.

"Get who?" Joey asked. "Where'd you come from?"

"The real killer," he whispered, loudly.

"Hey, Lenny, this is a private discussion," Cam said, looking over his shoulder. "Go back and sit down."

"Alright. But I'm tellin' ya. They always get their man. Yessir. They always do."

"Yeah, thanks for the insight," Cam said, as Lenny left and went back to his barstool at the counter.

They all looked at each other for a moment before continuing the conversation.

"There must be more to this investigation than this," Mason said, shaking his head.

"Like what?" Lloyd asked.

"Like what really happened," Mason continued, exasperated.

"That's what really happened," Lloyd said. "As far as any other allegations about Faron Chevalier, I'd need more to go on than you've given me so far."

"I don't understand this," Mason said. "You can't close the investigation of Faron Chevalier yet." He glanced at Noble for validation, but he just shrugged. "She's a murderer. And you all know that."

Noble nodded. At least he was showing some support, which Mason appreciated.

Cam leaned across the table. "You have no right to say that," he said, loudly.

"Oh, I have a right," Mason said. "She killed her husband for sure. In fact, I think she murdered all of them, and I'll prove it. I don't know how yet, but I will. All I can say is you'd better watch your back where she's concerned."

"You said that before. I can take care of myself. Stay out of my business."

"We'll see," Mason growled.

"Hey guys. What's going on?"

A tall man in a white apron came over to their table.

"Hey Rick. No worries," Cam said. "Me and the guys are just having a little discussion here."

"Well, maybe the guys want to take it outside," Rick said, firmly, glancing around the table.

"C'mon, Joey. I'm not hungry anymore," Mason said.

He pushed his chair back and stood. Joey did the same.

"Sorry you feel that way, Mason," Lloyd said. "If you come up with any more proof about your allegations about Faron, let me know. But as it stands right now, there's nothing to go on."

"We'll see," Mason said again.

He turned and stormed out of the restaurant with Joey close behind him. He had to get back to the cottage and come up with a new plan. The last thing he was going to do, despite what Cameron Talbert had said, was to quit following Faron around.

CHAPTER 16

Summer didn't feel much better than she had yesterday or even before that. Her current malaise had evidently started days ago. She stayed in bed all morning with the curtains drawn and a black, silk sleep mask covering her eyes. Any light at all caused a headache, she said. She'd nibbled on a whole piece of dry, wheat toast that she asked me to bring her for breakfast, but hadn't eaten anything other than that as far as I knew, even though it was the middle of the afternoon. I wasn't sure if that was good or bad with Noble around. I couldn't keep an eye on him all the time. Luckily, he'd left before lunch and hadn't yet come back.

He had returned to their bedroom later last night with a clean tray with a sandwich and fresh iced tea, she'd said, but she hadn't eaten much then either. I wished I could have told her what I suspected about poison, but I couldn't figure out a way to say it without sounding alarmist and strange to her. Telling her something I couldn't prove and that she wouldn't believe anyway wouldn't accomplish anything. So I just worried internally while trying to come up with a plan to stop him.

When Summer awoke from her nap in the early afternoon, she felt better and asked me to read to her. I was happy to oblige, even though I'd stashed my phone in my purse before checking on her, as I planned to take the canoe out on the lake and practice paddling by myself. I'd been reading up on how to do that and had practiced with a partner a few times before. But canoeing could wait. Entertaining Summer was way more important.

I walked to the nightstand and turned on a small, porcelain lamp which cast a dim, yellow glow through its elegant, vintage lampshade, turning the warm room into a cozy hideaway.

After helping her adjust her plump, oversized pillow so she could lean back against the headboard, I sat next to her bed in a comfortable wing chair and read aloud from a poetry anthology. After finishing a few poems, I stopped because she didn't seem to be listening.

"Would you like me to read something else?" I asked.

"What? No. I guess I'm too tired to listen anymore, that's all," she said.

"That's okay," I said. I closed the book and set it on the antique nightstand.

A soft rumble of thunder broke into the quiet of the afternoon just as a light wind blew in the window and ruffled the curtains. I walked over to draw the curtains aside and pull down the sash. As I did so, a sharp, cold rain rushed in and pricked my arms. I shoved the window shut and let the curtains fall back into place. I was glad I wasn't out on the lake in the sudden squall.

"Do you know where Noble is?" Summer asked as I walked back over and sat down in the wing chair. "I hope he's not outside, caught in the rain."

"No, I don't, but he took his car somewhere."

"Hmm," she said. "He probably had to go into town for something." She paused for a moment before continuing. "This must not be much fun for you, having me sick and all, not to mention the trauma of discovering Wade's body and finding out about Millie's death. I wish things had turned out differently."

"Don't worry about it," I said. "What's going on is out of your control."

"I know. This is so sad, though. Wade was such a nice

man, and Millie was loved by everyone in the town."

"It's too bad this happened," I said. "Life has a way of throwing in twists and turns when you least expect them." I felt that way about my life so far.

"That's true," she said. "But I wish we'd had a chance to play together as a trio like we used to, now that you're here. My violin is all tuned and ready to go because I was hoping to have a jam session after you arrived. But unfortunately, things turned out the way they did, and we never got around to it."

"Oh, I'm sorry. That would have been nice," I said. "I wish things had turned out differently, too. But, as things stand with my relationship with your husband, I don't think Noble would go for a reunion, anyway."

"You're probably right," Summer said.

I sat for a moment, recalling the past.

"Remember when we did a gig at that off-campus lounge, and a guy from my art history class got down on one knee and proposed to his girlfriend?" I asked.

"I do remember that. She said yes, and we played one of Noble's love songs so they could dance together. So romantic. Those were the days," Summer said, softly.

"Yes. Those were the days," I said, agreeing.

We stayed silent for a while, listening to the patter of rain on the roof.

"I still feel guilty about being laid up," Summer said eventually. "I told Noble I'd think of things we could do to entertain you when he asked me if you could come visit, and now look at me."

"Noble asked you what?" I asked.

"If we could invite you for a visit."

"Invite me? To the B&B?"

"Yes," she said.

"Noble was the one who wanted me to come?" I sat still, stunned.

"Well, I did, too," Summer said, quickly, obviously realizing her mistake in revealing Noble's request. "In fact, I really wanted you to come."

"So you didn't read about Gill's murder in an outdated newspaper in a waiting room this summer like you said?"

"Oh yes, I did. But I told Noble about the article, and that's when he made the suggestion that you come visit us."

I couldn't believe this.

"Wait a minute," I said. "Why would Noble treat me the way he has if he's the one who wanted me to come up here in the first place?"

"I don't know."

Summer shook her head, but then she grimaced and put her hand over her eyes.

"Are you okay? Can I help you?" I asked.

"No," she said. "Shaking my head gives me a headache, that's all. Anyway, I don't know what's going on with my husband. I feel bad that he's been acting so poorly. I'm as surprised as you are."

I didn't know what to think.

"What's really surprising to me is that Noble didn't know anything about Gill's death sooner," Summer said.

"Why is that?" I asked, confused.

"Well, because his sales job during the rest of the year, when he isn't teaching in the summer, brings him to Fenton City on and off. He was just there in the spring, and he never heard anything about Gill's murder."

"What?" My legs trembled, and my heart began to race.

"Noble was in Fenton City?"

"Yes. He sells paper to businesses there on his travels around the state throughout the year."

My mouth felt dry. I didn't know why, but I was really scared. Had Noble been in Fenton City when my husband, Gill, was murdered? And if so, what did that mean?"

I stood up, shaking.

"I'll get us some iced tea," I said. "I'll be back in a minute."

I made a beeline out the door before Summer could say anything and ran to my room, where I threw up in the bathroom until a welcome sense of peace washed over me. I sat on the floor, leaning back against the cool wall while dabbing my damp forehead with a washcloth. I was pretty sure I wasn't being poisoned, even if I was sure Summer was. I was simply terrified of Noble and of what I was beginning to think he was capable of doing or had done.

When I was able to stand, I did and washed my hands, rinsed out my mouth, and went downstairs to the kitchen. A fresh lake breeze blew in through the kitchen window along with pelts of rain, and I hurried to pull down the sash.

I thought I'd make sandwiches for Summer and me since neither one of us had eaten lunch. I pulled tomatoes out of the refrigerator and mixed together some tuna and mayo. Then I found some rye bread in the pantry and toasted four slices.

After rummaging through the drawers in the kitchen island to find a knife to slice the sandwiches and coming up empty, I went back to the pantry and found a block of knives on a shelf. One of the handles looked familiar. I pulled on the handle, and when the knife came out of the block, I gasped. The butcher knife was from a set in my kitchen at home. How had it gotten here? Did Summer own a similar set?

I stood stock still, staring at the implement in my hand. This was impossible, and yet there it was. I checked the other handles. They were different. The butcher knife was the only knife with a handle I recognized. Was it erroneously placed in the butcher block slot instead of the knife that actually matched the set? And who would do that if that were the case? I slid it back into the block and hurried out of the pantry. The coincidence with the knife was too frightening to think about, so I put the incident out of my mind and found a clean knife in the dishwasher to use.

Feeling dazed, I finished preparing lunch to the soothing drumming of rain on the roof before putting everything on a tray to bring up to Summer. As I walked up the stairs, I tried to gather my thoughts and reach a conclusion as to why my knife would be at the B&B. But I couldn't, so I continued to the bedroom and put the tray on a dresser there.

"Lunch is ready," I said, trying to sound chipper. "Do you feel like eating anything?"

Summer opened her eyes.

"Maybe a little," she said. "I'm really thirsty."

"Here. Have some iced tea," I said, walking over and handing her a glass.

I didn't intend to mention discovering my butcher knife in their pantry. Whatever explanation she might give wasn't good enough for me at the moment. I had my own suspicions, and I wanted to keep them to myself.

Summer took a sip and sighed. "Much better," she said. "I'll just keep this with me for a bit."

"Sure," I said. "Let me know when you feel like eating something."

"Okay," she said. She sipped her tea again. "Say, I have a question I've been meaning to ask."

"Shoot," I said. I sat down again in the chair next to her.

"I don't know how to put this, but did you and Wade hit it off really well when you first met?"

"Oh, well, I wouldn't say that, but he did hire me on the spot as a flute tutor."

"Yeah. Noble mentioned that."

"Did Noble say we hit it off?" I asked.

"Yes. He said Wade really liked you."

"Well, that's good," I said. I was beginning to feel uncomfortable. "Only enough to want me to help out at the music camp. Nothing more than that," I said. What could Noble have been thinking, saying something like that to Summer?

"Okay. I just wondered," she said.

She seemed ready to drop the subject, which was fine with me. As far as I was concerned, Noble had overstepped with his insinuations about me and about Wade, and I didn't like it. He sounded jealous again, and Wade wasn't alive to defend himself.

"You know, not to belabor the point, but since you arrived, I've found myself thinking about the old times a lot lately," Summer said, "especially about the three of us playing together as the Dixon trio. We had so much fun."

"Yes, we did," I said.

"Maybe I'm just nostalgic because Noble's been playing the old songs on the piano. Your presence probably induces memories for him, too."

"Could be," I said.

"I suppose we'll never be the same."

"That's the way life is," I said. "Nothing stays the same."

"You're right," Summer said. "Especially lately. At least Kasey's okay. I don't know what would have happened if she'd drowned in the bog in the same way as Wade and Millie. Cam would never have recovered. You saved him as much as you saved her."

"Well. I don't know about that, but I'm glad Kasey's okay, too."

Summer seemed to be in a maudlin mood, but I didn't blame her, given that she wasn't feeling well while trying to deal with everything that was going on, too. I couldn't help but wonder if something else was bothering her, though.

"Is everything okay between you and Noble?" I asked.

She sighed. "Well, now that you mention it, he's been aloof and not very nice to me for a while. I don't know what's going on with him, but I miss the way he used to be. I can't help thinking about it."

"Yes," I said. "I know what you mean."

I remembered the same thing happening between Noble and me a long time ago when we broke up. And I'd been afraid of him then because of his volatile emotions. Could Summer be experiencing the same thing from him? If so, the likelihood that he was poisoning her became even more probable.

"One of the reasons I was so glad you came to visit was because I wanted you here for company. I needed a friend."

"Well, you've got one," I said, sincerely.

"I know," she said, smiling. "I'm feeling better. Maybe I could try a little bit of a sandwich."

"Sure."

I got up and retrieved the sandwiches, which I placed in front of her on the tray. I took my own sandwich off the tray and sat down with the plate on my lap.

"This is good," she said, after eating for a while.

"Good," I replied.

"You know, I always wondered why you broke up with

Noble. I mean, I'm glad you did because then Noble and I got together. But to tell you the truth, I don't think he ever recovered from feeling jilted. He's very sensitive."

She looked at me earnestly. Her statement caught me off guard, and I wasn't sure what to say. I contemplated her question for a moment, trying to frame an appropriate answer. I thought of Noble as self-centered and egotistical rather than sensitive, but I wasn't going to say that. In my mind, he wasn't able to handle any type of rejection without having his ego shattered. But I had hurt him. I knew that.

"I didn't handle the breakup very well," I said. "Maybe I should have been more sensitive. I was young and impetuous, and I wasn't ready to commit to him. I didn't realize that until the last minute, and that ended up being to his detriment."

"Noble never has handled rejection very well," Summer said.

"I know. No one does, really," I said.

"That's true." Summer took another bite of her sandwich.

I hoped she understood. She seemed to. But her words gave credence to my feelings of trepidation about Noble. He didn't seem to be over me. In fact, he seemed to still be angry and jealous where I was concerned, and that wasn't good. In fact, it was scary.

The front door banged shut. I flinched. Noble was home.

"Would you like me to bring you anything else?" I asked, changing the subject quickly.

"No. I think I've eaten enough. I am feeling better, but I still have a bit of a stomachache. I don't want to eat too much. Here."

She picked up the tray. I stood and took the tray from her as I placed my plate next to hers.

"I'll bring this downstairs. Do you want to take a nap?"

She nodded.

"Alright. I'll close the door."

I turned off the lamp and headed for the hallway.

"Oh, and Faron."

"Yes?"

I stopped and turned around.

"I'm glad we talked."

"I'm glad we did, too," I said, smiling.

I continued on and stepped into the hallway before gently closing the door behind me and heading downstairs. When I reached the kitchen, I set the tray next to the sink, all the while looking around for Noble. I heard a noise in the parlor room and tiptoed over to peek in. Noble was at the piano, scribbling something on his notepad.

After a moment, he set the pad on top of the piano and began to play. It was a nice tune but somewhat melancholy. When he'd played about six notes, I gasped. I recognized the song. And it wasn't one he'd composed for us all to play together. The notes Noble played on the piano replicated the brief, bloodied score I'd found next to my first husband's dead body. How did Noble know the tune?

Reality slapped me hard in the face. I clapped my hand over my mouth to keep from screaming. Noble couldn't know what the tune sounded like. The police had confiscated the score and kept it secure and out of the public eye. Noble couldn't know the tune unless he was the one who put it next to Daniel's body.

Everything started to make sense—the misplaced knife, Noble's jealousy over my relationships, the yellow powder, Summer's discontent, and everything else. He still wanted me. And he'd do anything to get me. I swallowed and choked on my own fear. Noble heard me. He looked up and straight at me. His dark eyes narrowed into a piercing stare.

"Faron," he breathed.

He glanced at the piano keys and then back at me.

"This isn't what you think," he said, obviously realizing his error in playing the incriminating music.

"You," I said. "It was you all along."

"What do you mean?" he asked, quietly.

His voice had an eerie, sing-song cadence to it. He slowly stood, then stepped forward.

"No," I yelled. "Stay away from me."

He knew I recognized the tune. I could see it in his taut, drawn expression. He suddenly gritted his teeth and clenched his fists. His eyes glinted deviously.

"Faron," he said once more, gruffly this time. He took another step forward.

"You're a murderer!" I shouted.

I turned and ran for my life.

CHAPTER 17

I headed for the side door. I didn't know where I was going. I only knew I had to get away. Footsteps pounded behind me. He was chasing me. I ran faster. Noble was the killer.

I yanked the door open and ran outside, slamming the door behind me. A driving rain pattered on my head and stung my cheeks. Where should I run? My car? I didn't have my keys. The beach? Maybe. I glanced over my shoulder as I dashed toward the path through the woods. I didn't see Noble. Where was he? He'd been right behind me. I reached the path and glanced back again. He was running through the backyard holding something. Did he have a gun? Was he going to kill me?

I sprinted forward and raced down the muddy path. If I made it to the beach, what would I do then? I couldn't take the canoe or start the motorboat before Noble caught up to me. I'd be trapped. I abruptly turned into the woods at the first yellow flag instead and headed down the marked path toward the bog. I could make a beeline through there to the music camp and then on to Cam's cottage. I hoped Noble wouldn't surmise my intention. I turned my head and looked back at the path. He wasn't following me. Not yet, anyway.

I looked forward again, but not in time to see a fallen log that blocked the way. I tripped and fell flat on my face in the mud. Now what? I pushed myself up, panting, and glanced behind me again. Noble was at the beginning of the flagged path, and he started running toward me. He'd obviously seen me. I had to change my tactics. He could deduce that I was headed for Cam's place.

I dashed ahead as I tried to come up with a plan. My breathing came in short, stifled breaths, and my heart hammered against my chest like a battering ram. The rain poured down in heavy sheets and obscured my view. I glanced back again. Where was Noble? He must be hidden by the downpour. What if he was catching up to me? I ran faster.

When I finally reached the end of the path, I took a sharp left and prayed that he hadn't seen me. If I were careful and stayed near the edge of the woods, I could potentially make tracks to the lake. From there, I could wade over to the beach where I could commandeer the canoe and paddle to Cam's cottage. But that depended on Noble not seeing where I was headed. I zigzagged sideways into the woods and crouched behind a tree. If he came out of the path, I'd see him. But he wouldn't see me.

He suddenly appeared, running out of the woods and on down the path through the bog. My subterfuge had worked. I waited a moment to make sure he didn't double back before heading for the lake. I navigated through the woods for a while, but the underbrush was thick and prickly. Maybe I should head back to the B&B to grab my purse and make a getaway in my car. But Noble would see me on the path if he returned to look for me after not finding me anywhere in front of him. I couldn't take that chance, so I forged ahead through wet leaves and downed branches toward the lake.

My thoughts raced as I struggled on. How could Noble be the killer? I had loved him once enough to want to marry him. And now, he had sunk so low as to take other people's lives? What happened to him? Or had he always been this way, and I didn't know it? Maybe on some level, I had known what he was like and had fortuitously realized we couldn't make a go of things together. Possibly. Or had my insensitive rejection of him on the night before our impending marriage turned him into a cold-blooded monster? I shook my head to clear my mind. I couldn't think about this now. I had to survive.

Eventually, I gave up on the woods and stepped out into the whipping wind and rain. I sloshed through the moss and mire while hugging the edge of the tree line, where the ground was firmer. Noble wouldn't be able to spot me in the downpour if he backtracked down the path.

The rain plastered my hair against my face, and I couldn't see. I pushed my sopping tresses out of my eyes as I passed the newly fenced-in area and kept going. A boisterous Cove Lake beckoned in the distance if I could just get there. But could I canoe through the white-capped waves all the way to Cam's cottage? I'd find out when I got there. For now, I had to concentrate on reaching the lake.

I pushed on. How did I end up here, anyway? Why wasn't I home relaxing in my plush mansion in Fenton City? Or why wasn't I lounging by the pool at my luxurious home in Florida? Instead, I was slogging through a bog being chased by a murderer? Really? What was the disconnect here?

I thought about Gill and how he would have wanted me to be safe and secure at home with him. He loved me so much. I suddenly felt as though I was going to cry. Was the emotional wall I'd erected to keep from dealing with Gill's ghastly death crumbling? I couldn't let that happen. I banished my thoughts. I wasn't going to relive the horrifying moment I found Gill in that gruesome crime scene in our home. I shook my head and locked up my emotions again. No time for that. I had to work on survival.

But I couldn't help thinking that if Gill had still been alive, none of this would ever have happened, and I could have pursued my leisure life of wealth and happiness without ever seeing Noble again or knowing what he was really like. My past would have stayed the past. The only reason I was here in this dreadful situation was because Gill wasn't around to protect me anymore. Had that been Noble's plan—to murder Gill and lure me to the bed and breakfast? It seemed so. But I didn't want to know about Noble and what he was like. Unfortunately, I no longer had a choice. I had to confront the obvious or, by all appearances, lose my life.

I forged ahead. I wished I had on boots. My sandals were a poor substitute in this uneven terrain. I trudged on through the sludge and slippery muck and tried to keep from falling into the quivering morass. I pressed on further until I finally neared the waterfront.

Luckily, the rain began to let up as I pushed past the cattails onto a narrow slice of beach. I splashed into the shallows of the lake and waded sideways past the forest toward the beach at Hidden Glen. If I could just make it to the sand, I'd be golden because the canoe was overturned on shore near the forest. I could shove my intended transport into the lake and paddle to Cam's cottage and safety.

I stepped on a rock and slipped sideways. My sandal strap broke. I stopped and took both sandals off. When I looked up again, the hairs on the back of my neck stood up. I felt like I was being watched. I perused the lake and woods but didn't see anyone. Hopefully, Noble wasn't around, and my nerves had only conjured up an imagined danger. I waded on.

Finally, I reached the other edge of the forest and sloshed up to the beach. What luck. The canoe was still there, overturned right in front of me. I stopped for a moment and took a deep breath. I'd made it this far, but I had a ways to go to make it to Cam's cottage.

I tossed my sandals on the wet sand, and, after taking a few more breaths, went to work on the canoe. I hoped I had the strength to turn the boat over and push it into the lake. After several tries, I accomplished my goal and started to push. At least, the canoe was near the water. I pushed mightily until I finally shoved the canoe into the lake and stepped in after it. But where were the paddles?

My heart dropped. They were probably in the B&B. I couldn't go back there. What if Noble had returned? But then I remembered seeing one in the sailboat tied up at the dock. I pulled the canoe partially up on shore again and took off running.

The wind picked up as I ran across the beach and down the dock to the sailboat. I had to hurry if I was going to get to the cottage before the storm picked up again. The paddle was there. I carefully leaned in, grabbed it, and ran back to the canoe. After pushing the canoe into the water again, I hopped in and began to paddle.

Fat drops of rain plopped onto my cheeks, and the storm commenced again in earnest. The canoe veered left, so I paddled on the other side. But then it veered right. The wind blew the canoe even farther sideways, and the growing waves threatened to tip me over. This wasn't working. I set the paddle down and carefully moved forward to try again. When I did, the canoe went left, but not as much. I tried the other side and then alternated sides until I was heading in a somewhat straight line toward Cam's cottage.

He was probably there, warm and dry, and would welcome me when I finally got there. He'd probably make me some hot tea and ask me what was wrong. And then he'd listen to me in his compassionate way and make everything okay again. If only I could get there, I'd be fine. I was sure of that. But turbulent waves battered the canoe and occasionally sloshed over the sides, and I had to struggle to stay afloat, making my dreams of reaching the cottage seem more and more fantastical.

As I neared the music camp, a gust of wind tipped the canoe sideways, and a white-capped wave slammed into the side. I was going over. I flipped upside down and plunged deep into the cold lake, where I choked on water and tried to hold my breath. When I finally swam to the surface and gulped deep breaths of precious air, I realized the canoe was unnavagable. I couldn't paddle to Cam's cottage. I had to leave the canoe and swim to shore.

The waves were unrelenting as I battled through the churning water. I was already tired from running, and my legs didn't want to cooperate. I pulled myself forward with as much strength as I could muster using deep, freestyle strokes. But I kept sucking in water and choking. I glanced forward and caught a glimpse of the dock at the music camp. If I kept on at this pace, I'd soon be there.

I could run to Cam's from the music camp. All I had to do was reach the shore and then run to the path through the forest on the other side of the camp that led to Cam's cottage. It wouldn't take long, and I'd be safe. That's what I was going to do.

Suddenly, a cramp stabbed my calf, and I stopped mid-stroke. I went under, grabbing my leg, and swallowed a mouthful of lake water. I struggled to keep my head up while rubbing my calf. After a while, I felt some relief and started swimming again. But the cramp returned with a vengeance. I rolled over and started to backstroke. This worked better and gave my leg some relief. I backstroked until I finally reached the dock and pulled myself up on it. I laid there gasping for air and rubbing my painful calf. I had to get out of the rain and find shelter. The cramp still clutched my leg violently, and there was no way I'd be able to run all the way to Cam's cottage now. Besides, I was freezing and shivering violently.

I stood and shuffled down the dock and over a narrow strip of sand toward the music camp lodge, which stood at the top of a grassy slope behind a few trees. If I remembered correctly, Wade had told me that if I ever lost my key, I could find a spare one under the mat by the back door to the kitchen—not an original hiding place, but a functional one if the key was there. I hurried forward through the cold rain as fast as my sore leg and bare feet allowed. I could only hope that Noble wasn't here somewhere looking for me.

Just as I reached the back door, large pellets of hail pattered on my head and shoulders and stung my neck. I raised the mat. Success. I quickly retrieved the key and opened the back door. I closed the door after stepping inside and welcomed the resulting peace. Hail still pounded the lodge, but I was safe, and the noise was muted.

I turned on the light in the large storage room behind the kitchen. Then I walked through a swinging door and on through the kitchen, which had some illumination from the storage room light, to the front room. I plopped down on a bench at one of the long tables and closed my eyes. I was secure at last, for now anyway. At least I was out of the storm. I took a few deep breaths before crossing my arms and resting my head on my forearms.

The hail abruptly stopped, leaving only the soft tapping of raindrops, and the light drumming of rain on the roof slowed my breathing and calmed my racing heart. I'd just relax for a bit before deciding what to do next.

I awakened in the dim light of the lodge to a jangling sound and then a thump. How long had I slept? Not long, I supposed, since I was still as cold and wet as before. What was that sound? I looked toward the front door. A silhouette wavered, framed in the glass against the gray light of the storm outside. Someone was trying to get in. What if Noble came back to look for me?

I leaped from my seat and ran into the kitchen. I had to hide. But where? Covert footsteps tramped across the wood floor. I ducked behind the counter. Whoever was there was coming closer. A cupboard could hide me. But how could I remove the pots and pans without making noise? I couldn't. I moved awkwardly forward in my crouched position. A deep voice resonated throughout the lodge.

"Hello? Who's there?"

The voice was definitely Noble's. I had to keep him from seeing me. The footsteps came closer. Hiding under the sink would work. I remembered getting a glass of water once and noticing a large space there. But he was too near. He'd hear me if I moved toward the cupboard. I froze in fear, searching desperately for a way out. An empty, sprung mousetrap near the dishwasher caught my eye. I grabbed it off the floor, and, taking aim as best I could in the dim kitchen, threw it through the opening in the wall above the serving counter. A distant clatter rewarded my efforts. The footsteps stopped, and then seemed to change course. He must be going to investigate.

I took the opportunity to duck walk to the cupboard under the sink. I yanked open the door and quickly pushed dish detergent and sponges out of the way inside. Then I crawled in and contorted my body into a somersault position next to the drainpipe. I tugged on a dish towel hanging on the rack attached to the inside of the cupboard door and pulled it shut behind me, although a corner of the towel got stuck and kept the door from closing completely. I began to pull the caught corner in just as the kitchen light flickered and came on. I froze. Noble had returned.

"Who's there?" he asked, sharply.

My body shook so hard I was afraid he'd hear the cupboard rattling.

"Faron?"

I clapped my hand over my mouth to stifle a scream. How did he know it was me?

"I know you're in here," he said.

Footsteps again.

"Come out. Come out. Wherever you are," he said melodically.

The sing-song voice was back. I squeezed my eyes shut. The footsteps came closer. He turned the water on. Was he thirsty? Suddenly, the cupboard door sprang open, and Noble sprayed me with the spray nozzle from the sink hose. I screamed and covered my face.

"Ally, Ally, All in free," he said, like a little kid playing tag. "I found you."

I sat rigid, unable to think or talk. My body shook so hard I thought I'd fall apart. What should I do now?

"Come on out, Faron. I won't hurt you," Noble said.

He extended his hand toward me. I shook my head, and he pulled back. After a moment, I reluctantly unwound myself and wriggled out of the cupboard onto the cold floor. I stayed there on all fours, waiting for Noble to move away. When he didn't, I stood slowly to face him. I had no other choice. I clenched my fists and stared straight into his eyes, shaking violently. He stared back at me. His breathing was ragged.

"You can't hide from me," he said, quietly.

His eyes were bright and wild, and his black hair was straggly and wet. His beard and mustache were ratted, muddy, and scruffy, probably from chasing me through the bog earlier in the afternoon. He looked feral and brutish, and I trembled with fear when I suddenly realized what I was up against. I was trapped. And Noble had a gun.

CHAPTER 18

Noble stood still and continued to stare at me while holding his gun at his side.

"How'd you know I was here?" I asked, gasping.

I was terrified. Would he shoot me?

"Someone called me," Noble said, shrugging. "I drove my truck over."

He sounded normal and oddly conversational. I'd go along with him and see how things developed. But my nerves were on high alert even though I don't think I fully grasped this new reality. I knew he'd killed Daniel. And Noble knew that I knew.

"Called you? How did they know I was here?" I asked.

"They saw your canoe capsize."

"But why would someone call you?"

"I don't know," he said. He shifted his gaze away and then back. "The name Hidden Glen is on the side of the canoe."

None of this made any sense.

"But how did they see the name? There was no one around."

He ignored me and became more serious.

"Why did you run from me, Faron?" he asked. His voice was deep, and his eyes glinted with suspicion.

"Oh, no reason," I said, quickly, changing my focus.

I needed to think of something to placate him. He was obviously agitated.

"Did you think I would hurt you?" The sing-song voice was back. He waved the gun casually.

"No, of course not," I said.

"Well. You didn't say very nice things before you ran out," he said, smiling in a condescending way. "You called me a murderer, and you didn't give me a chance to explain."

"Yes. You're right," I said. "I was very rude. Please, forgive me."

I'd say what I had to in order to survive in my precarious situation, but no explanation Noble could give would convince me he wasn't a killer.

"That's more like it," he said. "Please have a seat. We can't go back to Hidden Glen now with Summer there, can we?"

I shook my head.

"No."

"We'll stay here for now. Sit down. Please," he said.

"Okay," I said, taking a seat at the table.

Our politeness with each other struck me as strange, but no stranger than anything else that had happened with him so far today. I shivered. My clothes were soaked, and my hair was dripping.

"Are you cold? Here, take this."

Noble unzipped his jacket and placed it around my shoulders. I pulled the jacket close about me and huddled into it, enjoying the welcome warmth.

"Thank you," I said.

"Of course," he said. "Let me start a fire to warm you."

He stuffed the gun in his pocket, then turned and walked toward the large, stone fireplace.

"Please don't," I said.

I didn't want to stay here any longer than I had to. He

turned to look at me.

"Alright," he said.

He walked back over and sat down across from me at the table. The arrogant way he stared at me made me shudder.

"What do you want?" I asked.

"What do you mean?

"I'll do anything you say. But I don't understand what you're doing here. What do you want?" I asked again.

"You. I want you," he said, simply.

I shook my head. He'd gotten right to the point. And he was dead serious. I could see it in his eyes.

"But what about Summer? What about Cove Pointe? And also, what about me? I'm not going to be part of your game," I said.

"You're already part of my game," he said, grinning.

"What do you mean by that?" I asked. "Do you think I'll live with you at Hidden Glen?"

"No. I have other plans."

"What other plans?"

"Come with me. I want to show you something."

I stiffened and remained still.

"I'd rather stay here," I said, quietly.

"Don't worry. You'll like this. I've waited a long time. Indulge me."

I trembled but forced myself to stand. I didn't want to make him mad. He waited until I was next to him and walked down the hall to the first music room. He held the door open for me to enter. He turned on the lights and shut the door after us. Then he pulled two chairs in front of it before walking over to the piano.

"Sit down, Faron," he said, softly, as he took a seat on the piano bench.

I lowered myself into a chair.

"No. Over here by me," he said.

I stood, shuffled closer to him, and sat down.

"I wrote this for you," he said. "I was going to play this song at our wedding as a surprise for you. Here. Let me play it for you now. I've waited a long time."

Noble began to play the most beautiful theme song I had ever remembered hearing. His body moved in time to the music, and his face contorted in ecstasy. He seemed transported. And then he played the coda. I gasped. I recognized the tune as the one he'd played at Hidden Glen before I ran out. It was the same short, melancholy tune that was left beside Daniel's bloody body.

I jumped up and ran for the door. I yanked a chair away and reached for the other. But before I could move it, Noble grabbed me.

"You're not going anywhere," he said, gruffly. "You're mine. The song is for you. It's my love song to you."

"No. I don't want it. I don't want you. Leave me alone," I yelled, struggling with him.

He held me tightly.

"Let me go," I yelled, wriggling and desperately attempting to remove myself from the tight clamp of his grip.

He held me rigidly until I finally gave up and stood still. After a moment, he loosened his grasp, leaned down, and picked up his jacket.

"Here. You dropped this," he said, solicitously.

"I don't want it," I said.

"Don't be silly," he said.

He wrapped the jacket around my shoulders again before pulling the second chair away and opening the door.

"Let's sit at the table by the fireplace again, and I'll get a fire started."

He obviously wasn't going to listen to me or let me leave, so I walked back to the front of the lodge with him. I glanced toward the door, but he was apparently keeping a close eye on me because he scolded me.

"I wouldn't do that, Faron," he said.

"Do what?"

"Try to run again. I won't let you get away this time."

I looked at his face and noted his grim expression. I believed him. I didn't make a move toward the door as I'd planned to. But before he could light a fire, I sat down at the table and asked him another question.

"What did you mean when you said you had other plans?" I asked.

He turned to look at me, then left the fireplace and walked over to me. He sat down across from me and folded his hands.

"I'm glad you asked me that," he said. "I've been intending to tell you, but I wanted to wait for the right time."

This didn't seem like the right time for anything to me, but I let him continue.

"I own a cabin in the wilderness farther north, and it's all set up for us."

"All set up for us?" I asked, puzzled.

"Yes. We can live there together, and no one will know."

"What? You're crazy."

"I'm not. I have this all planned out. We'll drive your car up there, and I'll get you situated. Then I'll hide your car in the woods and take the ferry back to Cove Pointe. Simple."

"Hide my car?" This was unbelievable. "Why?"

"To keep you from being located."

"What? You can't do this. Do you think I'll just stay there with you and never leave?" I asked redundantly. "And what do you mean by 'situated?'"

"Set up in the cabin. You'll love the area. The views are breathtaking. I'll come up on the weekends when Summer isn't well. We'll have a great life."

I stood there with my mouth open. So that's why Noble was poisoning Summer. So he could get away to be with me. Did he really think I'd go along with him? He continued.

"No one will ever know about our little hideaway but you and me. You're mine, Faron. You always have been. I just never got the chance to see you walk down the aisle."

He really was teetering on the edge of reality. How could I get through to him?

"Noble. You have to listen to me. This is not something you want to do. You'll go to prison for a long time."

"I don't think so," he said, offhandedly. "If you don't come with me, you'll go to prison for a long time. The authorities are already hot on your trail. They think you murdered Gill. You're on thin ice, babe. At this point, all you can do is hide, and I'm providing you with the perfect opportunity. Besides, once you get there, you'll never want to leave."

"This can't be happening," I said, flabbergasted. "Noble. I told you I was sorry I hurt you. But that was a long time ago. Can't you see how wrong this is?"

"No. This isn't wrong. This is right. This is the way things should have worked out between us. We'll be together. I love you, and you love me."

"I don't love you. I broke things off with you because I don't love you," I said, sharply.

"Don't say that. Don't say you don't love me," Noble

shouted, pounding his fist on the table.

"But I don't," I said, firmly, determined to stand my ground. "I told you that before."

"You do. You do."

"No, Noble, I don't. What we had was over a long time ago. You must know that."

"Don't say that. You came back. You came back to me because you love me."

"I didn't. I came here to spend time with Summer and to reminisce about old times. That's all. You know that," I reiterated, firmly.

I sat up straight, wary, and glanced behind me at the door. Noble wasn't just my jilted ex-fiancé anymore, stubbornly nursing an old wound; he was a dangerously unbalanced man I didn't recognize, and I was alone with him in the middle of nowhere. I slid off the bench and stood up.

"Sit down," he said, firmly.

"My foot fell asleep," I said. "I have to stand."

He glared at me but didn't insist further.

"You said you came here to spend time with Summer. What about Cam?" he growled.

"What about him?"

"You spend more time with him than with Summer."

"That's none of your business."

"It is now. But don't worry. I'll take care of Cam," he said, harshly. His eyes darkened.

"What do you mean?"

"He won't bother you anymore."

"He's not bothering me."

"Well, he's bothering me. He has no right to make moves on you like he has."

"Make moves on me? What do you mean? What's the matter with you?"

"No one else will ever love you, Faron. Not like I do, and not while I'm around. Don't you know that by now?"

"You can't tell me what to do or who to see. And you certainly can't tell Cam that."

"I don't intend to tell him. I intend to kill him," Noble said.

"What?"

I couldn't see for a moment. I felt like someone had hit me on the head with a rock. I dropped to my knees. Noble stood up and came around the table.

"Kill him?" I asked, fighting through the haziness that gripped my mind.

"Yes. That's why I brought my gun." He pulled the gun out of his pocket and leaned over, holding the gun closer to me. "Do you like it? It's new."

I didn't say anything. This couldn't be happening.

"I bought this one because I ditched the one I used before. But I'm sure it will work as well. I knew you were going to see Cam when you ran out on me."

The reality of Noble's murderous statement suddenly hit me full force.

"You can't. You can't kill Cam," I shrieked.

"There's no other way. I have to get rid of him. Same as the rest of them. I'm your real husband. No one else. It's time you realized that."

I stared up at him as I fought to suck in air. He stared back. What did he mean when he said, "Same as the rest of them?" My throat constricted and my heart pounded as the thin facade of my denial began to crack. A cold film of sweat slicked my arms and neck. I had to ask him what he meant. I struggled to form the words.

"Did you kill them?" I asked, slowly. "Did you kill all my husbands?"

He gave me a crooked smile.

"Tell me," I yelled.

He continued to stare at me with his cold, blank eyes. I held his gaze, trembling violently, but I had to know.

"Did you?" I asked again, in a whisper this time.

"Yes," he said.

I collapsed on the floor. I was conscious, but only barely. I laid there wondering if I was dead or alive.

"No, no, no." I couldn't fathom this. It was too much. "Daniel? You killed Daniel, too?" I choked out.

He'd already answered, and I knew he'd murdered him because I'd heard him playing the song he'd left next to Daniel's dead body. But I needed to hear him say it again. It wasn't real yet. Silence. And then the impossible word.

"Yes."

"Noooo." A disembodied voice shrieked through a tin tunnel of echoes.

Was the voice mine? Maybe. My body vibrated in a way I'd never experienced before, and a thick, yellow bile surged up into my mouth and out onto the floor. And then I wept with deep, heaving sobs that wrenched my gut and laid open my soul. I don't know how long. When I finally came to, I opened my eyes and searched for Noble. He stood over me, staring at nothing.

"How could you?" I asked. "How could you murder Daniel?"

Noble moved his gaze to me. "He took you away from me," he said, woodenly. "He had no right to do that. I couldn't bear it anymore."

I took stock of his words and then looked away. I felt nothing for him. And nothing he said could make me understand what he did. Something had changed him forever from the quiet music student I first met in college. I shivered to think my rejection of him could have led to such dire consequences.

"You'll get over it," Noble said.

"Get over it?" I said in disbelief. "This isn't something someone gets over."

"You will in time," he said. "And you have me now."

I didn't know what to say anymore. He obviously lived in a different realm and a different reality from mine or from anyone else's. I trembled as I realized Noble could do anything he wanted to do, and since no one but me knew what he was really like, I wouldn't be able to stop him. But I couldn't think about that now. I had to pull myself together and get away. I had to save Cam, and I had to save myself. But how?

There must be a way to escape. I thought for a moment before coming up with a plan. I'd run to Cam's place and tell him about Noble. Cam would believe me. I know he would. He'd get Noble locked up, and I could have a relationship with Cam as I'd planned. But if I left, Noble could still go after him and make good on his threat to kill him to keep him from being with me. I couldn't let that happen either. What should I do?

I stayed still for I don't know how long, with Noble standing over me. I was trapped. Eventually, I thought of another plan. I'd pretend to go along with him and escape when I had a chance. I struggled to push myself to my knees. Noble set his gun on the table and reached under my arms to help me stand.

"Alright. I'll go with you," I said, shakily, when I was upright. My knees wobbled, and Noble steadied me. "You were right about the authorities trying to pin the murders on me. I need someone to protect and take care of me. I'll go with you to the cabin."

"I knew you'd come around," he said, quickly, becoming more animated. "My truck's outside. We'll take it to the B&B and leave from there."

"Okay," I said, meekly, trying to sound humbled.

He smiled. "You won't regret this, Faron. We'll be so happy together." He turned slowly and pointed. "I'm parked near the willow tree by the curb," he said, glancing toward the door.

I took my chance. I lunged forward and grabbed the gun off the table.

"Faron," he yelled, grabbing my arm and reaching for the gun. "Give it back."

I ripped my arm away, then turned and pointed the gun at him with my finger on the trigger.

"Stay back," I shouted. "Stay away."

"Faron. Hand me the gun. You don't want to shoot me. You love me." He stepped forward.

"Don't move," I yelled.

"This is pointless," he said, taking another step closer.

"I'll shoot. I mean it," I said.

"You don't mean that," he said. "I know you. You'd never shoot anybody."

"I will," I shouted, as he edged nearer.

"No," he said. "You won't."

He reached for the gun. I kicked him hard in the shins and ran for the door. He tackled me, and I dropped the gun. It hit the ground hard. I pushed forward on the floor and seized the gun again.

"No," he said, gripping my hand and grabbing the gun himself.

I held on tight. He banged my hand on the floor, but I kept my grip on the gun. He pleaded with me. We struggled. And then the gun went off.

CHAPTER 19

A hesitant sunbeam peeked through the small window of my Cove Pointe jail cell, then beamed into life. Morning. I wasn't sure I wanted it to come. I had a terrible night, and who knew what the day would bring. But at any rate, the storm was over.

I threw off my itchy, gray blanket and padded over to look out the tiny window. At least I had on dry clothes. The crisp, cottony twill jumpsuit they gave me was better than the soggy outfit I'd been wearing, even if it was an ugly blue. I stood on my tiptoes and looked out. The big lake shimmered brilliantly across the street, quietly waking up with the town and reminding me of the world outside—the world I'd lost in an instant. I knew that after the gun went off yesterday, and I knew one other thing. Noble was dead.

The police showed up and arrested me at the music camp after Mason Snyder barged into the lodge, snatched the gun off the floor, and called them. How he knew I was there, I have no idea. But Noble was lying totally still in front of me, and there was no talking to Mason after he checked his pulse.

I just stayed sitting in the corner by the fireplace, where I'd gone in a nearly unconscious daze after the gunshot, until the police burst in, yanked me to my feet, and handcuffed me. They brought me here to this stark, gray, cobwebby cell after I used my one phone call to call Cam and tell him where I was. Cam could help me. I was sure he would. Hopefully, he'd listened to his voicemail by now. I turned and shuffled back to sit on my cot.

What was everyone else doing now? Was Summer okay? Her husband's death must have been a terrible shock, and she wasn't feeling well besides. And how was Kasey? Noble had been another music teacher of hers. And what about the rest of the town? Did everyone know their local business owner and friend was dead? I might be safer here than out there when everyone found out. I still don't know what happened exactly. I can only surmise that Noble's untimely death doesn't look good for me.

A guard brought breakfast a few hours later—toast, granola, and orange juice. The meager offering wasn't great, but I didn't want much more anyway. My stomach ached.

"Did my lawyer call?" I asked, hopefully.

The guard shook his head and left. Cam probably hadn't checked his voicemail yet, or maybe he had an early meeting at his firm. What could be going on in the outside world? Maybe I didn't want to know.

I ate what I could and set the tray on the floor near the cell door. Then I curled up under the blanket on my cot and closed my eyes. I laid there for several minutes, but I couldn't sleep despite how exhausted I still was from everything that had happened in the last day or two. And I really needed to see Cam. Where was he? I sat up and tossed the blanket against the wall. He wouldn't leave me all alone in this horrible place, would he? No. I had to believe he would come to see me. Who else could I call? I shivered as I realized I had no one else to contact.

Another cell door clanged shut, and I assumed other prisoners were in the jail along with me, but I couldn't see them. All the cells appeared to be on this side of the hallway. So all I saw through the bars was a few feet of space and a blank, white wall. I couldn't see staying here very long. It was too oppressive. Cam, where are you? What if he wasn't coming?

I stood and went over to look out the window again. People strolled up and down the street as though nothing had ever happened, enjoying the beautiful day. And nothing had happened to them. My life, however, had irrevocably changed. I looked away. I was different from them now. I wasn't free anymore.

Suddenly, footsteps echoed in the hall, and keys jangled loudly. Someone was coming. What did they want? Was a guard out there? I stood and held my breath.

"Faron, are you okay?"

"Cam."

I ran to the cell door, barely able to keep myself from ramming against it to reach him. The guard opened the door and stepped back, and I threw my arms around Cam's shoulders and hugged him tightly.

"You're here. You came. I can't believe it's you," I said.

I'd never felt such overwhelming relief in my life. The guard shut the door and left.

"Yes, of course I'm here," Cam said, holding me. "I came over as soon as they'd let me in. I had to file some paperwork on your behalf and prove that I'm allowed to act as your attorney, among a few other things. Now let's sit down, and you can tell me what happened."

He released me, pulled a wooden chair forward from against the wall, and sat down near my cot. I walked over and sat on the cot while taking deep breaths to keep from hyperventilating. My relief in seeing Cam had turned into fear that he would leave again. I was so thrilled that he had come to save me, and apparently didn't believe I had killed Noble, but my relief was tempered by the fact that he was obviously the only person I had left in the world. I needed him desperately.

"I didn't kill him," I said, breathlessly, when I could speak again.

"I know you didn't," Cam said. "How did it happen?"

"He threatened me. Or I mean he threatened you, or I mean. I don't know." How was I supposed to explain this? "I had to run from him," I said. "And when he caught up to me at the music camp, he had a gun, and he said he was going to kill you. So I grabbed the gun, and then he grabbed the gun. And then it went off." I stopped and put my hand on my heart.

Cam looked at me strangely. Had I said too much?

"Noble Dixon said he wanted to kill me?" Cam asked.

"Yes, and he had a gun," I said.

"Okay, well, how did he end up dead?"

I reached for the gun because I didn't want him to go after you, and he came after me. Then we fell on the floor and struggled, and that's when I heard the gunshot."

"You heard it? You didn't know the gun went off?"

"No."

"Geez." Cam sat back and rubbed his chin. "Wow. This is unbelievable. Noble Dixon came after you?"

I nodded. From the way Cam's eyes glazed over, I could tell he was having trouble accepting this new reality about Noble. I didn't think he'd believe me if I told him Noble was a serial killer and had admitted to killing my husbands, so I held off on that. Cam looked away from me. When he looked back, he was frowning.

"Okay. This is serious, Faron. I believe you, but I don't know how I'm going to persuade others to believe you. This is just a terrible accident due to unforeseen circumstances. I'm going to have to work up a case. That is, if you want me to."

My mouth dropped open.

"Of course I want you to. You're my only hope of getting out of here," I said.

"Okay. But I think you should know that I haven't worked on a trial in a long time. I lost the last trial I took on."

"That doesn't matter to me now," I said. "I know you're on my side. That's what counts."

"Well. Let me get this off my chest first," he said. "I was out of it at the last trial because of my personal grief over my lost family members at the time. I wasn't coping well, and my client suffered the consequences. He was a young husband and father accused of robbery, and he went to prison. I gave up being a defense attorney after that. But if you really want me to, I'll give it my best shot."

"I really want you to," I said, earnestly. "I need you."

"Okay then," he said, nodding. "We'll work on this together. I'll get more statements from you and work on your defense."

"Thank you so much," I said. "I know you'll get me out of here."

"I'll try," he said. "I'd better go and get to work on this."

"Alright," I said, standing along with him. "Oh, one other thing. How is everybody? Is Kasey okay?"

"Well. Of course, she's upset, but everyone is. It'll take some time to recover from this."

"How about Summer?" I asked.

"As I understand from Eleanor, Summer took the news hard, and she's not feeling well either. So hopefully, she'll recover."

"Thanks for telling me," I said.

"Alright. I'm going to get going," Cam said.

"Do you have to go already?" I asked. I didn't want to be

alone.

"I'd stay, but I have several people to talk to. A lot is happening outside of these walls. But I'll be back to see you as soon as I can, okay?"

I nodded. He looked at me for a moment.

"I'll do everything I can," he said.

"I know you will," I said.

He stood and walked to the cell door.

"Guard," he called out.

The guard came over and let him out. Cam turned and gave a short wave before disappearing from sight.

I sat down on my cot and thought about our meeting. Cam was definitely on my side, even though he was more distant toward me than I'd hoped. My new status as a prisoner probably had a lot to do with that. I wished that wasn't the case. I missed his closeness. But if anyone would champion my cause, he would. I laid back, feeling better but still sad. I closed my eyes again to finally get the full rest I needed.

Cam came back to see me the next afternoon. I was so happy to see him, I couldn't even speak. I hadn't realized how afraid I was that he wouldn't return. But there he was. The guard let him into my cell.

"Hi Faron," he said.

He pulled the chair up next to my cot again and sat down.

"Hi," I said, softly.

I had a bad night. The unbearable new reality of Noble's death and my resulting situation had kept me awake.

"How are you holding up?"

"Oh, you know," I said, despondently.

"Yeah," he said. "I thought you should know the media is all over this, so you're probably better off in here for a while than you would have been outside."

"That possibility had occurred to me," I said.

"I'm doing what I can to mitigate the coverage and keep your name in a good light. I'm on your side, but this is going to be a long haul," he said.

I nodded.

"And the fact that Gill was murdered earlier this year doesn't help anything," he said.

"Yes, I was thinking about that. What's going on with Gill's children in regard to the money and the house?" I asked. "Have you talked to Jay Morrison?"

"I have. I'm sure you realize your current situation doesn't help your case in that regard. But we'll have to wait and see what happens. I'm working with Jay to negotiate a fair outcome to the will and to keep your house in Florida."

"Oh good," I said. "Thank you."

"Will you hang in there for me?" he asked.

"I'll do my best," I said.

"Good. Let's get to work."

We spent the afternoon going over what happened with Noble at the music camp, discussing my recollections of how the gun went off, and working on strategies for my defense. When the light through the window faded into twilight, Cam packed up his briefcase and stood to go.

"I'll be back in a few days," he said.

I swallowed hard. The abandoned feeling that cropped up whenever he left made me melancholy.

"Promise?" I asked.

"I promise," he said.

Cam called to the guard that he was ready to leave and waved as he walked away down the hall. When he was no longer visible, I leaned forward in my sitting position, dropped my head into my hands, and locked up my heart until I saw him again.

***

When Paul Chevalier called with an invitation to his yacht on the big lake a few weeks after Faron was arrested, Mason jumped at the chance to meet with him. He briskly took down directions to the slip at the marina in Blue Haven and was now on his way over there.

After Faron had been locked up, Gill's oldest son demanded more and more frequent reports on what was going on in Cove Pointe and on what Mason continued to find out about her background. Paul intended to use Faron's unfortunate situation to his best advantage in regard to matters involving his father's estate and will, including a second home in Florida, and Mason needed to find out what he wanted now.

He arrived at the marina and parked, then headed toward the slips to find Paul's yacht. When he found his destination, he waved to the man on board and told him Paul was expecting him. A minute later, Paul came over and helped him board the boat. He took him inside to a comfortable salon-type room and poured marguerites for both of them before sitting down across from Mason on a plush sofa.

Paul had that same polished look about him that he always did with his slicked back, black hair and tortoiseshell glasses, but now he wore shorts and leather boat shoes without socks, which gave him a more casual look than Mason had been expecting. He still had that upper-crust look to him, though, which never failed to annoy Mason. He always seemed like he was looking down his nose at him, and he didn't like that. Mason took a tentative sip from the wide glass and nodded his approval before speaking.

"So what did you call me here for?" he asked bluntly.

He wanted to get right down to things. Paul had never asked him to his yacht before, and he wondered what was up. The man he'd waved to on the yacht walked in before Paul could answer.

"Mason, I'd like to introduce Jay Morrison. He's a lawyer involved with my father's case. Pour yourself a marguerita and have a seat," he said to Jay.

This guy looked more professional with his gray chinos and navy polo shirt, but the standoffish air was the same. He was probably as much of a snobby, stuffed shirt as Paul was.

Jay did as Paul asked before sitting near him on the sofa.

"So anyway, where was I? Oh yes. Why did I ask you here?" Paul continued. "Well, I have a small job for you."

"Yeah. What is it?" Mason asked, suddenly suspicious of the expectant way they were both looking at him.

"I need a guy to pick up some information for me. Are you interested?"

"Depends," Mason said. "Is this legal?"

Paul ignored him.

"I'll give you the name of the contact who has the information. All you need to do is pick up an envelope from this contact and deliver it to this address."

Paul leaned forward and held out a folded piece of paper. Mason hesitated before taking the paper and unfolding it.

"What's this about?" he asked. "Both these addresses are for legal offices."

Paul nodded. Mason looked at Jay.

"You're involved in Gill Chevalier's case?" he asked him.

"Yes," Jay answered.

"Is this information regarding that case or his widowed wife, Faron Chevalier's murder case?" Mason asked.

Jay shrugged. Mason looked at Paul.

"What do you say?" he asked him.

"Could be either one," Paul answered. "Will you do it? I'll make it worth your while."

Mason had a weird feeling, but the prospect of more money to pay his own legal bills from his divorce was too tempting.

"Yeah, alright. I'll do it," he said. "When?"

"As soon as possible," Paul said. "I'll make sure they're expecting you. And I need confirmation of the delivery from the delivery address. A note of receipt and a signature will do."

"Okay," Mason said. "Anything else?"

"No, unless you want to join us for an afternoon cruise."

"No, I'd better get going," Mason said.

He didn't trust these guys. The delivery address was to the prosecutor's office up north. He'd pick up the information, whatever it was, and deliver it promptly, but then he was washing his hands of the whole thing. This stunk worse than the fishy smell emanating from this boat slip.

Mason stood up and shook hands with them both, after which Paul walked him out, and Mason disembarked. He walked to his car and got in, then sat there thinking for a moment. What were these guys up to? Maybe he didn't want to know. But if Faron was on the receiving end of whatever they were doing, she'd better look out. From the looks of them, they weren't playing games. That's all he could say.

But he sure wasn't going to give her or her fancy lawyer friend, Talbert, a heads up on this one, even if it was probably under the radar. The authorities had finally caught up with Faron, and he wanted her new behind bars situation to stay that way. Mason started his car, drove out of the marina, and headed back to Cove Pointe.

***

Cam came back to see me on and off over the next few months, and we worked on my case. I'd never had such a stalwart protector and worker for my cause. He asked me questions and wrote things down to work on later. And he made light conversation in between making notes, which made me feel connected to him and the outside world. I waited for him to visit again the moment he left.

Between visits, my temperament went up and down. Some days, I was happy and sure we'd win and convinced I'd be out of here before you knew it. And other days, I sank down into the doldrums, wondering if I'd ever be free again. If Cam hadn't been there for me, I would have been totally lost.

I spent my days reading books from the jail's library and peering out the small window when I could. The big lake was so close and yet so far. At least I could see how beautiful it was, even if I couldn't go there to swim or sail or take the ferry to a far-off venue. Someday maybe, but not now.

One afternoon, late in the day, Cam asked me about my feelings as a child growing up as an orphan. I wasn't sure how to answer because I seldom talked about my childhood. But he seemed so earnest and interested that I opened up a little bit to him. He asked me another question, pausing as though trying to choose his words carefully.

"So was it hard being an orphan?" he asked.

"I don't know what you mean by hard," I said.

"Lonely, I suppose," he said.

"Hmm. Well, yes, I was lonely and wistful, too. I mean, you don't really miss something you never had, you know. But there's always a longing for what might have been."

He nodded, and his eyes glistened.

"That's the best way I can describe my feelings," I said.

"Did you ever try to find out who your birth parents were?"

"I did," I said, nodding. "But no one would tell me anything, and the court records about me were sealed." I shrugged. "So anyway, that's the way things go."

"Yeah," he said.

"The main problem growing up was being teased and misunderstood by other children who couldn't relate to my situation or my past. I gave up talking about myself a long time ago," I said.

"I'm glad you talked to me," Cam said.

I looked into his warm, caring eyes, and for a moment, I was transported away from my problems and fears. He was there for me. He cared. But the world was between us now. How I wished for my freedom and a chance to be with him again. Was that possible? I leaned toward him, raising my lips toward his, but something in his unyielding gaze and rock-solid posture stopped me from leaning further. I sat back, chagrined.

"I'm sorry, Faron," he said. "I need to keep our relationship professional for now."

I nodded. I understood. My life was on the line. But I missed him and his gentle touch. When he left me alone in my cell this time, I cried.

As the trial date neared, the leaves of the maples outside my cell window turned bright shades of red and orange. And the autumnal lake mirrored the moods of my soul—sometimes gray and turbulent, sometimes blue and peaceful and still.

Cam became extremely diligent as he pored over the evidence he planned to use and verified information. The only thing we disagreed about was testifying. I wanted to. But he didn't want me to. He thought I'd incriminate myself with the things I said, whether I meant to or not. I was convinced otherwise. I was sure I needed to testify in order to clear my name, and I welcomed the chance to do so. But he wouldn't hear of it. And because he was my lawyer and friend and I trusted him, I acquiesced.

By the time the trial date rolled around, I had put any qualms about not taking the stand out of my thoughts. I gave the thumbs up to Cam about his intentions in the courtroom, and on the night before the trial, we gave each other pep talks. I was certain we had a chance without my testimony. Well, I was pretty sure, anyway.

On the day of the trial, I walked into the wood-paneled courtroom and took my seat at the defense table next to Cam. He looked very intelligent and trustworthy in his blue suit and tie. My hopes for a positive outcome soared. He smiled and greeted me in a way that raised my spirits greatly. At least I was out of my cell and around people again, although the courtroom spectators didn't improve my mood the way Cam had. They looked kind of dour, and I was suddenly frightened. But then I glanced at Cam again and felt better.

When the jury walked in, I perused their faces and tried to get a feel for what they were like. But their expressions gave nothing away. I supposed the judge would enter the courtroom soon. I looked at Cam for approval again and returned his supportive smile before sitting back and waiting for the trial to begin.

CHAPTER 20

Mason Snyder stared directly at Cameron Talbert as he framed his answer to another question from Faron Chevalier's defense lawyer. He'd been sitting on the witness stand for much of the morning while Talbert peppered him with inane inquiries. And before that, he'd answered a myriad of questions from the prosecution. Mason was bored. But the information contained in his next answer was important to get across.

"I heard the gunshot when I was tying the motorboat to the dock. So I stepped out onto the dock and ran to the lodge," Mason told the courtroom. "The front door was unlocked. Faron was cowering in the corner by the fireplace behind Noble Dixon's body. She saw me and knew it was all over. I could see it in her eyes."

Cameron stared at him. Mason was pretty sure he'd hit a nerve with that one. But who cared? No self-respecting lawyer would have taken on Faron Chevalier's defense like he had anyway. Obviously, he wasn't a self-respecting lawyer.

"What did you do next?"

"I called the police, and they came and arrested her," Mason said.

"And all this happened after you called Noble Dixon from Joey Benson's cottage and told him to go to Cove Pointe Music Camp, as you previously testified?" Talbert prompted.

"Yes, but that was only after I saw the canoe tip over and watched someone swim to the dock there," Mason continued.

"Why did you call Mr. Dixon?"

"I was concerned about the individual."

"What did you think he could do?"

"I thought he might want to drive over and help the person since he lived near the music camp."

"And did he say he would?"

"Yes."

"Did you know the person in the canoe that capsized was Faron Chevalier?"

"No comment."

"Answer the question," Cameron said, sharply.

Mason looked at the judge whose stone-faced expression intimidated him.

"It looked like her," he said, after a moment.

"Yes or no," Cameron said.

Mason paused for a moment. "Yes."

"How did you know?"

"I saw her through my binoculars."

"Why were you using binoculars?"

"I'm a birdwatcher," Mason said, sarcastically. Who did this guy think he was?

"What was the weather like that day?"

"It was raining."

"Then how can you be sure the individual in the canoe was Faron?"

"I saw her earlier on the beach, too, when the rain let up."

"Had you been stalking Faron Chevalier?"

"Objection," the prosecution said.

"Sustained."

"Why did you take your motorboat to Cove Point Music Camp?"

"The canoe was floating in the lake, so I took the motorboat over, attached a towline and towed it to the music camp where the canoeist had swum to."

"And who was the canoeist?"

"Faron Chevalier." Mason sighed heavily.

"But you weren't stalking her?"

"Objection."

"Sustained."

"And that's when you heard the shot?" Cameron asked.

"Yes," Mason answered, curtly.

"Are you sure the shot came from inside the lodge?"

"Yes."

"Are you an expert in acoustics?"

"No."

"So you can't back up your assertion that the shot was from inside the lodge?"

"I know what I heard."

"But you're not a sound expert."

"No."

"No more questions, your honor," Cameron said.

"The witness may step down," the judge said.

Mason got up and left the witness stand. He glanced at the jury, then gave Talbert a scathing, sideways glance. Good luck with this screwy line of questioning, dude. He caught a glimpse of Faron as he walked back to his seat. She leaned over to talk to Cam and didn't look at him. That was fine with Mason. He'd done his part to keep her from talking to anybody much longer. The way things were going at the trial, she'd be behind bars for good soon.

Mason took his seat on a mahogany bench next to Joey and Tina in the back of the packed courtroom, which was filled to overflowing with angry residents of Cove Pointe. Noble Dixon had been a well-liked, upstanding member of the small community, and many of his friends had turned out for him. Mason was surprised at how many there were, given that the trial was being held in a courtroom in a larger town miles from Cove Pointe.

The contrast to Faron's empty turnout was stark and sad, cementing the relevance of her current situation. She had no one other than Cam, which seemed ominously strange and poignant. Why was she completely alone? The answer seemed to point to her as someone who was guilty of murder.

Tina leaned in sideways next to him and whispered. "Why is she wearing that tacky lavender blouse? I thought she had to wear a prison jumpsuit."

Mason sat back and regarded Tina, reevaluating his high opinion of her. Who cared what Faron was wearing? This was a murder trial with her freedom on the line. And since she was obviously the killer with contiguous concerns, she probably hadn't put much thought into her outfit.

"Got me," he said, turning away.

He scoffed. Women were women wherever you went. Sandy probably would have made an even nastier comment. He was glad he'd soon be rid of her. And Faron was on her way out of his purview, too. She wouldn't be a thorn in his side much longer.

Mason looked around and recognized a few reporters who had had a heyday covering Faron's murder trial, especially after all the publicity about the recent murder of Gill Chevalier, Faron's wealthy, third husband. Maybe he himself would be famous after his testimony today. Maybe they'd even interview him. Wouldn't that be something?

The judge called a recess for lunch, and Mason stood to leave with everyone else. Faron was talking adamantly to Cam, throwing her arms in the air and seeming to insist on something. He was just as adamant in return, shaking his head and even pounding his fist on the table, which seemed a little over the top for a strait-laced lawyer like he was. What could they be talking about? If he knew, Mason could probably make a lot of money selling the information to the media gathered here. But they were too far away to eavesdrop on.

A guard walked over and led Faron out of the courtroom. Cameron remained at the table with his head in his hands. Mason shook his head. Way to keep your cards close to your chest, counselor. Talbert shouldn't be giving away the fact that he was losing, and his actions clearly showed he thought he was.

Mason looked away and stepped into the aisle to follow the rest of the crowd out into the hall. When he got through the doors, he headed for the elevator, leaving Joey and Tina behind. Hopefully, the cafeteria served a good lunch. He could use something to eat.

***

I can't believe Cam wouldn't let me testify. After the private investigator's testimony, we needed something to pull us out of the hole. Even I could tell the trial wasn't going well, and I'm not a lawyer. But Cam was afraid the prosecution would grill me on cross-examination, and he didn't want that to happen. And he really wanted to do well by me because he'd lost a previous trial case, which was why he'd reverted to doing mostly contracts at his firm.

But I have to testify because the defense is in trouble. The prosecution keeps insinuating that I murdered Noble. But I didn't. The gun just went off. There's a difference, right? But my fingerprints were on the trigger, and their presence is a problem. That sick feeling of confusion I got when I realized Noble was dead is back. And I don't know if it will ever go away this time.

I'm so afraid I'll lose everything and everyone I've ever known because of Noble's death. Why? Because no one believes me, that's why. No one, but Cam, that is. But, like I said, he's having a hard time defending me, and I can't help but think he's vacillating in his support of me. I don't know what makes me feel that way. I just do. Is my lack of emotion the problem again? Maybe. But I don't feel anything for Noble despite the fact that he's dead. I can't cry if I don't feel like crying. But I appear to be the only one who isn't crying about him, and that doesn't seem to be in my favor.

We argued before lunch because Cam really doesn't want to lose another case. And he certainly doesn't want to lose mine, which is probably why he was so rigid and concerned about deviating from his plan. My testifying on my own behalf wasn't in his lexicon, but I'd have to change that. I still wanted Cam for myself. And I wanted him bad. I wouldn't have a chance with him if I ended up in jail.

I absolutely have to testify. That's the only way I can clear my name. And if I don't, who will? I don't see anyone on my side but Cam. The private investigator, whose name I'd found out was Mason Synder, seemed to have it in for me, too. I don't know why, and I don't know what I ever did to him. But finding out that he'd been watching me from a cottage on the other side of Cove Lake from Hidden Glen really irked me. No wonder I got a creepy feeling when I was on the beach at the B&B.

Anyway, the trial is about to start again. And when Cam came back from lunch, he told me he'd reconsidered. If I really wanted to take the stand, he'd let me. I guess he'd left the possibility open and probably talked it over with some of the other lawyers or maybe even the judge. I don't know. I don't know how these things work. All I know is I have a right to defend myself, and I'm going to do my best.

"All rise," the bailiff said when the judge came back into the courtroom.

We all stood and sat back down. Then Cam stood up again.

"The defense calls Faron Chevalier to the stand," he said.

I stood and walked to the witness stand, where I took my seat as properly as I could. I needed to testify in the best way I knew how if I was going to save myself. That's how I really felt. I was scared, too, but determined as well.

Cam walked up to stand in front of me after they'd sworn me in. I looked at him, and he nodded slightly, probably to give me courage.

"How did you know Noble Dixon?" he asked.

I took a deep breath.

"I was engaged to him six years ago," I answered.

Audible gasps filled the courtroom. I didn't realize our engagement was such a big deal. But I guess so. I glanced behind Cam at the spectators, wondering what had caused their noticeable reaction.

"And what happened with that engagement?"

I looked back at Cam. My eyelid twitched, and I rubbed it.

"Well, it ended. We called it off and went our separate ways."

I glanced around again and suddenly noticed two men who hadn't been in the courtroom before lunch. My heart skipped a beat.

"How did Noble feel about the engagement ending?"

"Objection. Defendant can't answer for the deceased."

"Sustained."

I put my hand to my heart and took another breath when I realized who the men were. My previous lawyer, Jay Morrison, and Gill's oldest son, Paul Chevalier, sat together in the back of the courtroom, staring at me. Why had they shown up? This trial was about Noble's murder, not Gill's.

"Okay then, how did you feel about the engagement ending?" Cam asked, obviously reorienting his question.

I swallowed hard before shifting my gaze back to Cam and answering.

"Sad. But I knew we weren't meant to be together," I said.

"Why was that?"

"I was in love with someone else."

Another audible gasp filled the courtroom along with an undulating hum of low murmurs. The judge pounded his gavel, and the crowd became silent.

"Did you marry someone else?" Cam continued.

"Yes."

More murmurs.

"How did Noble feel about that?"

"Objection."

"Sustained."

Cam looked like he was about ready to throw his arms up in frustration, but luckily, he didn't. He pressed his lips together until they nearly turned white, and then continued.

"Did you place the gun next to Noble's body at the music camp?" he asked.

"No."

"How did the gun get there?"

"Noble brought it with him." I turned to the jury. "It was his gun," I added.

"Okay. How did the gun get next to Noble's body?"

"I have no idea."

"Who shot the gun?" Cam asked.

"I didn't," I said, looking at the jury again.

"Who did?"

"I don't know. It just went off."

"But you didn't pull the trigger?"

"Objection."

"Sustained."

"Did you pull the trigger?"

"No."

"No more questions, your honor," Cam said, after turning to address the judge.

Cam turned away and didn't look back at me. Instead, he dropped his arms to his sides and walked slowly back to the defense table. He looked so defeated. That wasn't a good sign.

The prosecutor, a gray-haired, older man with a short, salt-and-pepper beard and a white mustache that curled up somewhat at the ends, stood sprightly and walked over to me.

"Good afternoon, Ms. Chevalier. How are you doing today?"

"Fine," I said, trying not to noticeably shudder. He sounded too chipper for my liking.

"Good. Good," he said.

"Let's start with some basic questions, shall we?"

I nodded.

"I would imagine a woman of your means and obvious breeding comes from a prestigious societal background with its requisite amenities and proper upbringing," he said. "Do you?"

"Objection," Cam said. "Leading the witness."

"Sustained."

"Do you come from an upper-class family?" the prosecutor asked.

"Objection," Cam said.

"Sustained."

"Where were you born?"

I stared at him, feeling my heart drop.

"I don't know. I mean, I'm not sure."

"You're not sure? Why is that?"

"Well, I, uh," I stammered. "I never knew my parents, and I grew up as an orphan. I don't have a birth certificate, so I don't know where I was born."

"I see. So you don't know who you are?" he asked with an innocent smile.

The murmurs in the courtroom this time were even louder. The judge pounded the gavel again.

"Objection," Cam said.

"Sustained."

"Can you prove who you are, Ms. Chevalier?"

"Objection," Cam called out.

"The witness will answer the question," the judge said.

"Yes, of course. I have other legal documentation."

"But you don't have an actual birth certificate?" he asked rhetorically.

"No."

"Does the name Giorgio Lockwell ring a bell?" he asked.

"No," I said. What was he talking about?

"Are you sure?"

"Yes."

"Have you ever seen this document?"

He showed me a yellowed newspaper clipping. I gasped when I looked at it more closely. I was sure it was the same one

I'd seen long ago in my foster mother's purse—the one about the woman who'd killed her husband and could have gone after her daughter, too.

"Well, I don't know," I said, wary. I didn't want to admit that the article looked familiar because I didn't know why he was asking. I perused the photo for a moment longer before handing the article back to him. "No. I don't think so."

The prosecutor turned to the judge.

"If it pleases the court, we'd like this entered into evidence. This is an article about Faron Chevalier's birth parents, the infamous crime family bank robbers, Giorgio and Cecilia Lockwell."

I gasped. "What?"

More loud murmurs overtook the courtroom. Did the spectators know more than I did? Who were these people?

"The article's accuracy was verified after tracing its origin to sealed court documents from years ago. When Faron was a toddler, Cecilia Lockwell, Faron's birth mother, shot and killed Giorgio Lockwell and then herself in a violent act of domestic violence."

"What?" I asked again, dazed.

The courtroom erupted in chaos. People shouted and stood.

"She killed Noble," someone yelled, pointing at me.

The judge pounded his gavel again.

"Objection," Cam shouted.

"Overruled." The judge took the article and looked at it after the furor subsided.

"This is admissible," he said.

"Thank you, your honor," the prosecutor said.

I sat rigid and shaking. This wasn't going the way I'd

planned.

"How did you end up in Cove Pointe, Ms. Chevalier?" the prosecutor asked.

I took a breath to calm myself. Was I just supposed to continue on as though nothing had happened after finding out who my parents were? I guess so.

"My former college roommate, Summer Dixon, asked me to come and stay at her bed and breakfast for a while," I said. I flicked a drop of perspiration off my forehead.

"Was that a usual occurrence?"

"Well, no, not really. It was the first time she asked me."

"Why did she ask you to visit now?"

"Just wanted to see me, I guess," I said. Where was he going with this?

"Did you come to Cove Pointe to visit Summer Dixon or to get away from publicity about your dead husband's murder?" he asked, smoothly.

This time, shouts erupted in the courtroom over the gasps and murmurs. The judge pounded his gavel over and over until everyone calmed down.

"Well, that was partly the reason, I suppose," I said, softly. A cold bead of sweat ran down my back.

"I'm sorry. I couldn't hear you. What was the reason you came to Cove Pointe?" he prompted.

"For peace and quiet," I said. I folded and unfolded my hands.

He smirked.

"Did you find peace and quiet here, Faron?"

"Not exactly," I said, lowering my eyes to keep from seeing the malevolent glint in his.

"Didn't you really come to Cove Pointe to murder your

estranged ex-fiancé, Noble Dixon?"

"Objection!" Cam yelled.

More shouts. Several people stood up and raised their fists.

"Order in the court," the judge said, pounding his gavel continuously. "Order in the court."

"No," I answered loudly, raising my voice to be heard over the din. "No."

My cheeks felt hot. And suddenly, a righteous anger mixed with a whirlpool of hurt and betrayal at being lied about and followed around and suspected of things I didn't do hit me full on. And a physical reaction to the unfairness of it all coursed through my body and erupted from my soul. I slammed my fist down on the witness stand.

"No!" I shouted. "No! Of course not!"

"No more questions, your honor," the prosecutor said.

He turned on his heels and walked back to the table for the prosecution. The courtroom fell completely silent. Everyone was looking at me.

"The witness may step down," the judge said.

I sat still for a moment, taking stock of my situation. I looked around at the faces of the spectators. They seemed punitive and angry. Then I stood slowly, drawing a breath to calm myself, and walked shakily past the jury. What had I just done by losing my cool in court? I glanced quickly at the jury but couldn't read their expressionless faces. Was that a good sign or not?

When I reached the defense table, I sat down next to Cam. He didn't look at me. That definitely wasn't good. We sat together in silence for a while. I remained motionless when the judge gave the jury instructions. Then he told them to leave and deliberate in the jury room until they reached a verdict.

I watched the jury leave. After they left, I couldn't feel my hands. My whole body was numb. That's how worried I was. My entire future was in the hands of twelve people. Why was the room still so quiet? I glanced behind me. The spectators had all left, too. Cam and I were alone except for the members of the prosecution who sat quietly at their table. I looked over at Cam.

"Please say something," I said.

"Like what?" he asked, quietly.

Cam's eyes said it all—those deep, woeful, sorrowful eyes. Were they really the same dancing blue eyes I'd seen when I first met him? What happened to the happy go lucky surfer dude I'd flirted with in the bookstore on my way to Cove Pointe? He wasn't that person anymore. Was it because of me? I hoped not. I liked the way he used to be.

"Say anything," I said. "I can't stand this silence from you."

"I'm sorry," he said. "I want to be supportive. We'll just wait and see what the jury comes back with."

"Are you hopeful?" I asked.

"There's always hope," he said. "By the way, I don't know who won the pie contest at the county fair, so I don't know who owes who dinner in regard to our bet. But if I owe you one, you can come over when we get out of here, and I'll cook, okay?"

I grinned in spite of myself. What a relief to hear him say something about our regular lives before the trial and outside of this horrible place.

"Okay," I said.

He gave me a half-hearted smile. We sat together, waiting. If I ever got out of here, Cam's the one I'd run to. He'd put his life on the line for me, and I knew that.

"Thank you," I said, quietly,

"For what?" he asked. "We don't know how this is going to turn out."

"For trying and for being there," I said. "For being my knight in shining armor."

"Don't be silly," he said. "You're worth it, Faron. I did my best. I just hope it's enough."

"I know," I said.

Just then, the bailiff walked in and talked to the judge. Shortly thereafter, everyone returned to the courtroom, and the jury came in and took their seats. So soon? I held my breath and then let out a deep sigh. What would the verdict be? When everyone was seated, the judge spoke.

"Have you reached a verdict?"

"Yes, your honor."

The foreperson handed a note to the bailiff, who gave it to the judge. I watched the judge with bated breath as he took the note and began to read.

"We, the jury, find the defendant guilty as charged," the judge said.

The courtroom remained silent. The judge had insisted that no one react to the verdict, and they didn't, not out loud anyway. I hung my head. This couldn't be real. My worst fears had come true. I couldn't even look at Cam. What would happen now? Where would I go? What would I do? I looked up when I felt a touch on my shoulder. Cam looked at me. His eyes glistened.

"I'm sorry, Faron," he said. "I did my best."

"I know," I said.

Tears rolled down his face as the guard came over to take me away.

"I'll get you out on appeal," Cam said.

"Okay," I said, nodding.

But I didn't hold out much hope. I leaned toward him, and he hugged me. We clung to each other, holding one another in a tight embrace. Eventually, Cam pulled away, and the guard took my arm. I stood and looked around at the people who remained in the courtroom, but no one looked back at me. The trial was over. That's all there was to it. Close the book on Faron. If I could only have one more chapter in my life. But then again, maybe not. Everyone knows the old saying, "Be careful what you wish for." But then again, maybe. I'd hate for it all to end here.

I let the guard lead me to the door. Then I looked back at Cam one more time. He gave me a casual wave like the ones he gave me when I first met him. I waved back. Bye, babe.

CHAPTER 21

Cam told me he'd get me out of jail on appeal, but he never did. I already knew my life was over when the gun went off in the music camp lodge, and I was right. But I didn't know how right.

So here I am now out of state on death row. The trial, my first one, I mean, was ten years ago in my estimation. But I tend to lose track of time in captivity. I'm about to be executed for Noble's murder, Gill's murder, and the murders of all the other men in my life. Serial killer extraordinaire. Black Widow, even. That's what they called me. That's what they say around here now, though it's not true. As Daniel always said, reality can change. And boy was he right. I went from building a new life for myself to losing everything in an instant.

My reality? I was tried and convicted for a murder I didn't commit. Welcome to my twilight zone.

Everything snowballed out of control after my first conviction. New charges went from state to federal, boom, just like that. Snap your fingers. More courtrooms, more trials, FBI involvement because of Gill's home in Florida being our primary residence, and me supposedly crossing state lines to kill him—what a crock—convictions for other murders. The whole shebang. And I didn't do it.

I shouldn't complain, and I won't. After all my time in prison reflecting on my actions in the past, I've accepted my fate. It's bad enough that I killed someone. And the fact that I didn't kill all of them doesn't really make a difference. I'm still guilty of one. I know that now.

But hadn't I shot Noble in self-defense? Or had I hesitated, perhaps only for a second, before pulling the trigger? Did I have the upper hand when Noble pleaded for his life? Or not? Did I make a choice? I only need to know for my own peace of mind.

The clicking of locks. The bang of a door. They're coming for me. They're coming for me now. Should I pray? Would it matter? I drop to my knees. No use. Judgment day has come and gone.

If only the first trial had gone differently, I probably wouldn't be here. But there's no use crying over spilled milk, as they say. The guilty verdict back then sealed my fate and started me on a downhill path through the legal system. I can't help but reminisce.

My fingerprints were on the trigger, but did that mean I was at fault? The gun was Noble's. He had planned to kill Cam. And he'd already shot my first husband, Daniel, with a different gun. He alluded to that when he showed it to me. But no one believed me. The similarities to Daniel's murder by gunshot were there, and they pointed to me, not to Noble. At least that's what the police determined. They said carrying a gun in Cove Pointe, as Noble did, wasn't illegal. Murdering someone with a gun, however, was illegal.

The stomping of boots on the floor. The sliding of bolts. They're almost here. They are here. The cell door slides open. I stand. They grasp my arms. I walk out of the cell with them and down the stark hallway. I won't cry. It's too late to cry. It's too late for anything. I close my eyes and shut them out. I let them lead me where I have to go.

How did my life get to this point? Oh, yeah. Everyone I ever knew, except Summer, who was probably too sick to protest and was hopefully still alive, and Cameron, who defended me in the courtroom in my first trial, determined I was guilty. Maybe Summer did, too. After all, her husband is dead, and I haven't seen her since I ran away from him at Hidden Glen.

I suppose I came to terms with never seeing her again after slews of sleepless nights and agonizing crying jags over everything I'd lost. If I had ever seen her again, I wouldn't have known what to say anyway. I'm sure everyone in Cove Pointe has moved on without me by now anyway. What's the point of bringing the past up again? But I have nothing else to do.

I glance at the guards next to me. They don't look back, which is probably just as well. I don't want to see the same disdainful stare I've seen so many times before.

The look in everyone's eyes when I tried to explain said everything. How many times could I proclaim my innocence before giving up and letting them convict me? I don't know. I didn't count them.

Cam believed me, or at least he didn't not believe me, to use the double negative. He'd told me he couldn't imagine I'd killed anyone, but his eyes glazed over when I tried to convince him that Noble was the killer. He just couldn't seem to get his head around the possibility, maybe because he'd known Noble to be someone who wouldn't have been capable of the things I told him about.

And so maybe that also explains why I haven't seen Cam since the first verdict. He told me he'd get me out on appeal, but he never did. And I guess he just gave up after a while. Noble was apparently right when he told me no one but him would ever love me. Maybe that was always true, or maybe he made that happen.

I look away from the guards and down at the floor. My

head begins to spin. Is the light getting dimmer? Or is my sight only fading as I realize my life has slipped away and is now about to end?

I told the police about the butcher knife from my set at home being in the kitchen pantry at Hidden Glen. I was sure that would prove my innocence and point to Noble as the real killer. But the police thought I brought the knife with me. They thought I'd used the knife on Wade instead of determining Noble had. But, if that was the case, why would I have told them where to find it? I mean, how conniving did they think I was that I could plant a knife in advance of killing someone so I could blame the murder on someone else? So ridiculous.

And then they proved the knife was used to stab both Gill and Wade to death. The coroner's report on Wade Kestin had come back soon after Millie's and listed Wade's death as due to stabbing with a sharp instrument. He was stabbed to death before he ended up in the quagmire. And once they found the murder weapon that I had ironically told them about, they kept me in jail on charges. Life became more serious after that.

But Noble must have killed Wade, not me. He had to have been the one lurking around the campfire on our music camp campout instead of the bog witch. He'd stayed at the B&B that night and had ample opportunity to see Wade in the bog picking blueberries and killing him then, probably out of jealousy over my relationship with Wade. But again, no one listened to anything I had to say.

I feel dizzy for a moment and lose my footing. I close my eyes. Maybe I could just take a quick nap. A guard grips my arm tightly and pulls me forward. No rest for the wicked, or so they say.

I don't think having no one to stand up for me other than

Cam, who acted as my lawyer, and no family to sit behind me during the trial was any help. My being all alone in the world was never more evident. Still, did that make me guilty? Apparently so.

And, although it didn't come up in the trial, did they really think I was strong enough to smother my second husband? Bryce was much bigger than me. But in the heat of passion and adrenaline, evidently, anything is possible.

And even though what I said about Noble's whereabouts didn't come up in the trial, either, I told everyone that he was in Fenton City at the time of all three of my husbands' murders. But that, too, didn't seem to make a difference despite the fact that he also told me he murdered them.

Paul Chevalier and Gill's other two kids certainly didn't buy my explanation, and neither did Jay Morrison, my previous supposed lawyer. I lost the house and the money, and everything. But what more proof that Noble was the killer did everyone need? Evidently something. The wide grin that contemptible private investigator, Mason Snyder, gave me from the back of the courtroom at my trial for Gill's murder said it all as to how he felt about my troubles. At least he wouldn't be following me around anymore as some sort of unshakable nemesis.

I open my eyes as the prison guards lead me through another door. This perp walk, or whatever you call it, is unbearable. Are we there yet? We round another corner and start down a short hallway. Guess not.

In a way, though, the verdict and the sentence make sense, especially given the close community of people in the small town of Cove Pointe, the kind of community I never had. If I had to choose between someone I knew and someone I didn't know as to who was telling the truth in this convoluted situation, I wouldn't believe me either.

The worst part is knowing that Cam listened to all the lies and distanced himself from me. He had no way of comprehending that Noble had been a threat to him and his daughter, no matter what I said to convince him. And I understand, even if I don't yet forgive his betrayal. At least Kasey still has a father and doesn't have to live with the crippling pain of losing one in the same way I had, which would have happened if Noble had carried out his sinister plan to kill Cam.

I shuffle through a door at the end of the hallway and swallow hard. I'm there. They lay me down. They strap me in. I see the IVs—one for each arm. I feel the pricks. My life is over. All over. Or at least it will be. Goodbye world. Goodbye everybody.

One last clarifying, horrifying thought sneaks through my consciousness and shatters my denial as I struggle to take one desperate, final breath because of me, and even to my immense relief Noble now has the distinct honor, out of all the men I loved and lost in my life to the murderous hands of a killer, to ultimately be the last one to die.

Terri Greening is a creative writer in the Great Lakes region. She enjoys yoga, gardening, nature parks, walking, and biking. She has a B.A. in journalism from Central Michigan University and an M.B.A. from Grand Valley State University.

www.ingramcontent.com/pod-product-compliance
Lightning Source LLC
Chambersburg PA
CBHW050732180626
46814CB00002B/717
9798891264755